V

BLUEBEARD'S EGG

BY MARGARET ATWOOD

Novels

The Edible Woman
Surfacing
Lady Oracle
Life Before Man
Bodily Harm
The Handmaid's Tale
Cat's Eye
The Robber Bride
Alias Grace

Short Stories

Dancing Girls
Bluebeard's Egg
Wilderness Tips

Short Fictions

Bones And Murder

Poetry

Poems: 1965–1975
Poems: 1976–1986
Morning In The Burned House

Criticism

*Survival: A Thematic Guide
To Canadian Literature*

For Children

Up In The Tree

Margaret Atwood

BLUEBEARD'S EGG

and Other Stories

VINTAGE

Published by Vintage 1996

2 4 6 8 10 9 7 5 3 1

Material in this collection has previously been published
as follows: 'Significant Moments in the Life of My
Mother' in *Queen's Quarterly*; 'Bluebeard's Egg' in
Chateleine and *North American Review*; 'The Salt
Garden' in *Ms*; 'Loulou; or, The Domestic Life of the
Language' in *Saturday Night*; 'The Whirlpool Rapids' in
the Toronto *Globe & Mail* Summer Fiction Issue and
Redbook (in a slightly different version); 'Unearthing
Suite' in a limited edition by Grand Union Press; 'Spring
Songs of the Frogs' in *Company* (England); 'Walking on
Water' in *Chateleine*; and 'In Search of the Rattlesnake
Plantain' in *Harper's*

First published in Great Britain by
Jonathan Cape Ltd, 1987

Vintage
Random House, 20 Vauxhall Bridge Road, London SW1V 2SA

Random House Australia (Pty) Limited
20 Alfred Street, Milsons Point, Sydney
New South Wales 2061, Australia

Random House New Zealand Limited
18 Poland Road, Glenfield,
Auckland 10, New Zealand

Random House South Africa (Pty) Limited
Endulini, 5A Jubilee Road, Parktown 2193, South Africa

Random House UK Limited Reg. No. 954009

A CIP catalogue record for this book
is available from the British Library

ISBN 0 09 974121 0

Printed and bound in Great Britain by
Cox & Wyman, Reading, Berkshire

For My Parents

CONTENTS

BLUEBEARD'S EGG

AND OTHER STORIES

SIGNIFICANT MOMENTS
IN THE LIFE OF
MY MOTHER

When my mother was very small, someone gave her a basket of baby chicks for Easter. They all died.

"I didn't know you weren't supposed to pick them up," says my mother. "Poor little things. I laid them out in a row on a board, with their little legs sticking out straight as pokers, and wept over them. I'd loved them to death."

Possibly this story is meant by my mother to illustrate her own stupidity, and also her sentimentality. We are to understand she wouldn't do such a thing now.

Possibly it's a commentary on the nature of love; though, knowing my mother, this is unlikely.

*   *   *

My mother's father was a country doctor. In the days before cars he drove a team of horses and a buggy around his territory, and in the days before snow ploughs he drove a team and a sleigh, through blizzards and rainstorms and in the middle of the night, to arrive at houses lit with oil lamps where water would be boiling on the wood range and flannel sheets warming on the plate rack, to deliver babies who would subsequently be named after him. His office was in the house, and as a child my mother would witness people arriving at the office door, which was reached through the front porch, clutching parts of themselves—thumbs, fingers, toes, ears, noses—which had accidentally been cut off, pressing these severed parts to the raw stumps of their bodies as if they could be stuck there like dough, in the mostly vain hope that my grandfather would be able to sew them back on, heal the gashes made in them by axes, saws, knives, and fate.

My mother and her younger sister would loiter near the closed office door until shooed away. From behind it would come groans, muffled screams, cries for help. For my mother, hospitals have never been glamorous places, and illness offers no respite or holiday. "Never get sick," she says, and means it. She hardly ever does.

Once, though, she almost died. It was when her appendix burst. My grandfather had to do the operation. He said later that he shouldn't have been the person to do it: his hands were shaking too much. This is one of the few admissions of weakness on his part that my mother has ever reported. Mostly he is portrayed as severe and in charge of things. "We all respected him, though," she says. "He was widely respected." (This is a word which has slipped a little in the scale since my mother's youth. It used to outrank *love.*)

It was someone else who told me the story of my grandfather's muskrat farm: how he and one of my mother's uncles fenced in the swamp at the back of their property and invested my mother's maiden aunt's savings in muskrats. The idea was that these muskrats would multiply and eventually be made into muskrat coats, but an adjoining apple farmer washed his spraying equipment upstream, and the muskrats were all killed by the poison, as dead as doornails. This was during the Depression, and it was no joke.

When they were young—this can cover almost anything these days, but I put it at seven or eight—my mother and her sister had a tree house, where they spent some of their time playing dolls' tea parties and so forth. One day they found a box of sweet little bottles outside my grandfather's dispensary. The bottles were being thrown out, and my mother (who has always hated waste) appropriated them for use in their dolls' house. The bottles were full of yellow liquid, which they left in because it looked so pretty. It turned out that these were urine samples.

"We got Hail Columbia for that," says my mother. "But what did we know?"

*   *   *

My mother's family lived in a large white house near an apple orchard, in Nova Scotia. There was a barn and a carriage-house; in the kitchen there was a pantry. My mother can remember the days before commercial bakeries, when flour came in barrels and all the bread was made at home. She can remember the first radio broadcast she ever heard, which was a singing commercial about socks.

In this house there were many rooms. Although I have been there, although I have seen the house with my own eyes, I still don't know how many. Parts of it were closed off, or so it seemed; there were back staircases. Passages led elsewere. Five children lived in it, two parents, a hired man and a hired girl, whose names and faces kept changing. The structure of the house was hierarchical, with my grandfather at the top, but its secret life—the life of pie crusts, clean sheets, the box of rags in the linen closet, the loaves in the oven—was female. The house, and all the objects in it, crackled with static electricity; undertows washed through it, the air was heavy with things that were known but not spoken. Like a hollow log, a drum, a church, it amplified, so that conversations whispered in it sixty years ago can be half-heard even today.

In this house you had to stay at the table until you had eaten everything on your plate. " 'Think of the starving Armenians,' mother used to say," says my mother. "I didn't see how eating my bread crusts was going to help them out one jot."

It was in this house that I first saw a stalk of oats in a vase, each oat wrapped in the precious silver paper which had been carefully saved from a chocolate box. I thought it was the most wonderful thing I had ever seen, and began saving silver paper myself. But I never got around to wrapping the oats, and in any case I didn't know how. Like many other art forms of vanished civilizations, the techniques for this one have been lost and cannot quite be duplicated.

"We had oranges at Christmas," says my mother. "They came all the way from Florida; they were very expensive. That was the big treat: to find an orange in the toe of your stocking. It's funny to remember how good they tasted, now."

*   *   *

When she was sixteen, my mother had hair so long she could sit on it. Women were bobbing their hair by then; it was getting to be the twenties. My mother's hair was giving her headaches, she says, but my grandfather, who was very strict, forbade her to cut it. She waited until one Saturday when she knew he had an appointment with the dentist.

"In those days there was no freezing," says my mother. "The drill was worked with a foot pedal, and it went *grind, grind, grind*. The dentist himself had brown teeth: he chewed tobacco, and he would spit the tobacco juice into a spittoon while he was working on your teeth."

Here my mother, who is good mimic, imitates the sounds of the drill and the tobacco juice: *"Rrrrr! Rrrrr! Rrrrr! Phtt! Rrrrr! Rrrrr! Rrrrr! Phtt!* It was always sheer agony. It was a heaven-sent salvation when gas came in."

My mother went into the dentist's office, where my

grandfather was sitting in the chair, white with pain. She asked him if she could have her hair cut. He said she could do anything in tarnation as long as she would get out of there and stop pestering him.

"So I went out straight away and had it all chopped off," says my mother jauntily. "He was furious afterwards, but what could he do? He'd given his word."

My own hair reposes in a cardboard box in a steamer trunk in my mother's cellar, where I picture it becoming duller and more brittle with each passing year, and possibly moth-eaten; by now it will look like the faded wreaths of hair in Victorian funeral jewellery. Or it may have developed a dry mildew; inside its tissue-paper wrappings it glows faintly, in the darkness of the trunk. I suspect my mother has forgotten it's in there. It was cut off, much to my relief, when I was twelve and my sister was born. Before that it was in long curls: "Otherwise," says my mother, "it would have been just one big snarl." My mother combed it by winding it around her index finger every morning, but when she was in the hospital my father couldn't cope. "He couldn't get it around his stubby fingers," says my mother. My father looks down at his fingers. They are indeed broad compared with my mother's long elegant ones, which she calls boney. He smiles a pussy-cat smile.

So it was that my hair was sheared off. I sat in the chair in my first beauty parlour and watched it falling, like handfuls of cobwebs, down over my shoulders. From within it my head began to emerge, smaller, denser, my face more angular. I aged five years in fifteen minutes. I knew I could go home now and try out lipstick.

"Your father was upset about it," says my mother, with an air of collusion. She doesn't say this when my father is present. We smile, over the odd reactions of men to hair.

I used to think that my mother, in her earlier days, led a life of sustained hilarity and hair-raising adventure. (That was before I realized that she never put in the long stretches of uneventful time that must have made up much of her life: the stories were just the punctuation.) Horses ran away with her, men offered to, she was continually falling out of trees or off the ridgepoles of barns, or nearly being swept out to sea in rip-tides; or, in a more minor vein, suffering acute embarrassment in trying circumstances.

Churches were especially dangerous. "There was a guest preacher one Sunday," she says. "Of course we had to go to church every Sunday. There he was, in full career, preaching hellfire and damnation"—she pounds an invisible pulpit—"and his full set of false teeth shot out of his mouth—*phoop*!—just like that. Well, he didn't miss a stride. He stuck his hand up and caught them and popped them back into his mouth, and he kept right on, condemning us all to eternal torment. The pew was shaking! The tears were rolling down our faces, and the worst of it was, we were in the front pew, he was looking right at us. But of course we couldn't laugh out loud: father would have given us Hail Columbia."

Other people's parlours were booby-trapped for her; so were any and all formal social occasions. Zippers sprang apart on her clothes in strategic places, hats were unreliable. The shortage of real elastic during the war demanded constant alertness: underpants then had buttons, and were more taboo and therefore more significant than they are now. "There you would be," she says, "right on the street, and before you knew it they'd be down around your galoshes. The way to do was to step out of them with one foot, then kick them up with your other foot and whip them into your purse. I got quite good at it."

This particular story is told only to a few, but other

stories are for general consumption. When she tells them, my mother's face turns to rubber. She takes all the parts, adds the sound effects, waves her hands around in the air. Her eyes gleam, sometimes a little wickedly, for although my mother is sweet and old and a lady, she avoids being a sweet old lady. When people are in danger of mistaking her for one, she flings in something from left field; she refuses to be taken for granted.

But my mother cannot be duped into telling stories when she doesn't want to. If you prompt her, she becomes self-conscious and clams up. Or she will laugh and go out into the kitchen, and shortly after that you will hear the whir of the Mixmaster. Long ago I gave up attempting to make her do tricks at parties. In gatherings of unknown people, she merely listens intently, her head tilted a little, smiling a smile of glazed politeness. The secret is to wait and see what she will say afterwards.

*   *   *

At the age of seventeen my mother went to the Normal School in Truro. This name—"Normal School"—once held a certain magic for me. I thought it had something to do with learning to be normal, which possibly it did, because really it was where you used to go to learn how to be a schoolteacher. Subsequently my mother taught in a one-room school house not far from her home. She rode her horse to and from the school house every day, and saved up the money she earned and sent herself to university with it. My grandfather wouldn't send her: he said she was too frivolous-minded. She liked ice-skating and dancing too much for his taste.

At Normal School my mother boarded with a family that contained several sons in more or less the same age group as the girl boarders. They all ate around a huge dining-room table (which I pictured as being of dark wood, with heavy carved legs, but covered always with a white linen tablecloth), with the mother and father presiding, one at each end. I saw them both as large and pink and beaming.

"The boys were great jokers," says my mother. "They were always up to something." This was desirable in boys: to be great jokers, to be always up to something. My mother adds a key sentence: "We had a lot of fun."

Having fun has always been high on my mother's agenda. She has as much fun as possible, but what she means by this phrase cannot be understood without making an adjustment, an allowance for the great gulf across which this phrase must travel before it reaches us. It comes from another world, which, like the stars that originally sent out the light we see hesitating in the sky above us these nights, may be or is already gone. It is possible to reconstruct the facts of this world—the furniture, the clothing, the ornaments on the mantelpiece, the jugs and basins and even the chamber pots in the bedrooms, but not the emotions, not with the same exactness. So much that is now known and felt must be excluded.

This was a world in which guileless flirtation was possible, because there were many things that were simply not done by nice girls, and more girls were nice then. To fall from niceness was to fall not only from grace: sexual acts, by girls at any rate, had financial consequences. Life was more joyful and innocent then, and at the same time permeated with guilt and terror, or at least the occasions for them, on the most daily level. It was like the Japanese haiku: a limited form, rigid in its perimeters, within which an astonishing freedom was possible.

There are photographs of my mother at this time, taken with three or four other girls, linked arm in arm or with their arms thrown jestingly around each other's necks. Behind them, beyond the sea or the hills or whatever is in the background, is a world already hurtling towards ruin, unknown to them: the theory of relativity has been discovered, acid is accumulating at the roots of trees, the bull-frogs are doomed. But they smile with something that from this distance you could almost call gallantry, their right legs thrust forward in parody of a chorus line.

One of the great amusements for the girl boarders and the sons of the family was amateur theatre. Young people–they were called "young people"–frequently performed in plays which were put on in the church basement. My mother was a regular actor. (I have a stack of the scripts somewhere about the house, yellowing little booklets with my mother's parts checked in pencil. They are all comedies, and all impenetrable.) "There was no television then," says my mother. "You made your own fun."

For one of these plays a cat was required, and my mother and one of the sons borrowed the family cat. They put it into a canvas bag and drove to the rehearsal (there were cars by then), with my mother holding the cat on her lap. The cat, which must have been frightened, wet itself copiously, through the canvas bag and all over my mother's skirt. At the same time it made the most astonishingly bad smell.

"I was ready to sink through the floorboards," says my mother. "But what could I do? All I could do was sit there. In those days things like that"– she means cat pee, or pee of any sort–"were not mentioned." She means in mixed company.

I think of my mother driven through the night, skirts dripping, overcome with shame, the young man beside her staring straight ahead, pretending not to notice anything. They both feel that this act of unmentionable urination has been done, not by the cat, but by my mother. And so they continue, in a straight line that takes them over the Atlantic and past the curvature of the earth, out through the moon's orbit and into the dark reaches beyond.

Meanwhile, back on earth, my mother says: "I had to throw the skirt out. It was a good skirt, too, but nothing could get rid of the smell."

* * *

"I only heard your father swear once," says my mother. My mother herself never swears. When she comes to a place in a story in which swearing is called for, she says "dad-ratted" or "blankety-blank."

"It was when he mashed his thumb, when he was sinking the well, for the pump." This story, I know, takes place before I was born, up north, where there is nothing underneath the trees and their sheddings but sand and bedrock. The well was for a hand pump, which in turn was for the first of the many cabins and houses my parents built together. But since I witnessed later wells being sunk and later hand pumps being installed, I know how it's done. There's a pipe with a point at one end. You pound it into the ground with a sledge hammer, and as it goes down you screw other lengths of pipe onto it, until you hit drinkable water. To keep from ruining the thread on the top end, you hold a block of wood between the sledge hammer and the pipe. Better, you get someone else to hold it for you. This is how my father mashed his thumb: he was doing both the holding and the hammering himself.

"It swelled up like a radish," says my mother. "He had to make a hole in the nail, with his toad-sticker, to ease the pressure. The blood spurted out like pips from a lemon. Later on the whole nail turned purple and black and dropped off. Luckily he grew another one. They say you only get two chances. When he did it though, he turned the air blue for yards around. I didn't even know he knew those words. I don't know where he picked them up." She speaks as if these words are a minor contagious disease, like chicken pox.

20

Here my father looks modestly down at his plate. For him, there are two worlds: one containing ladies, in which you do not use certain expressions, and another one—consisting of logging camps and other haunts of his youth, and of gatherings of acceptable sorts of men—in which you do. To let the men's world slip over verbally into the ladies' would reveal you as a mannerless boor, but to carry the ladies' world over into the men's brands you a prig and maybe even a pansy. This is the word for it. All of this is well understood between them.

This story illustrates several things: that my father is no pansy, for one; and that my mother behaved properly by being suitably shocked. But my mother's eyes shine with delight while she tells this story. Secretly, she thinks it funny that my father got caught out, even if only once. The thumbnail that fell off is, in any significant way, long forgotten.

* * *

There are some stories which my mother does not tell when there are men present: never at dinner, never at parties. She tells them to women only, usually in the kitchen, when they or we are helping with the dishes or shelling peas, or taking the tops and tails off the string beans, or husking corn. She tells them in a lowered voice, without moving her hands around in the air, and they contain no sound effects. These are stories of romantic betrayals, unwanted pregnancies, illnesses of various horrible kinds, marital infidelities, mental breakdowns, tragic suicides, unpleasant lingering deaths. They are not rich in detail or embroidered with incident: they are stark and factual. The women, their own hands moving among the dirty dishes or the husks of vegetables, nod solemnly.

Some of these stories, it is understood, are not to be passed on to my father, because they would upset him. It is well known that women can deal with this sort of thing better than men can. Men are not to be told anything they might find too painful; the secret depths of human nature, the sordid physicalities, might overwhelm or damage them. For instance, men often faint at the sight of their own blood, to which they are not accustomed. For this reason you should never stand behind one in the line at the Red Cross donor clinic. Men, for some mysterious reason, find life more difficult than women do. (My mother believes this, despite the female bodies, trapped, diseased, disappearing, or abandoned, that litter her stories.) Men must be allowed to play in the sandbox of their choice, as happily as they can, without disturbance; otherwise they get cranky and won't eat their dinners. There are all kinds of things that men are simply not equipped to understand, so why expect it of them? Not everyone shares this belief about men; nevertheless, it has its uses.

"She dug up the shrubs from around the house," says my mother. This story is about a shattered marriage: serious business. My mother's eyes widen. The other women lean forward. "All she left him were the shower curtains." There is a collective sigh, an expelling of breath. My father enters the kitchen, wondering when the tea will be ready, and the women close ranks, turning to him their deceptive blankly smiling faces. Soon afterwards, my mother emerges from the kitchen, carrying the tea pot, and sets it down on the table in its ritual place.

*   *   *

"I remember the time we almost died," says my mother. Many of her stories begin this way. When she is in a certain mood, we are to understand that our lives have been preserved only by a series of amazing coincidences and strokes of luck; otherwise the entire family, individually or collectively, would be dead as doornails. These stories, in addition to producing adrenalin, serve to reinforce our sense of gratitude. There is the time we almost went over a waterfall, in a canoe, in a fog; the time we almost got caught in a forest fire; the time my father almost got squashed, before my mother's very eyes, by a ridgepole he was lifting into place; the time my brother almost got struck by a bolt of lightning, which went by him so close it knocked him down. "You could hear it sizzle," says my mother.

This is the story of the hay wagon. "Your father was driving," says my mother, "at the speed he usually goes." We read between the lines: *too fast*. "You kids were in the back." I can remember this day, so I can remember how old I was, how old my brother was. We were old enough to think it was funny to annoy my father by singing popular songs of a type he disliked, such as "Mockingbird Hill"; or perhaps we were imitating bag-pipe music by holding our noses and humming, while hitting our Adam's apples with the edges of our hands. When we became too irritating my father would say, "Pipe down." We weren't old enough to know that his irritation could be real: we thought it was part of the game.

"We were going down a steep hill," my mother con-tinues, "when a hay wagon pulled out right across the road, at the bottom. Your father put on the brakes, but nothing happened. The brakes were gone! I thought our last moment had come." Luckily the hay wagon contin-ued across the road, and we shot past it, missing it by at least a foot. "My heart was in my mouth," says my mother.

I didn't know until afterwards what had really hap-pened. I was in the back seat, making bagpipe music, oblivious. The scenery was the same as it always was on car trips: my parents' heads, seen from behind, sticking up above the front seat. My father had his hat on, the one he wore to keep things from falling off the trees into his hair. My mother's hand was placed lightly on the back of his neck.

"You had such an acute sense of smell when you were younger," says my mother.

Now we are on more dangerous ground: my mother's childhood is one thing, my own quite another. This is the moment at which I start rattling the silverware, or ask for another cup of tea. "You used to march into houses that were strange to you, and you would say in a loud voice, 'What's that funny smell?'" If there are guests present, they shift a little away from me, conscious of their own emanations, trying not to look at my nose.

"I used to be so embarrassed," says my mother absentmindedly. Then she shifts gears. "You were such an easy child. You used to get up at six in the morning and play by yourself in the play room, singing away...." There is a pause. A distant voice, mine, high and silvery, drifts over the space between us. "You used to talk a blue streak. Chatter, chatter, chatter, from morning to night." My mother sighs imperceptibly, as if wondering why I have become so silent, and gets up to poke the fire.

Hoping to change the subject, I ask whether or not the crocuses have come up yet, but she is not to be diverted. "I never had to spank you," she says. "A harsh word, and you would be completely reduced." She looks at me sideways; she isn't sure what I have turned into, or how. "There were just one or two times. Once, when I had to go out and I left your father in charge." (This may be the real point of the story: the inability of men to second-guess small children.) "I came back along the street, and there were you and your brother, throwing mud balls at an old man out of the upstairs window."

We both know whose idea this was. For my mother, the proper construction to be put on this event is that my brother was a hell-raiser and I was his shadow, "easily influenced," as my mother puts it. "You were just putty in his hands."

"Of course, I had to punish both of you equally," she says. Of course. I smile a forgiving smile. The real truth is that I was sneakier than my brother, and got caught less often. No front-line charges into enemy machine-gun nests for me, if they could be at all avoided. My own solitary acts of wickedness were devious and well concealed; it was only in partnership with my brother that I would throw caution to the winds.

"He could wind you around his little finger," says my mother. "Your father made each of you a toy box, and the rule was—" (my mother is good at the devising of rules) "—the rule was that neither of you could take the toys out of the other one's toy box without permission. Otherwise he would have got all your toys away from you. But he got them anyway, mind you. He used to talk you into playing house, and he would pretend to be the baby. Then he would pretend to cry, and when you asked what he wanted, he'd demand whatever it was out of your toy box that he wanted to play with at the moment. You always gave it to him."

I don't remember this, though I do remember staging World War Two on the living-room floor, with armies of stuffed bears and rabbits; but surely some primal patterns were laid down. Have these early toy-box experiences—and "toy box" itself, as a concept, reeks with implications—have they made me suspicious of men who wish to be mothered, yet susceptible to them at the same time? Have I been conditioned to believe that if I am not solicitous, if I am not forthcoming, if I am not a never-ending cornucopia of entertaining delights, they will take their collections of milk-bottle tops and their mangy one-eared teddy bears and go away into the woods by themselves to play snipers? Probably. What my mother thinks was merely cute may have been lethal.

But this is not her only story about my suckiness and gullibility. She follows up with the *coup de grâce*, the tale of the bunny-rabbit cookies.

"It was in Ottawa. I was invited to a government tea," says my mother, and this fact alone should signal an element of horror: my mother hated official functions, to which however she was obliged to go because she was the wife of a civil servant. "I had to drag you kids along; we couldn't afford a lot of babysitters in those days." The hostess had made a whole plateful of decorated cookies for whatever children might be present, and my mother proceeds to describe these: wonderful cookies shaped like bunny rabbits, with faces and clothes of coloured icing, little skirts for the little girl bunny rabbits, little pants for the little boy bunny rabbits.

"You chose one," says my mother. "You went off to a corner with it, by yourself. Mrs. X noticed you and went over. 'Aren't you going to eat your cookie?' she said. 'Oh, no,' you said. 'I'll just sit here and talk to it.' And there you sat, as happy as a clam. But someone had made the mistake of leaving the plate near your brother. When they looked again, there wasn't a single cookie left. He'd eaten every one. He was very sick that night, I can tell you."

Some of my mother's stories defy analysis. What is the moral of this one? That I was a simp is clear enough, but on the other hand it was my brother who got the stomach ache. Is it better to eat your food, in a straightforward materialistic way, and as much of it as possible, or go off into the corner and talk to it? This used to be a favourite of my mother's before I was married, when I would bring what my father referred to as "swains" home for dinner. Along with the dessert, out would come the bunny-rabbit cookie story, and I would cringe and twiddle my spoon while my mother forged blithely on with it. What were the swains supposed to make of it? Were my kindliness and essential femininity being trotted out for their inspection? Were they being told in a roundabout way that I was harmless, that they could expect to be talked to by me, but not devoured? Or was she, in some way, warning them off? Because there is something faintly crazed about my behaviour, some tinge of the kind of person who might be expected to leap up suddenly from the dinner table and shout, "Don't eat that! It's alive!"

There is, however, a difference between symbolism and anecdote. Listening to my mother, I sometimes remember this.

* * *

"In my next incarnation," my mother said once, "I'm going to be an archaeologist and go around digging things up." We were sitting on the bed that had once been my brother's, then mine, then my sister's; we were sorting out things from one of the trunks, deciding what could now be given away or thrown out. My mother believes that what you save from the past is mostly a matter of choice.

At that time something wasn't right in the family; someone wasn't happy. My mother was angry: her good cheer was not paying off.

This statement of hers startled me. It was the first time I'd ever heard my mother say that she might have wanted to be something other than what she was. I must have been thirty-five at the time, but it was still shocking and slightly offensive to me to learn that my mother might not have been totally contented fulfilling the role in which fate had cast her: that of being my mother. What thumb-suckers we all are, I thought, when it comes to mothers.

Shortly after this I became a mother myself, and this moment altered for me.

* * *

While she was combing my next-to-impossible hair, winding it around her long index finger, yanking out the snarls, my mother used to read me stories. Most of them are still in the house somewhere, but one has vanished. It may have been a library book. It was about a little girl who was so poor she had only one potato left for her supper, and while she was roasting it the potato got up and ran away. There was the usual chase, but I can't remember the ending: a significant lapse.

"That story was one of your favourites," says my mother. She is probably still under the impression that I identified with the little girl, with her hunger and her sense of loss; whereas in reality I identified with the potato.

Early influences are important. It took that one a while to come out; probably until after I went to university and started wearing black stockings and pulling my hair back into a bun, and having pretentions. Gloom set in. Our next-door neighbour, who was interested in wardrobes, tackled my mother: " 'If she would only *do* something about herself,' " my mother quotes, " 'she could be *quite attractive.*' "

"You always kept yourself busy," my mother says charitably, referring to this time. "You always had something cooking. Some project or other."

It is part of my mother's mythology that I am as cheerful and productive as she is, though she admits that these qualities may be occasionally and temporarily concealed. I wasn't allowed much angst around the house. I had to indulge it in the cellar, where my mother wouldn't come upon me brooding and suggest I should go out for a walk, to improve my circulation. This was her answer to any sign, however slight, of creeping despondency. There wasn't a lot that a brisk sprint through dead leaves, howling winds, or sleet couldn't cure.

It was, I knew, the *zeitgeist* that was afflicting me, and against it such simple remedies were powerless. Like smog I wafted through her days, dankness spreading out from around me. I read modern poetry and histories of Nazi atrocities, and took to drinking coffee. Off in the distance, my mother vacuumed around my feet while I sat in chairs, studying, with car rugs tucked around me, for suddenly I was always cold.

My mother has few stories to tell about these times. What I remember from them is the odd look I would sometimes catch in her eyes. It struck me, for the first time in my life, that my mother might be afraid of me. I could not even reassure her, because I was only dimly aware of the nature of her distress, but there must have been something going on in me that was beyond her: at any time I might open my mouth and out would come a language she had never heard before. I had become a visitant from outer space, a time-traveller come back from the future, bearing news of a great disaster.

HURRICANE HAZEL

The summer I was fourteen, we lived in a one-room cabin, on a hundred acres of back-concession scrub farmland. The cabin was surrounded by a stand of tall old maples, which had been left there when the land was cut over, and the light sifted down in shafts, like those in pictures I had seen in Sunday school, much earlier, of knights looking for the Holy Grail, helmets off, eyes rolled up purely. Probably these trees were the reason my parents had bought the land: if they hadn't, someone else would have bought it and sold off the maples. This was the kind of thing my parents were in the habit of doing.

The cabin was of squared timber. It hadn't been built there originally, but had been moved from some other location by the people who had owned it before us, two high-school teachers who were interested in antiques. The logs had been numbered, then dismantled and put back together in the original order, and the cracks had been re-chinked with white cement, which was already beginning to fall out in places; so was the putty on the small panes of the windows. I knew this because one of my first jobs had been to wash them. I did this grudgingly, as I did most jobs around the house at the time.

We slept on one side of the room. The sleeping areas were divided off by parachutes, which my father had bought at the war-surplus store, where he often bought things: khaki-coloured pants with pockets on the knees, knife, fork, and spoon sets which locked together and snapped apart and were impossible to eat with, rain capes with camouflage markings on them, a jungle hammock with mosquito-netting sides that smelled like the inside of a work sock and gave you a kink in the back, despite which my brother and I used to compete for the privilege of sleeping in it. The parachutes had been cut open and were hung like curtains from lengths of thick wire strung from wall to wall. The parachutes inside the house were dark green, but there was a smaller orange one set up outside, like a tent, for my three-year-old sister to play in.

I had the cubicle in the southeast corner. I slept there on a narrow bed with wire coil springs that squeaked whenever I turned over. On the other side of the cabin, the living side, there was a table coated with ruined varnish and a couple of much-painted chairs, the paint now cracked like a dried mud flat so that you could see what colours had been used before. There was a dresser with plates in it, which smelled even mustier than the rest of the things in the cabin, and a couple of rocking chairs, which didn't work too well on the uneven boards of the floor. All this furniture had been in the cabin when we bought it; perhaps it was the schoolteachers' idea of pioneer décor.

There was also a sort of counter where my mother washed the dishes and kept the primus stove she cooked on when it was raining. The rest of the time she cooked outdoors, on a fireplace with a grate of iron rods. When we ate outside we didn't use chairs; instead we sat on rounds of logs, because the ground itself was damp. The cabin was in a river valley; at night there was heavy dew, and the heat of the morning sunlight made an almost visible steam.

My father had moved us into the cabin early in the

summer. Then he'd taken off for the forests on the north shore of the St. Lawrence, where he was doing some exploration for a pulp-and-paper company. All the time we were going through our daily routine, which revolved mainly around mealtimes and what we would eat at them, he was flying in bush planes into valleys with sides so steep the pilot had to cut the engine to get down into them, or trudging over portages past great rocky outcrops, or almost upsetting in rapids. For two weeks he was trapped by a forest fire which encircled him on all sides, and was saved only by torrential rains, during which he sat in his tent and toasted his extra socks at the fire, like wieners, to get them dry. These were the kinds of stories we heard after he came back.

My father made sure before he went that we had a supply of split and stacked wood and enough staples and tinned goods to keep us going. When we needed other things, such as milk and butter, I was sent on foot to the nearest store, which was a mile and a half away, at the top of an almost perpendicular hill which, much later, got turned into a ski resort. At that time there was only a dirt road, in the middle of what I thought of as nowhere, which let loose clouds of dust every time a car went past. Sometimes the cars would honk, and I would pretend not to notice.

The woman at the store, who was fat and always damp, was curious about us; she would ask how my mother was getting along. Didn't she mind it, all alone in that tumbledown place with no proper stove and no man around? She put the two things on the same level. I resented that kind of prying, but I was at the age when anybody's opinion mattered to me, and I could see that she thought my mother was strange.

If my mother had any reservations about being left alone on a remote farm with a three-year-old, no telephone, no car, no electricity, and only me for help, she didn't state them. She had been in such situations before, and by that time she must have been used to them. Whatever was going on she treated as normal; in the middle of crises, such as cars stuck up to their axles in mud, she would suggest we sing a song.

That summer she probably missed my father, though she would never say so; conversations in our family were not about feelings. Sometimes, in the evenings, she would write letters, though she claimed she could never think of what to say. During the days, when she wasn't cooking or washing the dishes, she did small tasks which could be interrupted at any time. She would cut the grass, even though the irregular plot in front of the house was over-grown with weeds and nothing would make it look any more like a lawn; or she would pick up the fallen branches under the maple trees.

I looked after my little sister for part of the mornings: that was one of my jobs. At these times my mother would sometimes drag a rocking chair out onto the bumpy grass and read books, novels of historical times or accounts of archaeological expeditions. If I came up behind her and spoke to her while she was reading, she would scream. When it was sunny she would put on shorts, which she would never wear when other people were around. She thought she had bony knees; this was the only thing about her personal appearance that she showed much awareness about. For the most part she was indifferent to clothes. She wanted them to cover what they were supposed to cover and to stay in one piece, and that was all she expected from them.

When I wasn't taking care of my sister, I would go off by myself. I would climb one of the maples, which was out of sight of the house and had a comfortable fork in it, and read *Wuthering Heights*; or I would walk along the old logging road, now grown up in saplings. I knew my way around in the weedy and brambly jungle back there, and I'd been across the river to the open field on the other side, where the next-door farmer was allowed to graze his cows, to keep down the thistles and burdock. This was where I'd found what I thought was the pioneers' house, the real one, though it was nothing now but a square depression surrounded by grass-covered ridges. The first year, this man had planted a bushel of peas, and he'd harvested a bushel. We knew this from the schoolteachers, who looked up records.

If my brother had made this discovery, he would have drawn a map of it. He would have drawn a map of the whole area, with everything neatly labelled. I didn't even attempt this; instead, I merely wandered around, picking raspberries and thimbleberries, or sunning myself in the tall weeds, surrounded by the smell of milkweed and daisies and crushed leaves, made dizzy by the sun and the light reflected from the white pages of my book, with grasshoppers landing on me and leaving traces of their brown spit.

Towards my mother I was surly, though by myself I was lazy and aimless. It was hard even to walk through the grass, and lifting my hand to brush away the grasshoppers was an effort. I seemed always to be half asleep. I told myself that I wanted to be doing something; by that I meant something that would earn money, elsewhere. I wanted a summer job, but I was too young for one.

My brother had a job. He was two years older than I was, and now he was a Junior Ranger, cutting brush by the sides of highways somewhere in northern Ontario, living in tents with a batch of other sixteen-year-old boys. This was his first summer away. I resented his absence and envied him, but I also looked for his letters every day. The mail was delivered by a woman who lived on a nearby farm; she drove it around in her own car. When there was something for us she would toot her horn, and I would walk out to the dusty galvanized mailbox that stood on a post beside our gate.

My brother wrote letters to my mother as well as to me. Those to her were informative, descriptive, factual. He said what he was doing, what they ate, where they did their laundry. He said that the town near their camp had a main street that was held up only by the telephone wires. My mother was pleased by these letters, and read them out loud to me.

I did not read my brother's letters out loud to her. They were private, and filled with the sort of hilarious and vulgar commentary that we often indulged in when we were alone. To other people we seemed grave and attentive, but by ourselves we made fun of things relentlessly, outdoing each other with what we considered to be revolting details. My brother's letters were illustrated with drawings of his tent-mates, showing them with many-legged bugs jumping around on their heads, with spots on their faces, with wavy lines indicating smelliness radiating from their feet, with apple cores in the beards they were all attempting to grow. He included unsavoury details of their personal habits, such as snoring. I took these letters straight from the mailbox to the maple tree, where I read them over several times. Then I smuggled them into the cabin under my T-shirt and hid them under my bed.

I got other letters too, from my boyfriend, whose name was Buddy. My brother used a fountain pen; Buddy's letters were in blue ball-point, the kind that splotched, leaving greasy blobs that came off on my fingers. They contained ponderous compliments, like those made by other people's uncles. Many words were enclosed by quotation marks; others were underlined. There were no pictures.

I liked getting these letters from Buddy, but also they embarrassed me. The trouble was that I knew what my brother would say about Buddy, partly because he had already said some of it. He spoke as if both he and I took it for granted that I would soon be getting rid of Buddy, as if Buddy were a stray dog it would be my duty to send to the Humane Society if the owner could not be found. Even Buddy's name, my brother said, was like a dog's. He said I should call Buddy "Pal" or "Sport" and teach him to fetch.

I found my brother's way of speaking about Buddy both funny and cruel: funny because it was in some ways accurate, cruel for the same reason. It was true that there was something dog-like about Buddy: the affability, the dumb faithfulness about the eyes, the dutiful way he plodded through the rituals of dating. He was the kind of boy (though I never knew this with certainty, because I never saw it) who would help his mother carry in the groceries without being asked, not because he felt like it but simply because it was prescribed. He said things like, "That's the way the cookie crumbles," and when he said this I had the feeling he would still be saying it forty years later.

Buddy was a lot older than I was. He was eighteen, almost nineteen, and he'd quit school long ago to work at a garage. He had his own car, a third-hand Dodge, which he kept spotlessly clean and shining. He smoked and drank beer, though he drank the beer only when he wasn't out with me but was with other boys his own age. He would mention how many bottles he had drunk in an offhand way, as if disclaiming praise.

He made me anxious, because I didn't know how to talk to him. Our phone conversations consisted mostly of pauses and monosyllables, though they went on a long time; which was infuriating to my father, who would walk past me in the hall, snapping his first two fingers together like a pair of scissors, meaning I was to cut it short. But cutting short a conversation with Buddy was like trying to divide water, because Buddy's conversations had no shape, and I couldn't give them a shape myself. I hadn't yet learned any of those stratagems girls were supposed to use on men. I didn't know how to ask leading questions, or how to lie about certain kinds of things, which I was later to call being tactful. So mostly I said nothing, which didn't seem to bother Buddy at all.

I knew enough to realize, however, that it was a bad tactic to appear too smart. But if I had chosen to show off, Buddy might not have minded: he was the kind of boy for whom cleverness was female. Maybe he would have liked a controlled display of it, as if it were a special kind of pie or a piece of well-done embroidery. But I never figured out what Buddy really wanted; I never figured out why Buddy was going out with me in the first place. Possibly it was because I was there. Buddy's world, I gradually discovered, was much less alterable than mine: it contained a long list of things that could never be changed or fixed.

All of this started at the beginning of May, when I was in grade ten. I was two or three years younger than most of the others in my class, because at that time they still believed in skipping you ahead if you could do the work. The year before, when I'd entered high school, I had been twelve, which was a liability when other people were fifteen. I rode my bicycle to school when other girls in my class were walking, slowly, langourously, holding their notebooks up against their bodies to protect and display their breasts. I had no breasts; I could still wear things

I'd worn when I was eleven. I took to sewing my own clothes, out of patterns I bought at Eaton's. The clothes never came out looking like the pictures on the pattern envelopes; also they were too big. I must have been making them the size I wanted to be. My mother told me these clothes looked very nice on me, which was untrue and no help at all. I felt like a flat-chested midget, surrounded as I was by girls who were already oily and glandular, who shaved their legs and put pink medicated make-up on their pimples and fainted interestingly during gym, whose flesh was sleek and plumped-out and faintly shining, as if it had been injected under the skin with cream.

The boys were even more alarming. Some of them, the ones who were doing grade nine for the second time, wore leather jackets and were thought to have bicycle chains in their lockers. A few of them were high-voiced and spindly, but these of course I ignored. I knew the difference between someone who was a drip or a pill, on the one hand, and cute or a dream on the other. Buddy wasn't a dream, but he was cute, and that counted for a lot. Once I started going out with Buddy, I found I could pass for normal. I was now included in the kinds of conversations girls had in the washroom while they were putting on their lipstick. I was now teased.

Despite this, I knew that Buddy was a kind of accident: I hadn't come by him honestly. He had been handed over to me by Trish, who had come up to me out of nowhere and asked me to go out with her and her boyfriend Charlie and Charlie's cousin. Trish had a large mouth and prominent teeth and long sandy hair, which she tied back in a pony tail. She wore fuzzy pink sweaters and was a cheerleader, though not the best one. If she hadn't been going steady with Charlie, she would have had a reputation, because of the way she laughed and wiggled; as it was, she was safe enough for the time being. Trish told me I would like Buddy because he was so cute. She also mentioned that he had a car; Charlie didn't have a car. It's likely that I was put into Buddy's life by Trish so that Trish and Charlie could neck in the back seat of Buddy's car at drive-in movies, but I doubt that Buddy knew this. Neither did I, at the time.

We always had to go to the early show—a source of grumbling from Trish and Charlie—because I wasn't allowed to stay out past eleven. My father didn't object to my having boyfriends, as such, but he wanted them to be prompt in their pick-up and delivery. He didn't see why they had to moon around outside the front door when they were dropping me off. Buddy wasn't as bad in this respect as some of the later ones, in my father's opinion. With those, I got into the habit of coming in after the deadline, and my father would sit me down and explain very patiently that if I was on my way to catch a train and I was late for it, the train would go without me, and that was why I should always be in on time. This cut no ice with me at all, since, as I would point out, our house wasn't a train. It must have been then that I began to lose faith in reasonable argument as the sole measure of truth. My mother's rationale for promptness was more understandable: if I wasn't home on time, she would think I had been in a car accident. We knew without admitting it that sex was the hidden agenda at these discussions, more hidden for my father than for my mother: she knew about cars and accidents.

At the drive-in Buddy and Charlie would buy popcorn and Cokes, and we would all munch in unison as the pale shadowy figures materialized on the screen, bluish in the diminishing light. By the time the popcorn was gone it would be dark. There would be rustlings, creakings, suppressed moans from the back seat, which Buddy and I would pretend to ignore. Buddy would smoke a few cigarettes, one arm around my shoulders. After that we would neck, decorously enough compared with what was going on behind us.

Buddy's mouth was soft, his body large and comforting. I didn't know what I was supposed to feel during these sessions. Whatever I did feel was not very erotic, though it wasn't unpleasant either. It was more like being hugged by a friendly Newfoundland dog or an animated quilt than anything else. I kept my knees pressed together and my arms around his back. Sooner or later Buddy would attempt to move his hands around to the front, but I knew I was supposed to stop him, so I did. Judging from his reaction, which was resigned but good-natured, this was the correct thing to do, though he would always try again the next week.

It occurred to me very much later that Trish had selected me, not despite the fact that I was younger and less experienced than she was, but because of it. She needed a chaperone. Charlie was thinner than Buddy, better-looking, more intense; he got drunk sometimes, said Trish, with an already matronly shake of her head. Buddy was seen as solid, dependable, and a little slow, and so perhaps was I.

After I had been going out with Buddy for a month or so, my brother decided it would be in my own best interests to learn Greek. By that he meant he would teach it to me whether I liked it or not. In the past he had taught me many things, some of which I had wanted to know: how to read, how to shoot with a bow, how to skip flat rocks, how to swim, how to play chess, how to aim a rifle, how to paddle a canoe and scale and gut a fish. I hadn't learned many of them very well, except the reading. He had also taught me how to swear, sneak out of bedroom windows at night, make horrible smells with

41

chemicals, and burp at will. His manner, whatever the subject, was always benignly but somewhat distantly pedagogical, as if I were a whole classroom by myself.

The Greek was something he himself was learning; he was two grades ahead of me and was at a different high school, one that was only for boys. He started me with the alphabet. As usual, I didn't learn fast enough for him, so he began leaving notes about the house, with Greek letters substituted for the letters of the English words. I would find one in the bathtub when I was about to take a bath before going out with Buddy, set it aside for later, turn on the tap and find myself drenched by the shower. (*Turn off the shower*, the note would read when translated.) Or there would be a message taped to the closed door of my room, which would turn out to be a warning about what would fall on me—a wet towel, a clump of cooked spaghetti—when I opened it. Or one on my dresser would announce a Frenched bed or inform me that my alarm clock was set to go off at 3 A.M. I didn't ever learn much real Greek, but I did learn to transpose quickly. It was by such ruses, perhaps, that my brother was seeking to head me off, delay my departure from the world he still inhabited, a world in which hydrogen sulphide and chess gambits were still more interesting than sex, and Buddy, and the Buddies to come, were still safely and merely ridiculous.

My brother and Buddy existed on different layers altogether. My brother, for instance, was neither cute nor a pill. Instead he had the preternatural good looks associated with English schoolboys, the kind who turned out to be pyromaniacs in films of the sixties, or with posters of soldiers painted at the time of World War One; he looked as if he ought to have green skin and slightly pointed ears, as if his name should have been Nemo, or something like it; as if he could see through you. All of these things I thought later; at the time he was just my brother, and I didn't have any ideas about how he looked. He had a maroon sweater with holes in the elbows, which my mother kept trying to replace or throw out, but she was never successful. He took her lack of interest in clothes one step further.

Whenever I started to talk like what he thought of as a teenager, whenever I mentioned sock hops or the hit parade, or anything remotely similar, my brother would quote passages out of the blackhead-remover ads in his old comic books, the ones he'd collected when he was ten or eleven: "Mary never knew why she was not POPULAR, until . . . Someone should tell her! Mary, NOW there's something you can do about those UGLY BLACKHEADS! *Later* . . . Mary, I'd like to ask you to the dance. (*Thinks:* Now that Mary's got rid of those UGLY BLACKHEADS, she's the most POPULAR girl in the class.)" I knew that if I ever became the most popular girl in the class, which was not likely, I would get no points at all from my brother.

When I told Buddy I would be away for the summer, he thought I was "going to the cottage," which was what a lot of people in Toronto did; those who had cottages, that is. What he had in mind was something like Lake Simcoe, where you could ride around in fast motorboats and maybe go water-skiing, and where there would be a drive-in. He thought there would be other boys around; he said I would go out with them and forget all about him, but he said it as a joke.

I was vague about where I was actually going. Buddy and I hadn't talked about our families much; it wouldn't be easy to explain to him my parents' preferences for solitude and outhouses and other odd things. When he said he would come up and visit me, I told him it was too far away, too difficult to find. But I couldn't refuse to give him the address, and his letters arrived faithfully every week, smeared and blobby, the handwriting round and laborious and child-like. Buddy pressed so hard the pen sometimes went through, and if I closed my eyes and ran my fingers over the paper I could feel the letters engraved on the page like braille.

I answered Buddy's first letter sitting at the uneven table with its cracked geological surface. The air was damp and warm; the pad of lined paper I was writing on was sticking to the tacky varnish. My mother was doing the dishes, in the enamel dishpan, by the light of one of the oil lamps. Usually I helped her, but ever since Buddy had appeared on the scene she'd been letting me off more frequently, as if she felt I needed the energy for other things. I had the second oil lamp, turned up as high as it would go without smoking. From behind the green parachute curtain I could hear the light breathing of my sister.

Dear Buddy, I wrote, and stopped. Writing his name embarrassed me. When you saw it on a blank sheet of paper like that, it seemed a strange thing to call someone. Buddy's name bore no relation to what I could really remember of him, which was mostly the smell of his freshly washed T-shirts, mixed with the smell of cigarette smoke and Old Spice aftershave. *Buddy*. As a word, it reminded me of *pudding*. I could feel under my hand the little roll of fat at the back of his neck, hardly noticeable now, but it would get larger, later, when he was not even that much older.

My mother's back was towards me but I felt as if she were watching me anyway; or listening, perhaps, to the absence of sound, because I wasn't writing. I couldn't think of what to say to Buddy. I could describe what I'd been doing, but as soon as I began I saw how hopeless this would be.

In the morning I'd made a village out of sand, down on

the one small available sandbar, to amuse my sister. I was good at these villages. Each house had stone windows; the roads were paved with stone also, and trees and flowers grew in the gardens, which were surrounded by hedges of moss. When the villages were finished, my sister would play with them, running her toy cars along the roads and moving the stick people I'd made for her, in effect ruining them, which annoyed me.

When I could get away, I'd waded down the river by myself, to be out of range. There was a seam of clay I already knew about, and I'd gouged a chunk out of it and spent some time making it into beads, leaving them on a stump in the sun to harden. Some of them were in the shape of skulls, and I intended to paint these later and string them into a necklace. I had some notion that they would form part of a costume for Hallowe'en, though at the same time I knew I was already too old for this.

Then I'd walked back along the river bank, climbing over the tangles of fallen trees that blocked the way, scratching my bare legs on the brambles. I'd picked a few flowers, as a peace offering to my mother, who must have known I'd deserted her on purpose. These were now wilting in a jam jar on the dresser: bladder campion, jewelweed, Queen Anne's Lace. In our family you were supposed to know the names of the things you picked and put in jars.

Nothing I did seemed normal in the light of Buddy; spelled out, my activities looked childish or absurd. What did other girls the age people thought I was do when they weren't with boys? They talked on the telephone, they listened to records; wasn't that it? They went to movies, they washed their hair. But they didn't wash their hair by standing up to their knees in an ice-cold river and pouring water over their heads from an enamel basin. I didn't wish to appear eccentric to Buddy; I wished to disguise myself. This had been easier in the city, where we lived in a more ordinary way: such things as my parents' refusal to buy a television set and sit in front of it eating their dinners off fold-up trays, and their failure to acquire an indoor clothes dryer, were minor digressions that took place behind the scenes.

In the end I wrote to Buddy about the weather, and said I missed him and hoped I would see him soon. After studying the blotchy X's and O's, much underlined, which came after Buddy's signature, I imitated them. I sealed this forgery and addressed it, and the next morning I walked out to the main road and put it in our loaf-shaped mailbox, raising the little flag to show there was a letter.

Buddy arrived unannounced one Sunday morning in August, after we had done the dishes. I don't know how he found out where we lived. He must have asked at the crossroads where there were a few houses, a gas station, and a general store with Coca-Cola ads on the screen door and a post office at the back. The people there would have been able to help Buddy decipher the rural-route number; probably they knew anyway exactly where we were.

My mother was in her shorts, in front of the house, cutting the grass and weeds with a small scythe. I was carrying a pail of water up the slippery and decaying wooden steps from the river. I knew that when I got to the top of the steps my mother would ask me what I wanted for lunch, which would drive me mad with irritation. I never knew what I wanted for lunch, and if I did know there was never any of it. It didn't occur to me then that my mother was even more bored with mealtimes than I was, since she had to do the actual cooking, or that her question might have been a request for help.

Then we heard a noise, a roaring motor noise, exaggerated but muffled too, like a gas lawnmower inside a tin garage. We both stopped dead in our tracks and looked at one another; we had a way of doing that whenever we heard any machine-made sound out on the main road. We believed, I think, that nobody knew we were there. The good part of this was that nobody would come in, but the bad part was that somebody might, thinking our place uninhabited, and the sort of people who would try it would be the sort we would least want to see.

The noise stopped for a few minutes; then it started up again, louder this time. It was coming in, along our road. My mother dropped her scythe and ran into the house. I knew she was going to change out of her shorts. I continued stolidly up the steps, carrying the pail of water. If I'd known it was Buddy I would have brushed my hair and put on lipstick.

When I saw Buddy's car, I was surprised and almost horrified. I felt I had been caught out. What would Buddy think of the decaying cabin, the parachute curtains, the decrepit furniture, the jam jar with its drooping flowers? My first idea was to keep him out of the house, at least. I went to meet the car, which was floundering over the road towards me. I was conscious of the dead leaves and dirt sticking to my wet bare feet.

Buddy got out of the car and looked up at the trees. Charlie and Trish, who were in the back seat, got out too. They gazed around, but after one quick look they gave no indication that they thought this place where I was living was hardly what they had expected; except that they talked too loudly. I knew though that I was on the defensive.

Buddy's car had a big hole in the muffler, which he hadn't had time to fix yet, and Charlie and Trish were full of stories about the annoyed looks people in the back-roads villages had given them as they'd roared through. Buddy was more reserved, almost shy. "You got my letter, eh?" he said, but I hadn't, not the one that announced this visit. That letter arrived several days later, filled with a wistful loneliness it would have been handy to have known about in advance.

Charlie and Trish and Buddy wanted to go on a picnic. It was their idea that we would drive over to Pike Lake, about fifteen miles away, where there was a public beach. They thought we could go swimming. My mother had come out by this time. Now that she had her slacks on she was behaving as if everything was under control. She agreed to this plan; she knew there was nothing for them to do around our place. She didn't seem to mind my going off with Buddy for a whole day, because we would be back before dark.

The three of them stood around the car; my mother tried to make conversation with them while I ran to the cabin to get my swimsuit and a towel. Trish already had her swimsuit on; I'd seen the top of it under her shirt. Maybe there would be no place to change. This was the kind of thing you couldn't ask about without feeling like a fool, so I changed in my cubicle of parachute silk. My suit was left over from last year; it was red, and a little too small.

My mother, who didn't usually give instructions, told Buddy to drive carefully; probably because the noise made his car sound a lot more dangerous than it was. When he started up it was like a rocket taking off, and it was even worse inside. I sat in the front seat beside Buddy. All the windows were rolled down, and when we reached the paved highway Buddy stuck his left elbow out the window. He held the steering wheel with one hand, and with the other he reached across the seat and took hold of my hand. He wanted me to move over so I was next to him and he could put his arm around me, but I was nervous about the driving. He gave me a reproachful look and put his hand back on the wheel.

I had seen road signs pointing to Pike Lake before but I had never actually been there. It turned out to be small and round, with flattish countryside around it. The public beach was crowded, because it was a weekend: teenagers in groups and young couples with children mostly. Some people had portable radios. Trish and I changed behind the car, even though we were only taking off our outer clothes to reveal our bathing suits, which everybody was going to see anyway. While we were doing this, Trish told me that she and Charlie were now secretly engaged. They were going to get married as soon as she was old enough. No one was supposed to know, except Buddy of course, and me. She said her parents would have kittens if they found out. I promised not to tell; at the same time, I felt a cold finger travelling down my spine. When we came out from behind the car, Buddy and Charlie were already standing up to their ankles in the water, the sun reflecting from their white backs.

The beach was dusty and hot, with trash from picnickers left here and there about it: paper plates showing half-moons above the sand, dented paper cups, bottles. Part of a hog-dog wiener floated near where we waded in, pallid, greyish-pink, lost-looking. The lake was shallow and weedy, the water the temperature of cooling soup. The bottom was of sand so fine-grained it was almost mud; I expected leeches in it, and clams, which would probably be dead, because of the warmth. I swam out into it anyway. Trish was screaming because she had walked into some water weeds; then she was splashing Charlie I felt that I ought to be doing these things too, and that Buddy would note the omission. But instead I floated on my back in the lukewarm water, squinting up at the cloudless sky, which was depthless and hot blue and had things like microbes drifting across it, which I knew were the rods and cones in my eyeballs. I had skipped ahead in the health book; I even knew what a zygote was. In a while Buddy swam out to join me and spurted water at me out of his mouth, grinning.

After that we swam back to the beach and lay down on Trish's over-sized pink beach towel, which had a picture of a mermaid tossing a bubble on it. I felt sticky, as if the water had left a film on me. Trish and Charlie were nowhere to be seen; at last I spotted them, walking hand in hand near the water at the far end of the beach. Buddy wanted me to rub some suntan lotion onto him. He wasn't tanned at all, except for his face and his hands and forearms, and I remembered that he worked all week and didn't have time to lie around in the sun the way I did. The skin of his back was soft and slightly loose over the muscles, like a sweater or a puppy's neck.

When I lay back down beside him, Buddy took hold of my hand, even though it was greasy with the suntan lotion. "How about Charlie, eh?" he said, shaking his head in mock disapproval, as if Charlie had been naughty or stupid. He didn't say Charlie and Trish. He put his arm over me and started to kiss me, right on the beach, in the full sunlight, in front of everyone. I pulled back.

"There's people watching," I said.

"Want me to put the towel over your head?" he said.

I sat up, brushing sand off me and tugging up the front of my bathing suit. I brushed some sand off Buddy too: his stuck worse because of the lotion. My back felt parched and I was dizzy from the heat and brightness. Later, I knew, I would get a headache.

"Where's the lunch?" I said.

"Who's hungry?" he said. "Not for food, anyways." But he didn't seem annoyed. Maybe this was the way I was supposed to behave.

I walked to the car and got out the lunch, which was in a brown paper bag, and we sat on Trish's towel and ate egg-salad sandwiches and drank warm fizzy Coke, in silence. When we had finished, I said I wanted to go and sit under a tree. Buddy came with me, bringing the towel. He shook it before we sat down.

"You don't want ants in your pants," he said. He lit a cigarette and smoked half of it, leaning against the tree trunk—an elm, I noticed—and looking at me in an odd way, as if he was making up his mind about something. Then he said, "I want you to have something." His voice was offhand, affable, the way it usually was; his eyes weren't. On the whole he looked frightened. He undid the silver bracelet from his wrist. It had always been there, and I knew what was written on it: *Buddy*, engraved in flowing script. It was an imitation army I.D. tag; a lot of the boys wore them.

"My identity bracelet," he said.

"Oh," I said as he slid it over my hand, which now, I could tell, smelled of onions. I ran my fingers over Buddy's silver name as if admiring it. I had no thought of refusing it; that would have been impossible, because I would never have been able to explain what was wrong with taking it. Also I felt that Buddy had something on me: that, now he had accidentally seen something about me that was real, he knew too much about my deviations from the norm. I felt I had to correct that somehow. It occurred to me, years later, that many women probably had become engaged and even married this way.

It was years later too that I realized Buddy had used the wrong word: it wasn't an identity bracelet, it was an identification bracelet. The difference escaped me at the time. But maybe it was the right word after all, and what Buddy was handing over to me was his identity, some key part of himself that I was expected to keep for him and watch over.

Another interpretation has since become possible: that Buddy was putting his name on me, like a *Reserved* sign or an ownership label, or a tattoo on a cow's ear, or a brand. But at the time nobody thought that way. Everyone knew that getting a boy's I.D. bracelet was a privilege, not a degradation, and this is how Trish greeted it when she came back from her walk with Charlie. She spotted the transfer instantly.

"Let's *see*," she said, as if she hadn't seen this ornament of Buddy's many times before, and I had to hold out my wrist for her to admire, while Buddy looked sheepishly on.

When I was back at the log house, I took off Buddy's identification bracelet and hid it under the bed. I was embarrassed by it, though the reason I gave myself was that I didn't want it to get lost. I put it on again in September though, when I went back to the city and back to school. It was the equivalent of a white fur sweater-collar, the kind with pom-poms. Buddy, among other things, was something to wear.

I was in grade eleven now, and studying Ancient Egypt and *The Mill on the Floss*. I was on the volleyball team; I sang in the choir. Buddy was still working at the garage, and shortly after school began he got a hernia, from lifting something too heavy. I didn't know what a hernia was. I thought it might be something sexual, but at the same time it had the sound of something that happened to old men, not to someone as young as Buddy. I looked it up in our medical book. When my brother heard about Buddy's hernia, he sniggered in an irritating way and said it was the kind of thing you could expect from Buddy.

Buddy was in a hospital for a couple of days. After that I went to visit him at home, because he wanted me to. I felt I should take him something; not flowers though. So I took him some peanut-butter cookies, baked by my mother. I knew, if the subject came up, that I would lie and say I had made them myself.

This was the first time I had ever been to Buddy's house. I hadn't even known where he lived; I hadn't thought of him as having a house at all or living anywhere in particular. I had to get there by bus and streetcar, since of course Buddy couldn't drive me.

It was Indian summer; the air was thick and damp, though there was a breeze that helped some. I walked along the street, which was lined with narrow, two-storey row houses, the kind that would much later be renovated and become fashionable, though at that time they were considered merely old-fashioned and inconvenient. It was a Saturday afternoon, and a couple of the men were mowing their cramped lawns, one of them in his undershirt.

The front door of Buddy's house was wide open; only the screen door was closed. I rang the doorbell; when nothing happened, I went in. There was a note, in Buddy's blotchy blue ball-point writing, lying on the floor: COME ON UP, it said. It must have fallen down from where it had been taped to the inside of the door.

The hallway had faded pink rose-trellis paper; the house smelled faintly of humid wood, polish, rugs in summer. I peered into the living room as I went towards the stairs: there was too much furniture in it and the curtains were drawn, but it was immaculately clean. I could tell that Buddy's mother had different ideas about housework than my mother had. Nobody seemed to be home, and I wondered if Buddy had arranged it this way on purpose, so I wouldn't run into his mother.

I climbed the stairs; in the mirror at the top I was coming to meet myself. In the dim light I seemed older, my flesh plumped and flushed by the heat, my eyes in shadow.

"Is that you?" Buddy called to me. He was in the front bedroom, lying propped up in a bed that was much too large for the room. The bed was of chocolate-coloured varnished wood, the head and foot carved; it was this bed, huge, outmoded, ceremonial, that made me more nervous than anything else in the room, including Buddy. The window was open, and the white lace-edged curtains—of a kind my mother never would have considered, because of the way they would have to be bleached, starched, and ironed—shifted a little in the air. The sound of the lawnmowers came in through the window.

I hesitated in the doorway, smiled, went in. Buddy was wearing a white T-shirt, and had just the sheet over him, pulled up to his waist. He looked softer, shorter, a little shrunken. He smiled back at me and held out his hand.

"I brought you some cookies," I said. We were both shy, because of the silence and emptiness. I took hold of his hand and he pulled me gently towards him. The bed was so high that I had to climb half onto it. I set the bag of cookies down beside him and put my arms around his neck. His skin smelled of cigarette smoke and soap, and his hair was neatly combed and still a little wet. His mouth tasted of toothpaste. I thought of him hobbling around, in pain maybe, getting ready for me. I had never thought a great deal about boys getting themselves ready for girls, cleaning themselves, looking at themselves in bathroom mirrors, waiting, being anxious, wanting to please. I realized now that they did this, that it wasn't only the other way around. I opened my eyes and looked at Buddy as I was kissing him. I had never done this before, either. Buddy with his eyes closed was different, and stranger, than Buddy with his eyes open. He looked asleep, and as if he was having a troublesome dream.

This was the most I had ever kissed him. It was safe enough: he was wounded. When he groaned a little I thought it was because I was hurting him. "Careful," he said, moving me to one side.

I stopped kissing him and put my face down on his shoulder, against his neck. I could see the dresser, which matched the bed; it had a white crocheted runner on it, and some baby pictures in silver stands. Over it was a mirror, in a sombre frame with a carved festoon of roses, and inside the frame there was Buddy, with me lying beside him. I thought this must be the bedroom of Buddy's parents, and their bed. There was something sad about lying there with Buddy in the cramped formal room with its heavy prettiness, its gaiety which was both ornate and dark. This room was almost foreign to me; it was a celebration of something I could not identify with and would never be able to share. It would not take very much to make Buddy happy, ever: only something like this. This was what he was expecting of me, this not very much, and it was a lot more than I had. This was the most afraid I ever got, of Buddy.

"Hey," said Buddy. "Cheer up, eh? Everything still works okay." He thought I was worried about his injury.

After that we found that I had rolled on the bag of cookies and crushed them into bits, and that made everything safer, because we could laugh. But when it was time for me to go, Buddy became wistful. He held on to my hand. "What if I won't let you go?" he said.

When I was walking back towards the streetcar stop, I saw a woman coming towards me, carrying a big brown leather purse and a paper bag. She had a muscular and determined face, the face of a woman who has had to fight, something or other, in some way or another, for a long time. She looked at me as if she thought I was up to no good, and I became conscious of the creases in my cotton dress, from where I had been lying on the bed with Buddy. I thought she might be Buddy's mother.

Buddy got better quite soon. In the weeks after that, he ceased to be an indulgence or even a joke, and became instead an obligation. We continued to go out, on the same nights as we always had, but there was an edginess about Buddy that hadn't been there before. Sometimes Trish and Charlie went with us, but they no longer necked extravagantly in the back seat. Instead they held hands and talked together in low voices about things that sounded serious and even gloomy, such as the prices of apartments. Trish had started to collect china. But Charlie had his own car now, and more and more frequently Buddy and I were alone, no longer protected. Buddy's breathing became heavier and he no longer smiled good-naturedly when I took hold of his hands to stop him. He was tired of me being fourteen.

I began to forget about Buddy when I wasn't with him. The forgetting was deliberate: it was the same as remembering, only in reverse. Instead of talking to Buddy for hours on the phone, I spent a lot of time making dolls' clothes for my little sister's dolls. When I wasn't doing that, I read through my brother's collection of comic books, long since discarded by him, lying on the floor of my room with my feet up on the bed. My brother was no longer teaching me Greek. He had gone right off the deep end, into trigonometry, which we both knew I would never learn no matter what.

Buddy ended on a night in October, suddenly, like a light being switched off. I was supposed to be going out with him, but at the dinner table my father said that I should reconsider: Toronto was about to be hit by a major storm, a hurricane, with torrential rain and gale-force winds, and he didn't think I should be out in it, especially in a car like Buddy's. It was already dark; the rain was pelting against the windows behind our drawn curtains, and the wind was up and roaring like breakers in the ash trees outside. I could feel our house growing smaller. My mother said she would get out some candles, in case the electricity failed. Luckily, she said, we were on high ground. My father said that it was my decision, of course, but anyone who would go out on a night like this would have to be crazy.

Buddy phoned to see when he should pick me up. I said that the weather was getting bad, and maybe we should go out the next night. Buddy said why be afraid of a little rain? He wanted to see me. I said I wanted to see him, too, but maybe it was too dangerous. Buddy said I was just making excuses. I said I wasn't.

My father walked past me along the hall, snapping his fingers together like a pair of scissors. I said anyone who would go out on a night like this would have to be crazy, Buddy could turn on the radio and hear for himself, we were having a hurricane, but Buddy sounded as if he didn't really know what that meant. He said if I wouldn't go out with him during a hurricane I didn't love him enough. I was shocked: this was the first time he had ever used the word *love*, out loud and not just at the ends of letters, to describe what we were supposed to be doing. When I told him he was being stupid he hung up on me, which made me angry. But he was right, of course. I didn't love him enough.

Instead of going out with Buddy, I stayed home and played a game of chess with my brother, who won, as he always did. I was never a very good chess player: I couldn't stand the silent waiting. There was a feeling of reunion about this game, which would not, however, last long. Buddy was gone, but he had been a symptom.

This was the first of a long series of atmospherically supercharged break-ups with men, though I didn't realize it at the time. Blizzards, thunderstorms, heat waves, hailstorms: I later broke up in all of them. I'm not sure what it was. Possibly it had something to do with positive ions, which were not to be discovered for many years; but I came to believe that there was something about me that inspired extreme gestures, though I could never pinpoint what it was. After one such rupture, during a downpour of freezing rain, my ex-boyfriend gave me a valentine consisting of a real cow's heart with an actual arrow stuck through it. He'd been meaning to do it anyway, he said, and he couldn't think of any other girl who would appreciate it. For weeks I wondered whether or not this was a compliment.

Buddy was not this friendly. After the break-up, he never spoke to me again. Through Trish, he asked for his identification bracelet back, and I handed it over to her in the girls' washroom at lunch hour. There was someone else he wanted to give it to, Trish told me, a girl named Mary Jo who took typing instead of French, a sure sign in those days that you would leave school early and get a job or something. Mary Jo had a round, good-natured face, bangs down over her forehead like a sheepdog's, and heavy breasts, and she did in fact leave school early. Meanwhile she wore Buddy's name in silver upon her wrist. Trish switched allegiances, though not all at once. Somewhat later, I heard she had been telling stories about how I'd lived in a cowshed all summer.

It would be wrong to say that I didn't miss Buddy. In this respect too he was the first in a series. Later, I always missed men when they were gone, even when they meant what is usually called absolutely nothing to me. For me, I was to discover, there was no such category as absolutely nothing.

But all that was in the future. The morning after the hurricane, I had only the sensation of having come unscathed through a major calamity. After we had listened to the news, cars overturned with their drivers in them, demolished houses, all that rampaging water and disaster and washed-away money, my brother and I put on our rubber boots and walked down the old, pot-holed and now pitted and raddled Pottery Road to witness the destruction first-hand.

There wasn't as much as we had hoped. Trees and

branches were down, but not that many of them. The Don River was flooded and muddy, but it was hard to tell whether the parts of cars half sunk in it and the mangled truck tires, heaps of sticks, planks, and assorted debris washing along or strewn on land where the water had already begun to recede were new or just more of the junk we were used to seeing in it. The sky was still overcast; our boots squelched in the mud, out of which no hands were poking up. I had wanted something more like tragedy. Two people had actually been drowned there during the night, but we did not learn that until later. This is what I have remembered most clearly about Buddy: the ordinary-looking wreckage, the flatness of the water, the melancholy light.

LOULOU;
OR, THE DOMESTIC LIFE
OF THE LANGUAGE

Loulou is in the coach-house, wedging clay. She's wearing a pair of running shoes, once white, now grey, over men's wool work socks, a purple Indian-print cotton skirt, and a rust-coloured smock, so heavy with clay dust it hangs on her like brocade, the sleeves rolled up past the elbow. This is her favourite working outfit. To the music of *The Magic Flute*, brought to her by CBC stereo, she lifts the slab of clay and slams it down, gives a half-turn, lifts and slams. This is to get the air bubbles out, so nothing will explode in the kiln. Some potters would hire an apprentice to do this, but not Loulou.

It's true she has apprentices, two of them; she gets them through the government as free trainees. But they make plates and mugs from her designs, about all they're fit for. She doesn't consider them suitable for wedging clay, with their puny little biceps and match-stick wrists, so poorly developed compared with her own solid, smoothly muscled arms and broad, capable but shapely hands, so often admired by the poets. *Marmoreal*, one of them said— wrote, actually—causing Loulou to make one of her frequent sorties into the dictionary, to find out whether or not she'd been insulted.

Once she had done this openly, whenever they'd used a word about her she didn't understand, but when they'd discovered she was doing it they'd found it amusing and had started using words like that on purpose. "Loulou is so geomorphic," one of them would say, and when she would blush and scowl, another would take it up. "Not only that, she's fundamentally chthonic." "Telluric," a third would pipe up. Then they would laugh. She's decided that the only thing to do is to ignore them. But she's not so dumb as they think, she remembers the words, and when they aren't watching she sneaks a look at the Shorter Oxford (kept in the study which really belongs to only one of them but which she thinks of as *theirs*), washing her hands first so she won't leave any tell-tale signs of clay on the page.

She reads their journals, too, taking the same precautions. She suspects they know she does this. It's her way of keeping up with what they are really thinking about her, or maybe only with what they want her to think they're thinking. The journals are supposed to be secret, but Loulou considers it her right and also a kind of duty to read them. She views it in the same light as her mother viewed going through the family's sock and underwear drawers, to sort out the clean things from the ones they'd already worn and stuffed back in. This is what the poets' journals are like. Socks, mostly, but you never know what you will find.

"Loulou is becoming more metonymous," she's read recently. This has been bothering her for days. Sometimes she longs to say to them, "Now just what in hell did you mean by that?" But she knows she would get nowhere.

"Loulou is the foe of abstract order," one would say. This is a favourite belief of theirs.

"Loulou is the foe of abstract ordure."

"Loulou is the Great Goddess."

"Loulou is the great mattress."

It would end up with Loulou telling them to piss off. When that didn't stop them, she would tell them they couldn't have any more baked chicken if they went on like that. Threatening to deprive them of food usually works.

Overtly, Loulou takes care to express scorn for the poets; though not for them, exactly—they have their points—but for their pickiness about words. Her mother would have said they were finicky eaters. "Who cares what a thing's called?" she says to them. "A piece of bread is a piece of bread. You want some or not?" And she bends over to slide three of her famous loaves, high and nicely browned, out of the oven, and the poets admire her ass and haunches. Sometimes they do this openly, like other men, growling and smacking their lips, pretending to be construction workers. They like pretending to be other things; in the summers they play baseball games together and make a big fuss about having the right hats. Sometimes, though, they do it silently, and Loulou only knows about it from the poems they write afterwards. Loulou can tell these poems are about her, even though the nouns change: "my lady," "my friend's lady," "my woman," "my friend's woman," "my wife," "my friend's wife," and, when necessary for the length of the line, "the wife of my friend." Never "girl" though, and never her name. *Ass* and *haunches* aren't Loulou's words either; she would say *butt*.

Loulou doesn't know anything about music but she likes listening to it. Right now, the Queen of the Night runs up her trill, and Loulou pauses to see if she'll make it to the top. She does, just barely, and Loulou, feeling vicarious triumph, rams her fist into the mound of clay. Then she covers it with a sheet of plastic and goes to the sink to wash her hands. Soon the oven timer will go off and one of the poets, maybe her husband but you never know, will call her on the intercom to come and see about the bread. It isn't that they wouldn't take it out themselves, if she asked them to. Among the four or five of them they'd likely manage. It's just that Loulou doesn't trust them. She decided long ago that none of them knows his left tit from a hole in the ground when it comes to the real world. If she wants the bread taken out when it's done but not overdone, and she does, she'll have to do it herself.

She wonders who will be in the kitchen at the main house by now: her first husband for sure, and the man she lived with after that for three years without being married, and her second husband, the one she has now, and two ex-lovers. Half a dozen of them maybe, sitting around the kitchen table, drinking her coffee and eating her hermit cookies and talking about whatever they talk about when she isn't there. In the past there have been periods of strain among them, especially during the times when Loulou has been switching over, but they're all getting along well enough now. They run a collective poetry magazine, which keeps them out of trouble mostly. The name of this magazine is *Comma*, but among themselves the poets refer to it as *Coma*. At parties they enjoy going up to young female would-be poets ("proupies," they call them behind their backs, which means "poetry groupies"), and saying, "I'd like to put you in a *Coma*." A while ago *Comma* published mostly poems without commas, but this is going out now, just as beards are going out in favour of moustaches and even shaving. The more daring poets have gone so far as to cut off their sideburns. Loulou is not quite sure whether or not she approves of this.

She doesn't know whether the poets are good poets, whether the poems they write in such profusion are any good. Loulou has no opinion on this subject: all that matters is what they are writing about her. Their poems get published in books, but what does that mean? Not money, that's for sure. You don't make any money with poetry, the poets tell her, unless you sing and play the guitar too. Sometimes they give readings and make a couple of hundred bucks. For Loulou that's three medium-sized casseroles, with lids. On the other hand, they don't have her expenses. Part of her expenses is them.

Loulou can't remember exactly how she got mixed up with the poets. It wasn't that she had any special thing for poets as such: it just happened that way. After the first one, the others seemed to follow along naturally, almost as if they were tied onto each other in a long line with a piece of string. They were always around, and she was so busy most of the time that she didn't go out much to look for other kinds of men. Now that her business is doing so well you'd think she would have more leisure time, but this isn't the case. And any leisure time she does have, she spends with the poets. They're always nagging her about working too hard.

Bob was the first one, and also her first husband. He was in art school at the same time she was, until he decided he wasn't suited for it. He wasn't practical enough, he let things dry out: paint, clay, even the left-overs in his tiny refrigerator, as Loulou discovered the first night she'd slept with him. She devoted the next morning to cleaning up his kitchen, getting rid of the saucers of mummified cooked peas and the shrivelled, half-gnawed chicken legs and the warped, cracked quarter-packages of two-month-old sliced bacon, and the bits of cheese, oily on the outside and hard as tiles. Loulou has always hated clutter, which she defines, though not in so many words, as matter out of its proper place. Bob looked on, sullen but appreciative, as she hurled and scoured. Possibly this was why he decided to love her: because she would do this sort of thing. What he said though was, "You complete me."

What he also said was that he'd fallen in love with her name. All the poets have done this, one after the other. The first symptom is that they ask her whether Loulou is short for something—Louise, maybe? When she says no, they look at her in that slightly glazed way she recognizes instantly, as if they've never paid proper attention to her or even seen her before. This look is her favourite part of any new relationship with a man. It's even better than the sex, though Loulou likes sex well enough and all the poets have been good in bed. But then, Loulou has never slept with a man she did not consider good in bed. She's beginning to think this is because she has low standards.

At first Loulou was intrigued by this obsession with her name, mistaking it for an obsession with her, but it turned out to be no such thing. It was the gap that interested them, one of them had explained (not Bob though; maybe Phil, the second and most linguistic of them all).

"What gap?" Loulou asked suspiciously. She knew her upper front teeth were a little wide apart and had been self-conscious about it when she was younger.

"The gap between the word and the thing signified," Phil said. His hand was on her breast and he'd given an absent-minded squeeze, as if to illustrate what he meant. They were in bed at the time. Mostly Loulou doesn't like talking in bed. But she's not that fond of talking at other times, either.

Phil went on to say that Loulou, as a name, conjured up images of French girls in can-can outfits, with corseted wasp-waists and blonde curls and bubbly laughs. But then there was the real Loulou—dark, straight-haired, firmly built, marmoreal, and well, not exactly bubbly. More earthy, you might say. (Loulou hadn't known then what he meant by "earthy," though by now she's learned that for him, for all of them, it means "functionally illiterate.") The thing was, Phil said, what existed in the space between Loulou and her name?

Loulou didn't know what he was talking about. What space? Once she'd resented her mother for having saddled her with this name; she would rather have been called Mary or Ann. Maybe she suspected that her mother would really have preferred a child more like the name—blonde, thin, curly-headed—but had disappointingly got Loulou instead, short, thick, stubborn-jawed, not much interested in the frilly dolls' clothes her mother had painstakingly crocheted for her. Instead, Loulou was fond of making mud pies on the back porch, placing them carefully along the railing where people wouldn't step on them and ruin them. Her mother's response to these pies was to say, "Oh, Loulou!" as if *Loulou* in itself meant mud, meant trouble and dismay.

"It's just a name," she said. "Phil is kind of a dumb name too if you ask me."

Phil said that wasn't the point, he wasn't *criticizing* her, but Loulou had stopped the conversation by climbing on top of him, letting her long hair fall down over his face.

That was early on; he'd liked her hair then. "Rank," he'd called it in a poem, quite a lot later. Loulou hadn't thought much of that when she looked it up. It could mean *too luxuriant* or *offensive and foul-smelling*. The effect of this poem on Loulou was to cause her to wash her hair more often. Sooner or later all the poets got into her hair, and she was tired of having it compared to horses' tails, Newfoundland dog fur, black holes in space and the insides of caves. When Loulou was feeling particularly enraged by the poets she would threaten to get a brush-cut, though she knew it would be pushing her luck.

When she has dried her hands, Loulou takes off her smock. Underneath it she's wearing a mauve sweatshirt with RAVING OPTIMIST stencilled across the front. The poets gave it to her, collectively, one Christmas, because a few weeks before one of them had said, "Why are you so grumpy, Loulou?" and Loulou had said, "I'm only grumpy when you pick on me," and then, after a pause, "Compared to you guys I'm a raving optimist." This was true, though they made fun of her for it. In a group they can laugh, but it's only Loulou who has seen them one at a time, sitting in chairs for hours on end with their heads down on their arms, almost unable to move. It's Loulou who's held their hands when they couldn't make it in bed and told them that other things are just as important, though she's never been able to specify what. It's Loulou who has gone out and got drunk with them and listened to them talking about the void and about the terrifying blankness of the page and about how any art form is just a way of evading suicide. Loulou thinks this is a load of b.s.: she herself does not consider the making of casseroles with lids or the throwing of porcelain fruit bowls as an evasion of suicide, but then, as they have often pointed out, what she's doing isn't an art form, it's only a craft. Bob once asked her when she was going to branch out into macramé, for which she emptied the dust-pan on him. But she matches them beer for beer; she's even gone so far as to throw up right along with them, if that seemed required. One of them once told her she was a soft touch.

The intercom buzzes as Loulou is hanging up her smock. She buzzes back to show she has heard, takes her hair out of the elastic band and smooths it down, looking in the round tin-framed Mexican mirror that hangs over the sink, and checks up on little Marilyn, her new apprentice, before heading out the door.

Marilyn is still having trouble with cup handles. Loulou will have to spend some time with her later and explain them to her. If the cup handles aren't on straight, she will say, the cup will be crooked when you pick it up and then the people drinking out of it will spill things and burn themselves. That's the way you have to put it for trainees: in terms of physical damage. It's important to Loulou that the production pieces should be done right. They're her bread and butter, though what she most likes to work on are the bigger things, the amphora-like vases, the tureens a size larger than anyone ought to be able to throw. Another potter once said that you'd need a derrick to give a dinner party with Loulou's stuff, but that was jealousy. What they say about her mostly is that she doesn't fool around.

Loulou flings her pink sweater-coat across her shoulders, bangs the coach-house door behind her to make it shut, and walks towards the house, whistling between her teeth and stomping her feet to get the clay dust off. The kitchen is filled with the yeasty smell of baking bread. Loulou breathes it in, revelling in it: a smell of her own creation.

The poets are sitting around the kitchen table, drinking coffee. Maybe they're having a meeting, it's hard to tell. Some nod at her, some grin. Two of the female poets are here today and Loulou isn't too pleased about that. As far as she's concerned they don't have a lot to offer: they're almost as bad as the male poets, but without the saving grace of being men. They wear black a lot and have cheek-bones.

Piss on their cheek-bones, thinks Loulou. She knows what cheek-bones mean. The poets, *her* poets, consider these female poets high-strung and interesting. Sometimes they praise their work, a little too extravagantly, but sometimes they talk about their bodies, though not when they are there of course, and about whether or not they would be any good in bed. Either of these approaches drives Loulou wild. She doesn't like the female poets—they eat her muffins and condescend to her, and Loulou suspects them of having designs on the poets, some of which may already have been carried out, judging from their snotty manner—but she doesn't like hearing them put down, either. What really gets her back up is that, during these discussions, the poets act as if she isn't there.

Really, though, the female poets don't count. They aren't

even on the editorial board of *Comma*; they are only on the edges, like mascots, and today Loulou all but ignores them.

"You could've put on more coffee," she says in her grumpiest voice.

"What's the matter, Loulou?" says Phil, who has always been the quickest on the uptake when it comes to Loulou and her bad moods. Not that Loulou goes in for fine tuning.

"Nothing *you* can fix," says Loulou rudely. She takes off her sweater-coat and sticks out her chest. *Marmoreal*, she thinks. So much for the female poets, who are flat-chested as well as everything else.

"Hey Loulou, how about a little nictitation?" says one of the poets.

"Up your nose," says Loulou.

"She thinks it's something dirty," says a second one. "She's confusing it with micturition."

"All it means is winking, Loulou," says the first one.

"He got it out of Trivial Pursuit," says a third.

Loulou takes one loaf out of the oven, turns it out, taps the bottom, puts it back into the pan and into the oven. They can go on like that for hours. It's enough to drive you right out of your tree, if you pay any attention to them at all.

"Why do you put up with us, Loulou?" Phil asked her once. Loulou sometimes wonders, but she doesn't know. She knows why they put up with her though, apart from the fact that she pays the mortgage: she's solid, she's predictable, she's always there, she makes them feel safe. But lately she's been wondering: who is there to make her feel safe?

* * *

It's another day, and Loulou is on her way to seduce her accountant. She's wearing purple boots, several years old and with watermarks on them from the slush, a cherry-coloured dirndl she made out of curtain material when she was at art school, and a Peruvian wedding shirt dyed mauve; this is the closest she ever comes to getting dressed up. Because of the section of the city she's going to, which is mostly middle-European shops, bakeries and clothing stores with yellowing embroidered blouses in the windows and places where you can buy hand-painted wooden Easter eggs and chess sets with the pawns as Cossacks, she's draped a black wool shawl over her head. This, she thinks, will make her look more ethnic and therefore more inconspicuous: she's feeling a little furtive. One of the poets has said that Loulou is to *subdued* as Las Vegas at night is to a sixty-watt light bulb, but in fact, with her long off-black hair and her large dark eyes and the strong planes of her face, she does have a kind of peasant look. This is enhanced by the two plastic shopping bags she carries, one in either hand. These do not contain groceries, however, but her receipts and cheque stubs for the two previous years. Loulou is behind on her income tax, which is why she got the accountant in the first place. She doesn't see why she shouldn't kill two birds with one stone.

Loulou is behind on her income tax because of her fear of money. When she was married to Bob, neither of them had any money anyway, so the income tax wasn't a problem. Phil, the man she lived with after that, was good with numbers, and although he had no income and therefore no income tax, he treated hers as a game, a kind of superior Scrabble. But her present husband, Calvin, considers money boring. It's all right to have some—as Loulou does, increasingly—but talking about it is sordid and a waste of time. Calvin claims that those who can actually read income-tax forms, let alone understand them, have already done severe and permanent damage to their brains. Loulou has taken to sending out her invoices and toting up her earnings in the coach-house, instead of at the kitchen table as she used to, and adding and subtracting are acquiring overtones of forbidden sex. Perhaps this is what has led her to the step she is now about to take. You may as well be hung, thinks Loulou, for a sheep as a lamb.

In addition, Loulou has recently been feeling a wistful desire to be taken care of. It comes and goes, especially on cloudy days, and mostly Loulou pays scant attention to it. Nevertheless it's there. Everyone depends on her, but when she needs help, with her income tax for instance, nobody's within call. She could ask Phil to do it again, but Calvin might make a fuss about it. She wants to be able to turn her two plastic shopping bags over to some man, some quiet methodical man with inner strength, and not too ugly, who could make sense of their contents and tell her she has nothing to worry about and, hopefully, nothing to pay.

Before Loulou found this particular accountant, she spent several afternoons window-shopping for one down at King and Bay. When it came right down to it, however, she was so intimidated by the hermetically sealed glass towers and the thought of receptionists with hair-dos and nail polish that she didn't even go in through the doors at any of the addresses she'd looked up in the Yellow Pages. Instead, she stood at street corners as if waiting for the light to change, watching the businessmen hurry past, sometimes in overcoats of the kind the poets never wear, solid-looking and beige or navy blue but slit provocatively up the back, or in three-piece suits, challengingly done up with hundreds of buttons and zippers, their tight tennis-playing butts concealed under layers of expensive wool blend, their ties waving enticingly under their chins like the loose ends of macramé wall hangings: one pull and the whole thing would unravel. The poets, in their track suits or jeans, seem easier of access, but they are hedged with paradox and often moody. The businessmen would be simple and unspoiled, primary reds and blues rather than puce and lilac, potatoes rather than, like the poets, slightly over-ripe avocadoes.

The sight of them filled Loulou with unspecific lust, though she found them touching also. She was like a middle-aged banker surrounded by sixteen-year-old virgins: she longed to be the first, though the first of what she wasn't sure. But she knew she knew lots of things they were unlikely to know: the poets, on their good days, have been nothing if not inventive.

Loulou doesn't think of the accountant she has now as a real one, by which she means a frightening one. He is not in a glass tower, he has no polished receptionist, though he does have a certificate on the wall and even a three-piece suit (though, Loulou suspects, only one). She discovered him by accident when she was down on Queen Street buying fresh chicken from A. Stork, the best place for it in her opinion, especially when you need a lot, as she did that day because all of the poets were coming for dinner. Heading for the streetcar stop with her sackful of tender flesh, Loulou saw a hand-lettered sign in the window of a dry-goods store: INCOME TAX, and underneath it some foreign language. It was the hand-lettered sign that did it for Loulou: badly lettered at that, she could do much better. On impulse she'd pushed open the door and gone in.

There was a tiny bald-headed man behind the counter, barricaded in with bolts of maroon cloth, a rack of cheesy-looking buttons on the wall behind him, but he turned out not to be the accountant. The accountant was in a separate room at the back, with nothing in it except a wooden desk of the sort Loulou associated with her grade-school teachers, and one other chair and a filing cabinet. He stood up when Loulou came in and offered to take her sack of chicken and put it somewhere for her. "No thanks," said Loulou, because she could see there was nowhere for him to put it—there was a fern on the filing cabinet, obviously on its last legs—and that he would merely get more flustered than he already was if she said yes; so she went through their first interview with a bag of still-warm cut-up chicken in her lap.

She's seen him twice since then. He takes more time with her than he really needs to, maybe because he's not what you would call all that busy. He also talks to her more than he needs to. By now, Loulou knows quite a lot about him. Getting started is harder than it used to be, he's told her. The dry-goods store belongs to his father, who gives him the office rent-free, in return for doing the accounts. The father is first-generation Czech, and he himself knows two other languages besides English. In this district—he spread his hands in a kind of resigned shrug while saying this—it helps. He does a couple of local bakeries and a hardware store and a second-hand jeweller's and a few of his father's old friends. Maybe when the recession is over things will pick up. He has volunteered, too, that his hobby is weight-lifting. Loulou has not asked whether or not he's married; she suspects not. If he were married, his fern would be in better shape.

While he talks, Loulou nods and smiles. She isn't sure how old he is. Young, she thinks, though he tries to make himself look older by wearing silver-rimmed glasses. She thinks he has nice hands, not like an accountant's at all, not spindly. The second time, he went out into the main store and came back with cups of tea, which Loulou found thoughtful. Then he asked her advice about a carpet. Already she felt sorry for him. He hardly ever goes out for lunch, she's discovered; mostly he just gets take-out from the deli across the street. She's considered bringing him some muffins.

These topics—carpets, weight-lifting, food—are easy for Loulou. What is more difficult is that he's decided she's not just a potter but an artist, and his idea of an artist does not at all accord with Loulou's view of herself. He wants her to be wispy and fey, impractical, unearthly almost; he talks, embarrassingly, about "the creative impulse." This is far too close to the poets for Loulou. She's tried to explain that she works with clay, which is hardly ethereal. "It's like mud pies," she said, but he didn't want to hear that. Nor could she find the words to make him understand what she meant: that when she's throwing a pot she feels exhilaration, exactly the same kind she felt as a child while making a terrible mess of her mother's back porch. If he could see her the way she really is when she's working, guck all over her hands, he'd know she's not exactly essence of roses.

The second time she saw him, the accountant said he envied her freedom. He would like to do something more creative himself, he said, but you have to make a living. Loulou refrained from pointing out that she seems to be doing a sight better at it than he is. She's much more tactful with him than she's ever been with the poets. The fact is that she's starting to enjoy his version of her. Sometimes she even believes it, and thinks she might be on the verge of learning something new about herself. She's beginning to find herself mysterious. It's partly for this reason she wants to sleep with the accountant; she thinks it will change her.

The poets would laugh if they knew, but then she's not about to tell them. She did announce his advent though, that first night, while the poets were all sitting around the table eating chicken and discussing something they called "the language." They do this frequently these days and Loulou is getting bored with it. "The language" is different from just words: it has this mystical aura around it, like religion, she can tell by the way their voices drop reverently whenever they mention it. That night they had all just finished reading a new book. "I'm really getting into the language," one said, and the others chewed in silent communion.

"I've got myself an accountant," Loulou said loudly, to break the spell.

"You've *got* him, but have you *had* him yet?" Bob said. The others laughed, all except Calvin, and began discussing the accountant's chances of escape from Loulou, which they rated at nil. They went on to detail the positions and locations in which Loulou could be expected to finally entrap him—under the desk, on top of the filing cabinet—and the injuries he would sustain. They pictured him fending her off with pens.

Loulou gnawed grimly at a chicken leg. They didn't believe any of this would happen, of course. They were too conceited: having known them, how could she stoop so low? Little did they know.

Loulou approaches the door of the dry-goods store, whistling Mozart between her teeth. Partly she's thinking about the accountant and what his body might be like under his suit, but partly she's thinking about tomorrow, when she has to start work on an order of twelve slab planters for one of her good customers. Either way, it's a question of the right placement of the feet. Like a Judo expert, which she is not, Loulou is always conscious of the position of her feet in relation to the rest of her.

The accountant is waiting for her, shadowy behind the dust-filmed glass of the door. It's after six and the store is closed. Loulou said, slyly, that she couldn't make it any earlier. She didn't want the little bald-headed man lurking around.

The accountant unlocks the door and lets her in. They go back through the smell of wool and freshly torn cotton into his office, and Loulou dumps out her bag of receipts (done up in bundles, with elastic bands: she's not without a sense of decency), all over his desk. He looks pleased, and says they certainly do have a lot of things to catch up on.

He brings in some cups of tea, sits down, picks up a newly sharpened pencil, and asks her how much of her living space can be written off as working space. Loulou explains about the coach-house. She doesn't use any of the actual house herself, she says, not for working, because the poets are always using it. Sometimes they live there too, though it depends.

"On what?" says the accountant, frowning a little.

"On whether they're living anywhere else," says Loulou.

When he hears that they don't pay rent, the accountant makes a tut-tutting sound and tells Loulou that she should not let things go on like this. Loulou says that the poets never have any money, except sometimes from grants. The accountant gets out of his chair and paces around the room, which is difficult for him because Loulou is taking up a lot of space in it. He says that Loulou is allowing herself to be imposed upon and she should get herself out of this situation, which is doing her no good at all.

Loulou may have felt this herself from time to time, but hearing the accountant say it right out in the open air disturbs her. Where would the poets go? Who would take care of them? She doesn't wish to dwell on this right now, it's far too complicated, and perhaps even painful. Instead she stands up, plants her feet firmly apart, intercepts the accountant as he strides past, and, with a tug here and a little pressure there, ends up with his arms more or less around her. She backs herself up against the desk for balance, puts one hand behind her, and upsets his cup of tea into the wastepaper basket. He doesn't notice a thing; luckily it isn't hot.

After a short time the accountant takes off his silver-rimmed glasses, and after another short time he says, in a voice half an octave lower than his normal one, "I wasn't expecting this." Loulou says nothing—she lies only when absolutely necessary—and starts undoing his vest buttons. When she's down to the shirt he lifts his head, glances around the room, and murmurs, "Not here." Which is just as well, because he hasn't got his carpet yet and the floor is painted concrete.

He leads her into the darkened dry-goods store and begins sorting through the bolts of cloth. Loulou can't figure out what he's doing until he selects a roll of dark-pink velvet, unfurls it, and lays it out on the floor behind the counter, with a little flourish, like a cloak over a mud puddle. Loulou admires the way he does this; he's too deft not to have done it before. She lies down on the pink velvet, reaches up for him, and after a few minutes of shaky-fingered fumbling with the clothes they make love, somewhat rapidly. This floor is concrete too and the pink velvet isn't very thick. Loulou worries about his knees.

"Well," says the accountant. Then he sits up and starts putting on his clothes. He does this very skilfully. Loulou wishes he would wait a few minutes—it would be friendlier—but already he's doing up his buttons. Maybe he's afraid someone will come in. He rolls up the pink velvet and inserts the bolt back into its proper slot on the shelf. They go back to his office and he locates his glasses and puts them on, and tells her he'll have some figures for her in maybe two weeks. He doesn't say anything about seeing her in the meantime: perhaps his image of her as a delicate artistic flower has been shaken. He kisses her good-bye, though. The last thing he says to her is, "You shouldn't let people take advantage of you." Loulou knows he thinks he's just done this very thing himself. He's like the poets: he thinks she can't see through him.

Loulou decides to walk back to her house, which is at

least a mile away, instead of taking the streetcar. She needs time to calm down. On the one hand she's elated, as she always is when she accomplishes something she's set out to do, but on the other hand she's disoriented. Is she different now, or not? Apart from the actual sex, which Loulou would never knock, and it was fine though a little on the swift side, what has it all boiled down to? She doesn't feel more known, more understood. Instead she feels less understood. She feels nameless. It's as if all those words which the poets have attached to her over the years have come undone and floated off into the sky, like balloons. If she were one of the poets, she would get something out of this: this is exactly the sort of thing they like to write about. A non-event, says Phil, is better to write about than an event, because with a non-event you can make up the meaning yourself, it means whatever you say it means. For the poets nothing is wasted, because even if it is, they can write about the waste. What she ought to do is throw them all out on their ears.

Loulou reaches her three-storey red-brick house and notes, as she always does, the mangy state of the lawn. The poets are divided on the subject of the lawn: some of them think lawns are bourgeois, others think that to say lawns are bourgeois is outdated. Loulou says she'll be damned if she'll cut it herself. The lawn is a stand-off. She goes up the front walk, not whistling, and unlocks her front door. In the hallway the familiar smell of the house envelops her, but it's like a smell from childhood. It's the smell of something left behind.

The poets are in the kitchen, sitting around the table, which is littered with papers and coffee cups and plates with crumbs and smears of butter on them. Loulou looks from one poet to another as if they are figures in a painting, as if she's never seen them before. She could walk out of this room, right this minute, and never come back, and fifty years later they would all still be in there, with the same plates, the same cups, the same crumby butter. Only she doesn't know where she would go.

"We're out of muffins," says Bob.

Loulou stares at him. "Piss on the muffins," she says at last, but without conviction. He looks tired, she thinks. He is showing signs of age, they all are. This is the first time she's noticed it. They won't go on forever.

"Where've you been?" says Calvin. "It's past seven-thirty." This is his way of saying they want their dinner.

"My God, you're helpless," says Loulou. "Why didn't you just phone out for some pizza?" To her knowledge they have never phoned out for pizza. They've never had to.

She sits down heavily at the table. The life she's led up to now seems to her entirely crazed. How did she end up in this madhouse? By putting one foot in front of the other and never taking her eyes off her feet. You could end up anywhere that way. It isn't that the accountant is normal, any more than the poets are; nor is he a possible alternative. She won't even sleep with him again, not on purpose anyway. But he is other, he is another. She too could be other. But which other? What, underneath it all, is Loulou really like? How can she tell? Maybe she is what the poets say she is, after all; maybe she has only their word, their words, for herself.

"*Pizza*," Bob is beginning, in an injured tone. "Pig of a dog. . . ." But the others shut him up. They can see that something is wrong, and they very much don't want to know what.

"Reify the pizza," says Calvin to Phil. "You use phone. Is modern western invention of technology." Now they're pretending to be foreigners of some kind. This is a game they play more frequently when there is tension in the air than when there isn't.

"Insert finger in possible small hole," says Calvin. "Twist wrist."

"With anchovies then," says Bob, not joining in. Loulou hears their voices coming to her across space, as if they're in another room. What she sees is the grain of the wood in the table right by her hand.

"Loulou thinks *to reify* means *to make real*," says Phil to everyone, when he's hung up the phone. They're always talking about her in the third person like that, telling each other what she thinks. The truth is that she's never heard the word before in her life.

"So what is it, smartass?" says Loulou with an effort, squeezing out a little belligerence to set them at ease.

"If Loulou didn't exist, God would have to invent her," says Bob.

"God, hell," says Phil. "*We* would. We did it the first time, right?"

This is going too far for Loulou. Nobody invented her, thank you very much. They make things up about her, but that's a whole other story. "Up your nose," says Loulou.

"To reify is to make into a thing," says Phil, "which, as I'm sure most of us will agree, is hardly the same."

Loulou looks around the room. They are all in place, they're all watching her, to see what she will say next. She sticks out her chin at them. "Why not?" she says. "What's the big difference?" and they relax, they laugh, they give each other little punches on the shoulder as if they're part of a team and they've just scored a point. That, they tell each other, is just like Loulou, and suddenly she sees that this is what they require of her, possibly all they require: that she should be *just like Loulou*. No more, but certainly no less. Maybe it's not so bad.

UGLYPUSS

Joel hates November. As far as he's concerned they could drop it down the chute and he wouldn't complain. Drizzle and chill, everyone depressed, and then the winter to go through afterwards. The landlord has turned down the heat again, which means Joel has to either let his buns solidify and break off or use the electric heater, which means more money, because the electricity's extra. The landlord does this to spite him, Joel, personally. Just for that, Joel refuses to move. He tells other people he likes the building, which he does: it's a golden oldie, a mansion that's seen better days, with an arched entrance-way and stained glass. But also he won't give the old rent-gouger the satisfaction. Becka could handle him, when she was still living here. All she'd had to do was lean over the banister while the old bugger was standing below, and use her good voice, the furry one, and up went the temperature; a trick that's not possible for Joel.

He'd like to be someplace warm, but who can afford it? Too bad they made grants taxable, not that he's likely to get another one the ways things are going.

Things are not going too well. He's beginning to think street theatre should stay in California: up here you can only do it three months of the year, and some of that is too hot, they steam inside those outsize masks. Even directing is no picnic. Last summer he got a sunburn, on the top of his head, where he's beginning to go bald. It was right after this that Becka caught him in the bathroom, standing with his back to the mirror, looking at his head from behind with a plastic violet-framed hand mirror, hers. She wouldn't let up on that for weeks. "Checked out your manly beauty this morning?" "Thought about Hair-Weeve?" "You'd look cute as a blonde. It would go with the skull." "Chest wigs yet?" "You could cut off some of your beard and glue it on the top, right?" Maybe he had it coming; he remembered getting onto her about spending twenty-five dollars at the hairdresser's once, soon after she'd moved in with him. It was her twenty-five dollars, but they were supposed to be sharing expenses. He'd called it an indulgence. She remembered that he remembered, of course. She has a memory like a rat-trap: full of rats.

Joel's fingers are cold. The apartment is like a football game in the rain. He puts down the black Bic ball-point with which he hasn't written anything for the past half hour, stretches, scratches his head. He recalls, for an instant and with irritation, the Italian calligraphy pen Becka affected for a while: an affectation that has gone the way of all the others. Then he turns back to square one.

The piece they're working on is for two weeks from now: the Crucifixion according to Solemate Sox, with management as Judas. They're going to do it right beside the picket lines, which will cheer the picketers up, or that was the general idea. Joel isn't too sure about this piece, and there's been a certain amount of debate about it within the group. The concept was Becka's: she justified it by saying they should pick symbolism the workers can tune into, and most of these workers are Portuguese, they'll know all about Judas, you only have to look at the statues on their lawns, all those bleeding plaster Jesuses and Virgin Marys with their creepy-looking babies. Though for the same reason some of the others felt that Christ as a large knitted sock, in red and white stripes, might turn out to be too much for them. There could be a communications breakdown. Joel himself had been uneasy, but he'd voted on Becka's side, because they'd still been trying to work it out then and he knew what hell there would be to pay if he'd come out against her. Just another example, she would have said, of how he would never let her express herself.

He hopes it won't rain: if it does, the giant sock will get waterlogged, among other things. Maybe they should scrap it, try for another approach. Whatever they do, though, they'll probably have the assistant manager and the old boy himself coming outside and accusing them of anti-Semitism. This happens to Joel a lot; it's escalated after the piece on Lebanon and arms sales to South Africa they did outside the Beth Tzedec on Yom Kippur. Possibly the portable canvas mass grave, filled with baby dolls and splashed with red paint, had been going too far. A couple of the troupe members had wondered whether it was in bad taste, but Joel had said that bad taste was just an internalized establishment enforcer.

Joel doesn't believe in pulling punches. And if you punch, they punch back. It's getting so he can hardly go to parties any more. Though it's not all parties he should avoid, only certain kinds, the kinds where he will find his own second cousins and men he went to *shul* with, who are now dentists or have gone into business. Even before the Lebanon piece, they were none too polite. At the last party, a woman he didn't know at all, an older woman, came up to him and said, "Instead of shaking your hand I should kick you in the stomach."

"What for?" said Joel.

"You know what for," the woman said. "You've got a nerve. Eating our food. Better you should choke."

"Don't you think there should be an open discussion of the situation?" said Joel. "Like they do in Israel?"

"Goys have no right," said the woman.

"So who's a goy?" said Joel.

"You," said the woman. "You're not a real Jew."

"All of a sudden you're some kind of self-appointed committee on racial purity?" said Joel. "Anyway, read the Torah. They used to stone the prophets."

"Shmuck," said the woman.

Joel tries not to let it get to him: he's got his credentials ready. You want murdered relatives? he'll tell them. I've got.

Then how can you betray them? they'll say. Spitting on the dead.

You think they'd agree with what's happening? he'll say. Two wrongs don't make a right.

Then there's a silence in him, because that's a thing no one will ever know.

Joel's head hurts. He gets up from his desk, sits down in the chair he thinks in, which is like the one at home that his father used to lie in to read the paper, a La-Z-Boy recliner, covered in black naugahyde. Joel bought his at least third-hand from the Goodwill, out of nostalgia and a wish for comfort; though Becka said he did it to affront her. She could never stand any of his furniture, especially the Ping-Pong table; she was always lobbying for a real dining-room table, though, as Joel would point out with great reasonableness, it wouldn't have a double function.

"You're always talking about bourgeoise," she'd say, which wasn't true. "But that chair is the essence. Eau de bourgeoise." She pronounced it in three syllables: *boor-joo-ice*. Maybe she did this on purpose, to get at him by mutilating the word, though the only time he'd corrected her (the *only* time, he's sure of that), she'd said, "Well, excuse me for living." Could he help it if he'd spent a year in Montreal? And she hadn't. He couldn't help any of the things that he had and she hadn't.

Early on, he thought they'd been engaging in a dialogue, out of which, sooner or later, a consensus would emerge. He thought they'd been involved in a process of mutual adjustment and counter-adjustment. But viewed from here and now, it was never a dialogue. It was merely a degrading squabble.

Joel decides not to brood any more about boring personal shit. There are more important things in the world. He picks up this morning's paper, from where it lies in segments on the floor, in which he knows he will read distorted and censored versions of some of them; but just as he's settling down to the purblind and moronic "Letters to the Editor" section, the phone rings. Joel hesitates before answering it: maybe it will be Becka, and he never knows which angle she'll be coming at him from. But curiosity wins, as it often does where Becka is concerned.

It isn't Becka though. "I'm going to cut your nuts off," says a male voice, almost sensuously, into his ear.

"To whom do you wish to speak?" says Joel, doing his best imitation of an English butler from a thirties film. Joel watches a lot of late movies.

This isn't the first phone call like this he's had. Sometimes they're anti-Semites, wanting to cut his Jewish nuts off; sometimes they're Jews, wanting to cut his nuts off because they don't think he's Jewish enough. In either case the message is the same: his nuts must go. Maybe he should introduce the two sides and they could cut each other's nuts off; that seems to be their shtick. He likes his where they are.

Joel's elocution throws the guy and he mumbles something about dirty Commie bastards. Joel tells him that Mr. Murgatroyd is not home at the moment; would he care to leave his name and number? The coward hangs up, and so does Joel. He's sweating all over. He didn't when this first started happening, but the ones at two A.M. have been getting to him.

Joel doesn't want to turn into one of those paranoids who dive under the sofa every time there's a knock at the door. No Gestapo here, he tells himself. What he needs is some food. He goes out to the kitchen and rummages through the refrigerator, finding not much. Of the two of them, it was Becka who'd done most of the shopping. Without her, he's reverted to his old habits: pizza, Kentucky Fried, doughnuts from the Dunkin' Doughnuts. He knows it's unhealthy, but he indulges in unhealth as a kind of perverse rebellion against her. He used to justify his tastes by saying that this was what the average worker eats, but he knew even at the time that he was using ideology to cover for addiction. He must be getting middle-aged though, because he's still taking the vitamin pills Becka used to foist on him, threatening him with beri-beri, constipation, and scurvy if he dodged. He recalls with some pain her roughage phase.

The truth is that even Becka's normal cooking, good though it was, made him nervous. He always felt he was in the wrong house, not his, since he'd never associated home with edible food. His mother had been such a terrible cook that he'd left the dinner table hungry more evenings than not. At midnight he would prowl through his mother's apartment, stomach growling so loud you'd have thought it would wake her up, on bare criminal feet into the kitchen. Then followed the hunt for the only remotely digestible objects in the place, which were always baked goods from stores like Hunt's or Woman's Bakery, apple turnovers, muffins, cupcakes, cookies. She used to hide them on him; they'd never be in the refrigerator or the breadbox, not once she'd figured out that it was him who'd been eating them at night. Carefully, like a safe-cracker turning a sensitive combination lock, he'd dismantle the kitchen, moving one pot at a time, one stack of dishes. Sometimes she'd go so far as to stash them in the living room; once, even in the bathroom, under the sink. That was stooping pretty low. He remembers the sense of challenge, the mounting excitement, the triumph when he would finally uncover those familiar sweet oily brown-paper bags with their tightly screwed tops and their odour, faintly stale. He has an image of himself, in his pyjamas, crouching beside the cache he's just dragged out from under the easy chair, cramming in the Chelsea buns, gloating. Next day she'd never mention it. Once or twice he failed, but only once or twice. She never mentioned that, either.

Now, prodding the shambles in his own refrigerator, Joel can't find anything to eat. There's half a pint of yoghurt, but it's left over from Becka and, by now, questionable. He decides to go out. He locates his jacket finally, which is in the nest of clothing at the bottom of the hall closet. Things somehow don't stay hung up when he hangs them. The jacket has *Bluejays* across the back and is ravelling at the cuffs; it has grease on it from where he crawled under the car, years ago, trying to prove to someone or other that he knew why it was leaking; a futile exercise. The car had been completely irrational; there was never a plausible explanation for any of the things it did, any of the parts that fell off it. Joel felt that driving it was like thumbing your nose at the car establishment, at car snobbery, at the Platonic idea of cars; he refused to trade it in. This was the car that finally got stolen. "They were doing us all a favour," said Becka.

Becka once threatened to burn his Bluejays jacket. She said if he had to wear a stupid macho label, at least he could pick a winner; which goes to show how much she knows about it. Expos she could live with. By that time he'd started ignoring her; the text anyway, not the subtext. In so far as that was possible.

As he's doing up the zipper the phone rings. Joel thinks it may be another nut-cutter; he should get a telephone-answering machine, the kind you can listen in on. But this time it really is Becka. The small sad voice tonight, the one he never trusts. She's more believable when she's being loud.

"Hi, Becka," he says, carefully neutral. "How are things going?" She was the one who walked out, though "walked" is too mild a description of it, so if there's conciliation to be done she can do it. "You want something?" he adds.

"Don't be like that," she says, after a short evaluating pause.

"Like what?" he says. "What am I being like that's so terrible?"

She sighs. He's familiar with these sighs of hers: she sighs over the phone better than any woman he's ever known. If he hadn't been sighed at by her so often, if he didn't know the hidden costs, he'd fall for it. She dodges his question, though; once she'd have met it head-on. "I thought maybe I could come over," she says. "So we could talk about it."

"Sure," says Joel, sliding into an old habit: he's never refused an offer to talk about it. But also he knows where talking about it leads. He pictures Becka's body, which she always holds back as the clincher; which is what he calls lush and she calls fat. Some of their first arguments were over this difference of opinion. "I'll be here," he says. If it's an offer, why turn it down?

But after he puts down the phone he regrets his easy acquiescence. So they go to bed. So what? What's it expected to prove? Is she working up to another move, back in? He's not sure he feels like going through the whole wash and spin cycle once again. Anyway, he's hungry. He types out a note—writing would be too intimate—saying he's been called out suddenly, to an important meeting, and he'll talk to her later. He doesn't say *see*. He opens the back door, which is the one she'll use, and tapes the note to it, noticing as he does so that someone has thrown an egg at his door: the remains are oozing down the paintwork, partly solidified, the broken shell is on the sidewalk.

Joel goes back in, closes the door. It's dark out there. Someone has taken a lot of trouble, going around to the back like that; someone who knows exactly who lives behind his door. It wasn't just a random shot, someone who happened to be passing by with an egg in his hand and got a sudden urge to hurl it. He has choices: maybe it's one of the nut-slicers, an idea he doesn't relish. Maybe it's the landlord: that's what he thought last week, when he found a nail hammered through the back tire of his bicycle. He doesn't think it's anyone official. He's suspected the RCMP of bugging his phone, more than once, he knows that squeaky-clean sound on the line, and no doubt he's on their list, most people who do anything at all in this country are. But eggs they wouldn't bother with.

Or maybe it's Becka. Throwing an egg at his door, then phoning him to make up because she feels guilty about something she'll never confess to him she's done, that's her style. "What egg?" she'll say to him if he asks, making her innocent chipmunk eyes, and how will he ever know? Once, when they were at a party together, they heard a gossipy story about a woman who'd recently split up with a man they both knew. She'd gone to the post office and filled out a change-of-address card in his name, redirecting all his mail to a town somewhere in the middle of Africa. At the time, and because he didn't like the guy much, Joel had found this hilarious. Becka hadn't, though she'd listened to the story more carefully than he had, and had asked questions. It strikes him now that she'd been filing it away for future reference. Now he tries to remember the rest of the story, the other things the woman had done: intercepting the man's shirts on the way back from the laundry and cutting off all the buttons, sending funeral wreaths to his new girl friend. Joel is safe on both counts: no laundered shirts, no new girl friend. It's just the mail he'll have to watch.

Now he's wondering whether going out is such a good idea. Becka still has a key, which he'll have to do something about pretty soon. Maybe she'll be in his apartment, waiting for him, when he gets back. He decides to take his chances. When she finds he isn't there, she can stay or she can go, it's up to her. (Leaving it up to her has always been one of his best tactics. It drives her mad.) Either way, he's made his move. He's shown her he's not eager. Any effort put out this time around is going to be hers.

As he searches for his wallet in the jumble of paperbacks, papers, and socks beside the bed, Uglypuss brushes against his legs, purring. He scratches her between the ears and pulls her up slowly by the tail, which he's convinced cats like. ("Cut that out, you'll break its spine," Becka would protest. But Uglypuss was his goddamn cat, to begin with.)

"Uglypuss," he says. He's had her almost as long as he's had his La-Z-Boy recliner and his Ping-Pong table: she's been through a lot with him. She turns her odd face up at him, half orange, half black. divided down the nose, a Yin and Yang cat, as Becka used to say during her organic-cereal and body-mind-energy phase.

She follows him to the door, the front one this time; he'll leave through the communal vestibule, walk down the steps, where there are street lights. She meows, but he doesn't want her going out, not at night. Even though she's spayed, she wanders, and sometimes gets into fights. Maybe the toms can't tell she's a girl; or maybe they think she is, but she disagrees. He used to make pointed analyses of Uglypuss's sexual hang-ups, to Becka, over breakfast. Whatever the reason, she gets herself messed up: her ears are nicked, and he's had it with the antibiotic ointment, which she licks off anyway. He thinks of distracting her with food, but he's out of cat kibble, which is one more reason for going out. He takes the container of dubious yoghurt out of the refrigerator and leaves it on the floor, opened for her.

*   *   *

Joel wipes his mouth, pushes the plate away. He's stuffed down everything: Weiner schnitzel, home fries, the lot. Now he's full and lazy. The back room of the Blue Danube used to be one of his favourite places to eat, before he moved in with Becka, or rather, she moved in with him. It's inexpensive and you get a lot for your money, good quality too. It has another advantage: other people who want cheap food come here, art students, in pairs or singly, out-of-work actors or actresses, those on the prowl but not desperate or rich or impervious enough to go to singles bars. Joel wouldn't want to pick up the kind of girl who would go to singles bars.

Becka never liked this place, so he gradually eased out of the habit of coming here. The last time they ate together it was here, though: a sure sign, for both of them, that the tide had turned.

Becka had come back from the washroom and plunked herself down opposite him, as though she'd just made an earth-shattering discovery. "Guess what's written in the women's can?" she'd asked.

"I'll bite," said Joel.

"Women make love. Men make war," she said.

"So?" Joel said. "Is the lipstick pink or red?"

"So it's true."

"That's supposed to be an insight?" said Joel. "It's not *men* that make war. It's *some* men. You think those young working-class guys want to march off and be slaughtered? It's the generals, it's the . . ."

"But it's not women, is it?" said Becka.

"That's got nothing to do with anything," Joel said, exasperated.

"That's what I mean about you," said Becka. "It's only your goddamned point of view that's valid, right?"

"Bullshit," he said. "We aren't talking about points of view. We're talking about *history*."

As he said this, the futility of what he was trying to do swept over him, as it sometimes does: what's the point of continuing, in a society like this one, where it's always two steps forward and two back? The frustration, the lack of money, the indifference, and on top of that the incessant puerile bickering on the left over who's more pure. If there was a real fight (he thinks "guns" but not "war"), if it was out in the open, things would be clearer; but this too can be seen as a temptation, the impulse to romanticize other people's struggles. It's hard to decide what form of action is valid. Do you have to be dead to be authentic, as the purists seem to believe? Though he hasn't noticed any of them actually lining up for the firing squads. Maybe he's chosen the wrong mode; maybe street theatre doesn't fit in up here, where the streets are so neat and clean and nobody lives on them, in shacks or storm sewers or laid out on mats along the sidewalks. Sometimes he thinks maybe they're all just play-acting, indulging in a game of adult dress-up that accomplishes nothing in the end.

But these moods of his seldom last long. "Wars are fought so those in power can stay there," he said to Becka, trying to be patient.

"You don't think you're ever going to *win*, do you?" Becka said softly. She can read his mind, but only at bad times.

"It's not about winning," Joel said. "I know whose side I'd rather be on, that's all."

"How about being on mine?" Becka said. "For a change."

"What the shit are you talking about?" said Joel.

"I'm not hungry," said Becka. "Let's go home."

It's the word *home* that echoes in the air here for Joel now, plaintively, in a minor key. Home isn't a place, Becka said once, it's a feeling. Maybe that's what's the matter with it, Joel answered. For him, when he was growing up, home was the absence of a thing that should have been there. Going home was going into nothingness. He'd rather be out.

He looks around the room, which is smoke-filled, bare-walled, his gaze passing over couples, resting longer on women by themselves. Why not admit it? He's come out tonight because he's looking for it, as so many times before: someone to go home with, to her home, not his, in the hope that this unknown place, yet another unknown place, will finally contain something he wants to have. It's Becka's phone call that's done it: she has that effect on him. Every move to encircle him, pin him down, force him into a corner, only makes him more desperate to escape. She never came right out and said so, but what she wanted was permanence, commitment, monogamy, the works. Forty years of the same thing night after night was a long time to contemplate.

He sees a girl he knows slightly, remembers from the summer, when they were doing the Cannibal Monster Tomato play down near Leamington, for the itinerant harvesters. (Cold-water shacks. Insecticides in the lungs. No medical protection. Intimidation. It was a good piece.) The girl was a minor player, someone who carried a sign. As he recalls, she was getting laid by one of the troupe; that was the only explanation he could think of at the time for her presence among them. He hopes he was right, he hopes she's not too political. Becka wasn't political when he first met her. In those days she was doing art therapy at one of the nuthouses, helping the loonies to express themselves with wet newspaper and glue. She'd had a calmness, a patience that he's since realized was only a professional veneer, but at the time he'd settled into it like a hammock. He'd enjoyed trying to educate her, and she'd gotten into it to parrot him or please him. What a mistake.

In recent years, he's come to realize that the kind of women that ought to turn him on—left-leaning intellectual women who can hold up their end of a debate, who believe in fifty-fifty, who can be good pals—aren't the kind that actually dó. He's not ashamed of this discovery, as he would have been once. He prefers women who are soft-spoken and who don't live all the time in their heads, who don't take everything with deadly seriousness. What he needs is someone who won't argue about whether he's too macho, whether he should or shouldn't encourage the capitalists by using under-arm deodorant, whether the personal is political or the political is personal, whether he's anti-Semitic, anti-female, anti-anything. Someone who won't argue.

He pushes back his chair and walks over, ready for rejection. They can always tell him to go away. He doesn't mind that much, he never tries to force the issue. There's no sense in being obnoxious, and he doesn't want to be with anyone who doesn't want to be with him. He's never seen the point of rape.

This girl has reddish hair, parted in the middle and drawn back. She's crouched over her noodles, pretending to be absorbed in a large but paperbacked book that's propped open beside her plate. Joel goes through the openers: "Hi, good to see you again. Mind if I join you?"

She glances up, with that little frown he's seen on their faces so often, that coming-out-of-the-trance face, *Oh, you startled me*, as if she hasn't been aware of his approach. She's been aware. She recognizes him, hesitates, deciding, then she smiles. She's grateful, he sees, for the company: it must be all over with what's-his-name. Relieved, he sits down. Even though he knows no one is really watching him, it still makes him feel like an idiot to be sent away, like a puppy that's made a mess.

Now for the book: that's always a good way in. He turns it so he can see the title. *Quilt-Making Through History*. That's a hard one: he knows nothing and cares less about quilt-making. He guesses that she's the kind of girl who would read about it but would never actually do it; though opening up with a statement to this effect would be far too aggressive. It's a mistake to begin by putting them down.

"Like a beer," he says, "or are you a vegetarian?"

"As a matter of fact I am," she says, with that superior tight mini-smile they give you. She hasn't got the joke. Joel sighs; they're off to a roaring start.

"Then I guess you mind if I smoke?" he says.

She relents; evidently she doesn't want to drive him away. "You go ahead," she says. "It's a big room." She doesn't add that it's full of smoke already, and he likes her better.

He thinks of saying, "Live around here?" but he can't, not again. "Tell me about yourself" is out too. Instead he finds himself shifting almost immediately, much sooner than he usually does, into social realism. "This day has been total shit," he says. He feels this, it's not fake, the day *has* been total shit; but on another level he knows he wants sympathy, and on yet another one he's aware it's a useful ploy: if they feel sorry for you, how can they turn you down?

Becka used to accuse him of having a detachable prick. In her version, he unscrewed it, put it on a leash, and took it out for walks, like a dachshund without legs or a kind of truffle-hunting pig (her metaphor). According to her, it would stick itself into any hole or crevice it could find, anything vaguely funnel-shaped, remotely female. In her more surrealistic inventions (when she was still trying to live with what she called this habit of his, before she switched to *compulsion*, when she was still trying to be humorous about it), he'd find himself stuck somewhere, in a mouse-hole or a dead tree or an outside faucet, unable to get loose, because his prick had made a mistake. What could you expect, she said, from a primitive animal with no eyes?

"If I got you a sheep and a pair of rubber boots, would you stay home more?" she said. "We could keep it in the garage. If we had a garage. If it wasn't too boor-joo-ice to have a garage."

But she was wrong, it isn't the sex he's after. It isn't only the sex. Sometimes he thinks, in the middle of it, that really he'd rather be jogging around the block or watching a movie or playing Ping-Pong. Sex is merely a social preliminary, the way a handshake used to be; it's the first step in getting to know someone. Once it's out of the way, you can concentrate on the real things; though without it, somehow you can't. He likes women, he likes just talking with them sometimes. The ones he likes talking with, having a laugh with, these are the ones that become what he refers to privately as "repeaters."

"How come I'm not enough for you?" Becka said, soon after the first two or three, when she'd figured it out. He wasn't a very good liar; he resented having to conceal things.

"It's not important," he said, trying to comfort her; she was crying. He still loved her in a simple way then. "It's no more important than sneezing. It's not an emotional commitment. You're an emotional commitment."

"If it's not important, why do you do it?" she said.

He wasn't able to answer that. "This is just the way I am," he said finally. "It's part of me. Can't you accept it?"

"But this is just the way *I* am," she said, crying even more. "You make me feel like nothing. You make me feel I'm worth nothing to you. I'm not even worth any more than a sneeze."

"That's blackmail," he said, pulling away. He couldn't stand to have love and fidelity extracted from him, like orange juice or teeth. No squeezers. No pliers. She should have known she was the central relationship: he'd told her often enough.

This girl's name, which he's forgotten but which he digs out of her by pretending to almost remember it, is Amelia. She works, of course, in a bookstore. Looking more closely, he can see she's not quite as young as he first thought. There are tiny shrivellings beginning around her eyes, a line forming from the nostril to the corner of her mouth; later it will extend down to her chin, which is small and pointed, and she will develop that peevish, starved look. Redheads have delicate skin, they age early. She has a chain around her neck, with a glass pendant on it containing dried flowers. He guesses she'll be the kind of girl who has prisms hanging in her window and a poster of a whale over the bed, and when they get to her place, she does.

Amelia turns out to be one of the vocal kind, which he likes: it's a tribute, in a way. He's surprised, too: you couldn't have told it by looking at her, that almost prissy restraint and decorum, the way she tightened her little bum, moved it away when he put his hand on it as she was unlocking the door. Joel doesn't know why he always expects girls with pierced ears and miniature gold stars in them, high cheekbones and frail rib cages, to be quiet in' bed. It's some antiquated notion he has about good taste, though he should know by now that the thin ones have more nerve-endings per square inch.

Afterwards she goes back to being subdued, as if she's faintly ashamed of herself for those groans, for having clutched him like that, as if he's not a semi-stranger after all. He wonders how many times she's gone home with someone she barely knows; he's curious, he'd like to ask, "You do this often?" But he knows from past experience they're likely to find this insulting, some kind of obscure slur on their moral standards; even if, like himself, they do. Sometimes, especially when they're younger, he feels he ought to tell them they shouldn't behave like this. Not all men are good risks, even the ones who eat at the Blue Danube. They could be violent, into whips or safety pins, perverts, murderers; not like him. But any interference from him could be interpreted as patriarchal paternalism: he knows that from experience too. It's their own lookout; anyway, why should he complain?

Amelia lies against him, head on his biceps, red hair spilling across his arm, her mouth relaxed; he's grateful for her simple physical presence, the animal warmth. Women don't like the term "muff," he knows that; but for him it's both descriptive and affectionate: something furry that keeps you warm. This is the kind of thing he needs to get him through November. She's even being friendly, in a detached sort of way. He can't always depend on them to be friendly afterwards. They've been known to hold it against him, as if it's something he's done all by himself, to them instead of with them; as if they've had nothing to do with it.

He likes this one well enough to suggest that maybe they could watch the late show on TV, which isn't an experience he'd want to share with just anyone. Sex yes, late movies no. He wonders if she's got any food in the house, some cake maybe, which they could eat right off the plate while watching, licking the icing from each other's fingers. He's hungry again, but more than that, he wants the feeling of comfort this would bring. There's something about lemon icing in a dark room. But when she says without any undertones that, no, she'd like some sleep, she needs to get up early to go to her fitness class before work, that's all right with him too. He puts on his clothes, lighthearted; this whole thing has cheered him up a lot. He has that secret feeling of having gotten away with it again, in the bedroom window and out again without being caught: no sticky flypaper here. He remembers, briefly, the day he figured out his mother was hiding the cookies, not so he wouldn't find them, but so he would, and how enraged, how betrayed he'd been. He'd seen the edge of her green chenille bathrobe whisking back around the corner; she'd been standing in the hall outside the kitchen, listening to him eat. She must have known what a rotten cook she was, and this was her backhanded way of making sure he got at least some food into him. That's what he thinks now, but at the time he merely felt he'd been controlled, manipulated by her all along. Maybe that was when he started to have his first doubts about free will.

Amelia has turned on her side and is almost asleep. He kisses her, says he'll let himself out. He wonders if he likes her well enough to see her again, decides he probably doesn't. Nevertheless he makes a note of her phone number, memorizing it off the bedside phone; he'll jot it down later, out in the kitchen, where she won't notice. He never knows when a thing like that will come in handy. Any port in a storm, and when he's at a low point, a trough in the graph, he needs to be with someone and it doesn't much matter who, within limits.

He pisses into her toilet, flushes it, noting the anti-nuke sticker on the mirror, the pots of herbs struggling for existence on the windowsill. Then he goes into the kitchenette and turns on the light, taking a quick peek into the refrigerator in passing, on the off-chance she's got something unhealthy and delicious in there. But she's a tofu girl, and reluctantly he's out the door.

He's not thinking about Becka. He doesn't remember her till his key's in the lock, when he has a sudden image of her, waiting on the other side, black hair falling around her face like something in a Lorca play, large wounded eyes regarding him, some deadly instrument in her hand: a corkscrew, a potato peeler, or, more historically, an ice-pick, though he doesn't own one. Cautiously he opens the door, eases through, is relieved when nothing happens. Maybe it's finally over, after all. It occurs to him that he's forgotten to buy cat food.

His relief lasts until he hits the living room. She's been here, all right. He gazes at the innards of his La-Z-Boy, strewn across the floor, its wiry guts protruding from what's left of the frame, at the hunks of soft foam from the sofa washing against the fireplace as if it's a shore, as if Becka has been a storm, a hurricane. In another corner he finds all his Ping-Pong balls, lined up in a row and stomped on; they look like hatched-out turtle eggs. Some of his underwear is lying in the fireplace, charred around the edges, still smouldering.

He shrugs. Histrionic bitch, he thinks. So he'll replace it: there's nothing here that can't be duplicated. She won't get to him that easily. She hasn't touched the typewriter, though: she knows exactly how far she can go.

Then he sees the note. *Want Uglypuss back! It's in a garbage can. Start looking.* The note is pinned to the big orange art-shop candle on the mantlepiece, one of the first things she gave him. It's as if he's finally had a visit from Santa Claus, who has turned out to be the monster his mother was always warning him against when he showed symptoms of wanting a Christmas like some of the other kids on the block. *Santa Claus brings you lumps of coal and rotten potatoes. What do you need it for?*

But this was no Santa Claus, it was Becka, who knows just where to slide in the knife. Dead or alive, she doesn't say. She's never exactly loved Uglypuss, but surely she wouldn't murder. He fears the worst, but he can't assume it. He'll have to go and see. He hears the claws scrabbling on metal, the plaintive wails, the mounting panic, as he does up his zipper again. Finally he knows she'll stop at nothing.

He walks in a widening circle through the streets around his house, opening every can, digging through the bags, listening for faint meows. He shouldn't be spending time on something this trivial, this personal; he should be conserving his energy for the important things. What he needs is perspective. This is Becka controlling him again. Maybe she was lying, maybe Uglypuss is safe and sound at her new place, purring beside the hot-air register. Maybe Becka is making him go through all this for nothing, hoping he'll arrive on her doorstep and she can torture him or reward him, whichever she feels like at the moment.

"Uglypuss!" he calls. He tells himself he's in a state of shock, it will hit him tomorrow, when the full implications of a future without Uglypuss will sink in. At the moment though he's thinking: *Why did I have to give it that dumb name!*

*   *   *

Becka walks along the street. She has often walked along this particular street. She tells herself there is nothing unusual about it.

Both of her hands are bare, and there's blood on the right one and four thin lines of it across her cheek. In her right hand she's carrying an axe. Actually it's smaller than an axe, it's a hatchet, the one Joel keeps beside the fireplace to split the kindling when he lights the fire. Once she liked to make love with him on the rug in front of the fireplace, in the orange glow from the candle. That was until he said there was always a draft and he'd rather be in bed, where it was warmer. After a while she figured out that he didn't really like being looked at; he had an odd sort of modesty, as if he felt his body belonged to him alone. Once she tried flattering him about it, but this was a bad move, you weren't supposed to compare. So then it was under the covers, like a married couple. Before that she used to bug him about keeping the axe in the living room, she wanted him to leave it on the back porch and split the kindling out there instead; she told him she didn't like getting splinters.

It was looking at the axe that finally did it. Joel was gone when he said he'd be there. She didn't know exactly where he'd gone but she knew in general. He was always doing that to her. She waited for an hour and a half, pacing, reading his magazines, surrounded by a space that used to be hers and still felt like it. The heat was off, which meant Joel had been antagonizing the landlord again. She thought about lighting a fire. Uglypuss came and rubbed against her legs and complained, and when she went into the kitchen to put out some food, there was the yoghurt she'd bought herself, opened on the floor.

She asked herself how long she was going to wait. Even if he came back soon, he'd have that smug look and the smell of it still on him. She'd have the choice of ignoring it, in which case he won, or saying something, in which case he won also, because then he could accuse her of intruding on his privacy. It would be just another example, he'd say, of why things couldn't work out. That would make her angry—they could, they could work out if he'd only try—and then he would criticize her for being angry. Her anger would be a demonstration of the power he still holds over her. She knows it, but she can't control it. This time was once too often. It was always once too often.

Becka walks quickly, head a little down and forward, as if she has to push to make her way through the air. Her hair blows back in the wind. It's beginning to drizzle. In her left hand she's carrying a green plastic garbage bag, screwed shut and knotted at the top. The street she's on is Spadina, a street she remembers from childhood as the place where she would be taken by her grandfather when he wanted to pay visits to some of his old cronies. She'd be shown off by him, and given things to eat. That was before the Chinese mostly took over. It's well enough lighted, even at this time of night, bamboo furniture, wholesale clothing, restaurants, ethnic as they say; but she's not buying or eating, she's just looking, thanks, for a garbage can, someplace to dump the bag. An ordinary garbage can is all she asks; why can't she find one?

She can't believe she's done what she's just done. What horrifies her is that she enjoyed it, the axe biting into the black Naugahyde of that ratty chair of his, into the sofa, the stuffing she'd pulled out and thrown around, it might as well have been Joel. Though if he'd been there he would have stopped her. Just by being there, by looking at her as if to say, *You mean you really can't think of anything more important to do?*

This is what he's turned me into, she thinks. I was never this mean before, I used to be a nice person, a nice girl. Didn't I?

Today, before calling him, she'd been sick of the taste of the inside of her own mouth. She'd had enough of solitude, enough freedom. A woman without a man is like a fish without a bicycle. Brave words, she'd said them once herself. That was before she figured out she wasn't a fish. Today she thought she still loved him, and love conquers all, doesn't it? Where there's love there's hope. Maybe they could get it back, together. Now, she doesn't know.

She thinks about stuffing the garbage bag into a mailbox, the parcel kind, or a newspaper stand. She could put in the quarter, open the box, take out the newspaper, leave the bag. Someone would find it quicker that way. She is not heartless.

But suddenly there's a garbage can, not a plastic one but old-style metal, in front of a Chinese fruit-and-vegetable store. She goes over to it, leans the hatchet against it, sets down the bag, tries to lift the lid. Either it's stuck or her hands are numb. She bangs it against a telephone pole; several people look at her. At last the lid comes loose. Luckily the can is half empty. She drops the bag in. Not a sound: she sprayed in some boot water-proofer, which was about the only thing she could think of: breathing the fumes makes you dizzy. Kids at high school used to get high on it. The stupid cat clawed its way through the first two garbage bags, before she thought of tying it up in one of Joel's shirts and spraying it with boot water-proofer to quiet it down. She doesn't know if it went unconscious; maybe it just couldn't get through Joel's shirt and decided not to fight a losing battle. Maybe it's catatonic. To coin a phrase. She hopes she hasn't killed it. She pokes the bag a little: there's a wiggle. She's relieved, but she doesn't relent and let it loose. Why should she have all the grief? Let him have some, for a change.

This is what will really get to him, she knows: this theft. His kidnapped child, the one he wouldn't let her have. *We're not ready yet* and all that crap. Crap! He'd always thought more of the cat than he did of her. It used to make her sick, to watch the way he'd pick it up by the tail and run it through his hands, like sand, and the cat loved it, like the nauseating masochist it was. It was the kind of cat that drooled when you stroked it. It fawned all over him. Maybe the real reason she couldn't stand it was that it was a grotesque and stunted furry little parody of herself. Maybe this was what she looked like, to other people, when she was with him. Maybe this was what she looked like to him. She thinks of herself lying with her eyes closed and her mouth slack and open. Did he remember what she looked like at those moments, when he was with others?

She doesn't close the lid on the garbage can. She leaves the hatchet where it is, walks away. She feels smaller, diminished, as if something's been sucking on her neck. Anger is supposed to be liberating, so goes the mythology, but her anger has not freed her in any way that she can see. It's only made her emptier, flowing out of her like this. She doesn't want to be angry; she wants to be comforted. She wants a truce.

She can remember, just barely, having had confidence in herself. She can't recall where she got it from. Go through life with your mouth open, that used to be her motto. Live in the now. Encounter experience fully. Hold out your arms in welcome. She once thought she could handle anything.

Tonight she feels dingy, old. Soon she will start getting into the firming cream; she will start worrying about her eyelids. Beginning again is supposed to be exciting, a challenge. Beginning again is fine as an idea, but what with? She's used it all up; she's used up.

Still, she would like to be able to love someone; she would like to feel inhabited again. This time she wouldn't be so picky, she'd settle for a man maybe a little worn around the edges, a second, with a few hairline cracks, a few pulled threads, something from a fire sale, someone a little damaged. Like those ads for adoptable children in the *Star*: "Today's Child." Today's lover. A man in a state of shock, a battered male. She'd take a divorced one, an older one, someone who could only get it up for kinky sex, anything, as long as he'd be grateful. That's what she wants, when it comes right down to it: a gratitude equal to her own. But even in this she's deluding herself. Why should such a man be any different from the rest? They're all a little damaged. Anyway, she'd be clutching at a straw, and who wants to be a straw?

She should never have called him. She should know by now that over is over, that when it says *The End* at the end of a book it means there isn't any more; which she can never quite believe. The problem is that she's invested so much suffering in him, and she can't shake the notion that so much suffering has to be worth something. Maybe unhappiness is a drug, like any other: you could develop a tolerance to it, and then you'd want more.

People came to the end of what they had to say to one another, Joel told her once, during one of their many sessions about whether they should stay together or not; the time he was trying for wisdom. After that point, he said, it was only repetition. But Becka protested; Becka hadn't come to the end of what she had to say, or so she thought. That was the trouble: she never came to the end of what she had to say. He'd push her too far and she'd blurt things out, things she couldn't retrieve, she would make clumsy mistakes of a kind she never made with other people, the landlord for instance, with whom she was a miracle of tact. But with Joel, the irrevocable is always happening.

He once told her he wanted to share his life with her. He said he'd never asked anyone that before. How she melted over that, how she lapped it up! But he never said he wanted her to share her life with him, which, when it happened, turned out to be a very different thing.

What now, now that she's done it? Time will go on. She'll walk back to the row house in Cabbagetown she shares with two other women. This is about all she can afford; at least she has her own room. She hardly ever sees the other two women; she knows them mostly by their smells, burnt toast in the mornings, incense (from one of them, the one with the lay-over boy friend) at night. The situation reeks of impermanence. She got the place by answering an ad in the paper, *Third woman needed, share kitchen, no drugs or freaks,* after moving out of the apartment she still thinks of as her own, and after a miserable week with her mother, who thought but did not say that it served her right for not insisting on marriage. What did she expect anyway, from a man like that? Not a real job. Not a real Jew. Not real.

When she gets to the house she'll be worn out, her adrenalin high gone, replaced by a flat grey fatigue. She'll put on her most penitential nightgown, blue-flowered flannelette, the one Joel hates because it reminds him of landladies. She'll fix herself a hot-water bottle and climb into a bed which does not yet smell like hers and feel sorry for herself. Maybe she should go out hunting, sit in a bar, something she's never done, though there's always a first time. But she needs her sleep. Tomorrow she has to go to work, at her new job, her old job, mixing poster paints for the emotionally disturbed, a category that right now includes her. It doesn't pay well and there are hazards, but these days she's lucky to have it.

She couldn't stay with the troupe, even though she'd done such a good job of the headless corpses for the El Salvador piece in the spring, even though it was her who'd come up with Christ as a knitted sock. It would be disruptive for the troupe, they both agreed on that, to have her there; the tension, the uneven balance of conflicting egos. Or words to that effect. He was so good at that bullshit, the end result of which was that she'd been out of a job and he hadn't, and for a while she'd even felt noble about it.

Becka's four blocks away from the garbage can now, and it's raining in earnest. She stands under an awning, waiting for the rain to slow down, trying to decide whether or not to give in and take the streetcar. She wants to walk all the way back, to get rid of this furious energy.

It's time for Joel to be coming home. She pictures him

opening the door, throwing his jacket on the floor; she sees what he will find. Now she feels as if she's committed a sacrilege. Why should she feel that way? Because for at least two years she thought he was God.

He isn't God. She can see him, in his oily Bluejays jacket, running through the streets, panting because he'll be out of breath, he'll have eaten too much for dinner, with whatever slut he'd picked up, plunging his hands into chilly garbage, calling like a fool: *Uglypuss!* People will think he's crazy. But he will only be mad with grief.

Like her, leaning her forehead against the cold shop window, staring through the dark glass, yellowed by those plastic things they put there to keep the sun from fading the colours, at the fur-coated woman inside, tears oozing down her cheeks. She can't even remember now which garbage can she put the damn thing in, she couldn't find it again if she looked. She should have taken it home with her. It was her cat too, more or less, once. It purred and drooled for her, too. It kept her company. How could she have done that to it? Maybe the boot spray will make it feeble-minded. That's all he'll need, a feeble-minded cat. Not that anyone will be able to tell the difference.

In her either, if she goes on like this. She wipes her nose and eyes on her damp sleeve, straightens. When she gets home she'll do some Yogic breathing and concentrate on the void for a while, trying once more for serenity, and take a bath. *My heart does not bleed*, she tells herself. But it does.

TWO STORIES ABOUT EMMA

THE WHIRLPOOL RAPIDS

There are some women who seem to be born without fear, just as there are people who are born without the ability to feel pain. The painless ones go around putting their hands on hot stoves, freezing their feet to the point of gangrene, scalding the linings of their throats with boiling coffee, because there is no warning anguish. Evolution does not favour them. So too perhaps with the fearless women, because there aren't very many of them around. I myself have known only two. One was a maker of television documentaries and was one of the first to shoot footage in Vietnam. There would be the beach, they said, and the line of jungle, with the soldiers advancing towards it, and in front of them, walking backwards, would be this woman. Providence appears to protect such women, maybe out of astonishment. Or else, sooner or later, it doesn't.

I'm told the fearlessness goes away when these women have babies. Then they become cowards, like the rest of us. If the baby is threatened they become ferocious, of course, but that is not out of the ordinary.

The other woman I knew, and still know—her luck has held—is Emma, who has always intrigued me. I think of

Emma as a woman who will do anything, though that isn't how she thinks of herself. The truly fearless think of themselves as normal.

This, as far as I've been able to tell, is how she got like that.

*   *   *

When she was twenty-one, Emma nearly died. Or so she was told, and since four of those with her actually did die, she had to believe it. At the time she hadn't felt anywhere near dead.

It was a freak accident, and the fact that she was there at all was an accident too, the result of a whim and of knowing someone. Emma always knows a lot of people. The person she knew for this occasion was a man, a boy really, about her own age. He didn't qualify as a boyfriend, he was just one of the group she'd hung out with the previous year, at university. In the summers he worked for a travel agency, a good one that specialized in organizing out-of-the-ordinary tours: bicycle trips through France, African game parks, that sort of thing. This boy, whose name was Bill, was one of the tour leaders. Because of his prowess with bicycles he had well-developed leg muscles, clearly visible that day, as he was wearing shorts and a T-shirt. It may have been these bicycle muscles that saved him, in the event.

Emma did not have bicycle muscles. She was never a slug physically, and only in recent years has she felt the need to pay any special attention to her shape. At that time she had good biceps, the result of lifting heavy trays. She was working as a waitress in the coffee shop of a tourist motel in Niagara Falls. The motel had a neon sign outside that showed two entwined hearts, one red, one blue, and it had hearts printed at the top of the menu, which Emma found somewhat gruesome in association with food. The motel was slanted towards newlyweds, and even had a Bridal Suite, wallpapered in red, with a Magic Fingers bed and a machine that made instant coffee for two.

Emma says she has never been able to understand the association of Niagara Falls with honeymoons. What is the sight of all that water falling over a cliff supposed to do for you sexually? Possibly it makes men feel more potent: she thinks she should ask about this sometime. And brides may become quivery and weak-kneed in the face of such brute inhuman force, a quality they wistfully hope that their bridegrooms may prove to possess. Though these days, surely they know by the time they make it as far as the altar. No more pigs in pokes.

Or perhaps it's the vulgarity of the town itself, its transience, its tinsel-and-waxworks tawdriness, fitting contrast to the notion of Eternal Love, which, despite the jokes she's made about it at various times in her life, Emma has never ceased to believe in.

At that point she didn't know it. She wasn't thinking of love, but of making enough money to get her through her last year at university without going too far into hock. Niagara Falls was a good enough place for that: the satiated tip well.

Thus she had what Bill the bicycle adept was looking for: accessibility. If she had been elsewhere, none of this would have happened.

There was nothing remarkable about Bill; he was merely one of those agents of Fate who have intruded on Emma's life from time to time and then departed from it, mission accomplished. Like many fearless people, Emma believes in Fate.

Bill was a nice boy; nice enough so that when he ambled into Emma's coffee shop one day and told her that he wanted her body, Emma took it as a joke and did not resent it. Really he wanted her to come on a test run, he said. The travel agency he was working for was doing a pilot project on a new kind of tour: down the Whirlpool Rapids below Niagara Falls, on a big rubber raft. They'd done the run nine times so far, and it was perfectly safe, but they weren't ready to open the tour to the public until they'd had one more test. It was only travel agency people and their friends going, he said, and they were short of bodies: there had to be a full contingent for the thing to work, they needed forty people for the weight and balance. It struck him as the kind of thing that might appeal to Emma.

Emma was flattered by this image of herself, and readily accepted it as a true one: a physically brave young woman, a bit of a daredevil, willing to put on a life jacket at a moment's notice and sit on a large inflated platform of rubber and swirl down the dangerous Niagara Whirlpool Rapids. It would be like roller coasters, which she'd always found compelling. She would join the ranks of those who had, in the past, wished to challenge Niagara Falls: the tightrope walkers, and those who'd had themselves bolted into padded barrels and flung into the river above the drop; even the suicides, whom Emma lumped in with the challengers, because if you were not in some way gambling, why not just use a gun? In all of these attempts, it seemed to Emma, there was an element of religious trial: walking barefoot over the coals, ordeal by water. All of these people were flinging themselves on the mercy, of something or other. Certainly not just a river. Save me, Lord; show me I'm important enough to deserve it. Possibly it was this, Emma thought, looking back on it afterwards, that had prompted her: a desire to risk the self that was really a form of arrogance.

Emma said yes at once and arranged for her next day off to coincide with the tenth rubber-raft test run. On the morning of the day, which was a Monday, Bill picked her up from the run-down frame house she rented with three other girls and drove her across the Rainbow Bridge to the launching site, which was on the American side. It turned out afterwards–some reporter dug it up–that the Canadian officials had refused permission, considering the enterprise too hazardous, but even if Emma had known this it probably wouldn't have stopped her. Like many of her countrypeople, she considered her fellow Canadians to be a lacklustre bunch; wasn't it the Canadians who'd turned up their noses at the telephone when Alexander Bell first invented it?

The raft was black and enormous, and seemed, resting at its moorings, very stable. Emma was given an orange life jacket, and buckled herself into it, helped by Bill. Then they scrambled on board and found seats at the front end. They were among the first to arrive and had to wait for the others. Emma began to feel slightly let down and to wonder why she'd come. The raft was too big, too solid; it was like a floating parking lot.

But once they'd moved out into the current, the rubber surface under her began to ripple, in large waves of contraction, like a giant throat swallowing, and spray came in upon them, and Emma knew that the rapids, which had looked so decorative, so much like cake frosting from a distance, were actual after all. There were some dutiful thrilled noises from the other passengers, and then some genuine noises, less thrilled. Emma found herself clutching Bill's arm, a thing she wouldn't ordinarily have done. The sky was an unnatural blue, and the shore–dotted with the white-clad or pastel figures of tourists, which appeared static and painted, like a design on wallpaper– was very far away.

There was a lot of talk later about why the tenth run should have failed so badly, after the other nine had gone without a hitch. Some attempts were made to pin it on the design of the raft; others said that, owing to an unseasonal amount of rain during the preceding week, the water level had been too high and the current far swifter than usual. Emma could not remember wondering why, at the time. All she saw was the front of the raft tipping down into a trough deeper than any they'd yet hit, while a foaming wall of water rose above them. The raft should have curved sinuously, sliding up the wave. Instead it buckled across the middle, the front half snapping towards the back, like the beak of a bird closing. Emma and Bill and the other people in the front row shot backwards over the heads of the rest, who were jumbling in a heap at the bottom of the V, now submerging. (Emma didn't exactly see this at the time; she deduced it later. Her impressions were of her own movement only, and of course it was all very fast.)

Something struck her on the side of the head—a foot in a boot, perhaps—and she was underwater. Later she learned that the raft had flipped and a man had been trapped underneath it and drowned, so it was just as well that she had been flung clear. But underwater she did not think. Something else made her hold her breath and struggle towards the surface, which she could see above her, white and silver, so her eyes must have been open. Her head rose up, she gasped air and was sucked under.

The water tumbled and boiled and Emma fought it. She was filled almost to bursting with an energy that came from anger: *I refuse to die in such a stupid way*, was how she formulated this afterwards. She thinks she shouted, at least once: "No!" Which was a waste of breath, as there was nobody around to hear her. There were rocks, and she collided with several and was bruised and scraped, but nothing more hit her head, and after what seemed like an hour but was really only ten minutes the current was less and she found she could keep her head above the water and actually swim. It was hard to move her arms. She propelled herself towards the shore, and, finally, dragged herself up onto a small rocky beach. Her running shoes were gone. She must have kicked them off, though she couldn't remember doing it; or maybe they had been torn off. She wondered how she was going to get over the rocks without shoes.

The sky was even bluer than it had been before. There were some blue flowers also, weeds of some kind, cornflowers, growing among the rocks. Emma looked at them and did not feel anything. She must have been cut, her clothes were certainly ripped, there was a lump on the side of her forehead, but she didn't notice any of this at the time. Two people, a man and a woman, in summery clothes, came sauntering towards her along a path.

"What country am I in?" Emma asked them.

"Canada," said the man.

They walked past her and continued their stroll, as if they didn't notice anything unusual about her. Probably they didn't. The news of the accident had not yet reached them, so they didn't realize there had been one.

Emma, in her turn, did not find their behaviour out of place. *That's good then*, she thought to herself. She wouldn't have to go back over the bridge and through Immigration, which was lucky, because her purse had been swept away and so she did not have her birth certificate with her. She began to walk upstream, slowly, because of her bare feet. There was an unusual number of helicopters around. She thumbed a lift to the motel—she doesn't know why she elected to go there instead of to her house—and by the time she got there, the accident had been on the news and everyone thought she was dead.

She was taken to the hospital and treated for shock, and interviewed on television. Her picture was, briefly, in the papers. Bill came to see her and described his own experience to her. He had reached a point, under the water, at which he had given up, and the water had become very peaceful and very beautiful. This was how Emma realized that she herself hadn't been at all close to death. But Bill's bicycle-muscled legs had kicked by

117

themselves, like a wounded frog's, and brought him back.

For a while Emma felt closer to Bill than she did to anyone, but this feeling passed, although they still send each other Christmas cards. There was never any possibility of a romance: they were, after the accident, too much like twins, and then too much like strangers. Intimacy brought about by shared catastrophe can only go so far.

Emma has told me that she learned several things from this experience. First, that the number nine is luckier than the number ten, a superstition she has retained to this day. Second, that many more people than she'd thought would have known about her death, had it occurred, and been affected by it in some way; but third, that they wouldn't have been affected very deeply or for very long. Soon she would have become just a name, the name of a woman who had died young, in a tragic accident, some time ago. It was for this reason, perhaps, that Emma never had any of those wistful longings for death, those flirtations with the pale horseman, that afflict so many women in their twenties. She never thought to herself, a little hopefully, a little melodramatically, that maybe she wouldn't see thirty, that some unspecified but graceful disease would carry her off. Not her. She was determined to live, no matter what.

Nor was she ever tempted, after that, to give up anything—a man, an apartment, a job, even a vacation—in the mistaken conviction that by doing so she would be helping along the happiness of others. Because she found out early how very little difference she makes in the general scheme of things, she has clenched her teeth, ignored whimpers and hints and even threats, and done what she wanted, almost always. For this she has been called selfish and unfeeling. I think it has been to her credit that on these occasions she has not trotted out the story of her near-death by drowning as a justification for her sometimes dubious behaviour.

But the most obvious effect of the accident on Emma was her strong subsequent belief—it amounted to an article of religious faith—that she was invulnerable. She didn't merely feel this, she knew it, as firmly as she knew that her hand was her hand. She had been thrown into the Whirlpool Rapids of Niagara Falls and had lived; therefore nothing could touch her. She walked in a bubble of charmed air, which at times she imagined she could almost see, shimmering around her like mist; like, in fact, the mist that rose from the Falls themselves. If an arrow had been shot at her, it would have bounced off. No doubt about it, at least for Emma.

Little by little this belief faded. It was strongest right after the accident, but evaporated year by year, until by now nothing is left of it but a faint phosphorescence. Her friends call it optimism, this conviction of hers that everything will work out for her somehow.

WALKING ON WATER

Several years after the Whirlpool Rapids, at her most fearless, Emma was in a boat, going up the Nile. This was during her world-travel phase. She didn't have a lot of money at the time, so it wasn't a very high-class boat. The best place to be was on the deck. There was an interior where you could sit down, but it was smoke-filled and smelled of many previous passengers, not all of them happy. So Emma stayed outside, which was no pain as she could see the landscape better from there. She had on a floppy denim hat to guard against sunstroke.

She was travelling alone.

A medium-sized, possibly thirtyish Arab, puzzled by the cultural discrepancies that had placed a young woman on a boat, wearing peculiar clothing and not enough of it and gazing pensively over the rail, unaccompanied except for a shoddy-looking rucksack, began making advances to her. She did not respond, except by frowning and moving farther away from him. He smiled: he had many gold teeth. He offered her money, not very much.

"Go away," said Emma.

The man interpreted this as encouragement. Perhaps it was a mistake to have spoken to him at all. He laid a hand on her arm, which was bare to the elbow. She took the hand off, not too abruptly—she didn't want to offend, merely to disengage—and moved to the railing on the opposite side of the boat. Some other men were watching, friends of this one probably; she thought they were egging him on. He followed her and put his arm around her waist.

"If you don't leave me alone," she said to him loudly, "I'll jump off this boat."

The other men were laughing. He tried to kiss her, in an exaggerated courtly way he had probably seen in old American movies, attempting to bend her over backwards. But he was several inches shorter than Emma and couldn't budge her. By now he was putting on a show for the others, without any hope of real success. Emma took hold of his hand and bent the little finger back, to make him let go, a trick she remembered from schoolyards. Then she clambered over the railing, looking, she was aware, a little awkward in the long wraparound skirt she was wearing in deference to the local horror of legs. She jumped overboard. The Nile was muddy and opaque, and she had a brief instant of loss of faith as she was going down. What she thought was: *Crocodiles*. But there weren't any, and the men yelled, and the boat stopped and backed up and retrieved her, as she'd known it would. The men on the boat were respectful after that, keeping their distance and discussing her in low voices, and, she hoped, with awe. It was a gesture they understood. They hadn't believed a young Western woman travelling alone could ever have been serious enough about what they considered her honour to risk death for it.

Emma sat on the deck, dripping, drying her hair in the sun, her hat—which had oddly enough stayed on her head—steaming beside her. She felt a little cheap, pulling a trick like that—though it was clearly the only thing to do, under the circumstances—because she knew she hadn't been risking anything at all. She'd never had any intention of dying.

You may think from what I've said that Emma is a sort of tomboy, willing to exchange cigarettes and backslaps with men, but otherwise impervious to them. On the contrary: Emma, although tall, is always falling in love, a venture that for her seems to be a lot like skydiving: you leap impulsively into thin air, and trust that your parachute will open.

The men she falls in love with are usually married, and awful as well, or this is what Emma's friends think. We try to produce nice men for her, men with whom she could settle down, as she keeps saying with what may be fake wistfulness that she would like to do. But these kindly or courteous or even solvent men don't interest Emma. She wants exceptional men, she says, men she can look up to, and so she adores, one after another, men who have excelled in their fields, frequently through ruthless egoism, back-stabbing and what Emma calls dedication, which often means that when the chips are down they have no real time for anyone else, including Emma. Why she can't spot this kind of man a mile off, especially after all that practice, I don't know. But as I've said, she's fearless. The rest of us have more self-protection.

At this time of her life—the world-travel time—Emma was in love with Robbie, who had been her professor at college. Robbie was twenty years older than Emma, a stocky red-bearded Scot whose grumpiness was legendary. Emma mistook it for shyness. She thought he was more spiritually mature than she was, and therefore difficult to understand. She also thought that Robbie, sooner or later, would realize that Emma, and not his wife of fifteen years, mother of his two sons, was his true soul mate. This was towards the beginning of Emma's career. Later she dropped the marriage motif, or at least did not say so much about it. But the men did not become any less awful.

Robbie was a leading man in his field, which was not large. He was an archaeologist, specializing in burials. In fact he was writing a book on comparative tombs, which took him here and there about the world. This was convenient for Emma. Robbie was never averse to having her join him, as long as she paid her own way. Among Robbie's other sins, the rest of us felt, was his exploitation of the liberated woman theme. He was always lecturing Emma about how she could be more liberated. But Emma loved him despite this.

During the early, idyllic stage of their relationship, when Robbie had become for Emma the only man in the world who did not stop at the belt and then continue on again at the bottoms of the trousers, when she still believed in fidelity and eternity, when she was convinced Robbie would eventually marry her, Emma almost killed Robbie. She didn't do it on purpose.

They were on a Caribbean island: St. Eunice, one of the lesser-known ones. This vacation was Robbie's idea. He'd been doing tombs in Mexico, but he'd cut that short to make a detour here, in order to join Emma.

"Look how I'm sacrificing my career for you," he said as a joke, though Emma suspected he partly meant it. There were no tombs on St. Eunice worth bothering about, said Robbie.

They did spend an afternoon at a local cemetery, where the graves were covered in poured concrete and fenced in, to keep off the goats, said Robbie, and wilting real flowers and bleaching plastic ones stood in glass jam jars. Propitiations to the dead, said Robbie. Emma said it looked like Newfoundland. Robbie had never been to Newfoundland, and sulked: He didn't like the thought of Emma having been to places he hadn't. Emma, to restore his good humour—it was too hot to be angry—said she'd never actually been there, she'd only seen pictures of it. Then he brightened up, pointed to an odd maze pattern painted on one of the cement graves, and told her that mazes had originally been the entrances or exits to burial mounds. They were to confuse the dead, so they'd never get out. Similar patterns occurred on doors and doorsteps in some cultures, he said, but in those cases the maze was to keep the dead from getting in.

This conversation occupied their time between the graveyard and the house, where Robbie, excited by his own erudition, made love to Emma in the middle of the afternoon, which she was still young enough to find novel.

They were staying in a house that belonged to a friend of a friend of Robbie's. The house was stone and stucco, with latticed windows and a ceiling fan in the West Indian style, and a wide verandah running all the way around it. Trumpet vines shaded the patio, and there was a cool sea breeze.

But apart from each other there wasn't much to do. They were there for two weeks, and by the end of the first one Emma was feeling the need for some time apart from Robbie, although she still loved him as much as ever, of course. But, like a volatile gas, he did have a way of expanding to fill the space available.

Emma, who was physically adventurous, more so than Robbie, began to go for long walks. Sometimes she would climb up cliffs, or make her way along slippery ledges visible only at low tide. Occasionally Robbie would go with her on these walks, but more often he would stay at the house, sitting on the verandah, writing up his notes.

Near the house where Emma and Robbie were staying there was a beach, and across from it, about a third of a mile away, there was an island called Wreck Island. A pleasure liner had run aground there: you could still see what was left of the hull. When the wreck happened, and after the passengers were rescued, many of the local people took their boats out, at the right moment—for the currents in the channel could be choppy and treacherous—and made off with items from the liner. The woods, Emma was told, were full of toilets that had never been installed, chandeliers, huge bowls from the liner's kitchen, too big for cooking.

Emma heard this story in the local beach bar, where she also heard that there was an underwater ridge running out to Wreck Island. You could see it as a darker line if you stood on a hill overlooking the bay. Local tradition had it that at low tide it was possible to walk from one island to the other, along the ridge. The water would come about up to your neck, they said. A man in trouble with his neighbour over a woman had done this within living memory; the neighbour later commandeered a rowboat at knife point, rowed across, and beat the shit out of him, but the ridge-walker had come out of it the hero and was known afterwards as Jesus Christ, because he had walked on water.

Emma, hearing this tale, got the notion into her head that she too would like to walk out to Wreck Island. She couldn't explain why. To Robbie, she put it down to boredom: she'd already explored everything in the immediate vicinity, and wouldn't it be a challenge to walk out to the island? She wouldn't have said "a challenge" if she hadn't had an ulterior motive, which was to persuade Robbie to make the walk with her. She wasn't totally foolhardy, and though she still believed in her invulnerability she didn't mind companionship and a little back-up. She knew that Robbie didn't really want to go, but she also knew that he wouldn't be able to resist the word *challenge*. She made it clear that she was going herself in any case, and in the end he agreed to accompany her. He said she'd need someone to keep an eye on her, in case she got into trouble.

Emma chose their gear carefully: bathing suits, with T-shirts over them, because of the sun; running shoes, because the ridge was part coral; floppy denim sun hats, which Emma bought specially at a local boutique, Emma's hot pink, Robbie's blue, both printed with images of starfish. She smeared sun block on Robbie's nose—he liked being fussed over—and some on her own. She felt they should each carry a plastic water bottle slung over the shoulder and under the arm, in case they got thirsty. She also provided them with long walking sticks, for balance and for feeling their way ahead under the water.

Emma got the tide tables from one of the yacht people, of whom there were many in the beach bars. At low tide, about ten in the morning, they set out. News of the attempt had circulated, and there were a few well-wishers there to see them off. A group of others, shyer, Emma thought, were loitering at a distance, to watch.

Emma went first. Finding the ridge was no difficulty. The water was up to her armpits—Jesus Christ must have been a short man—and the footing wasn't bad, though she kept a lookout for the dark burr shapes of sea urchins. At its narrowest the ridge seemed to be about a foot wide, and dropped off steeply on either side. It must have been an old geological formation, a lava upwelling harder than the surrounding bed. Many of these islands, she knew, were volcanic.

A quarter of the way out, Emma realized that the water was much colder than it was when you just went swimming in it. Also, the current in the channel between the islands was stronger than she'd thought. The truth was that she hadn't given it much attention at all: the current wasn't something she'd included in her mental picture of this little stroll. The tide had been at pause mark when they'd begun, but now that they'd hit the halfway point it had begun to run in again. Going over the ridge it would be faster. She decided they wouldn't try to walk back, but would signal someone from the main island to come out and get them. Until now she hadn't thought about the mechanics of getting back. This was typical of Emma. She was a one-way specialist: she disliked going backwards.

She felt the waves were steepening, and it was harder to keep her footing, though by using her stick she was managing it. Her calf muscles were beginning to ache with the constant strain of pulling against the water. She had to concentrate, which was why she didn't look around earlier, to see where Robbie was. Now she did.

At first she didn't see him at all. He wasn't on the ridge behind her, where he should have been. What she did see was that the hill overlooking the bay was black with people. They were sitting quietly, as if at a play, intent on the performance going on before them.

The performance was Robbie drowning. Emma saw him now: he'd been swept off the reef and was being carried through the channel by the current, out to sea. All she could see was his light blue sun hat and a little of the head underneath. As she watched, an arm came up, flailed weakly, sank again. She heard a faint sound: Robbie calling. Why hadn't she heard him before?

She raised her stick into the air and shook it at the hillside. "Do something!" she yelled. She pointed at Robbie with the stick, as if it were a magic wand and she could command him to stop, lift, float backwards. She felt helpless. She felt tricked. She knew that she could not swim after him and rescue him: if she did that, they would both be lost. She had to keep walking, or the water would soon be too high.

In the end, they sent Horace out after Robbie in his decrepit rowboat. Nobody else would chance it, as the turn of the tide was known to be the most ridiculous moment for going out into Wreck Bay channel, and there weren't any motorboats handy. Everybody sane kept their motorboats and their sailboats and even their rowboats around at the other side of the island where there was a safe harbour, but Horace was thought to be "soft," and he was also stubborn: he liked to have his rowboat there, where he could keep watch on it. He was also, luckily for Robbie, strong as an ox. Feeble-minded or not, he behaved on that occasion a lot better than anyone else, including Emma. He rowed after Robbie, fished him out, and rowed him back to shore. The crowd cheered, and Robbie went into shock.

Emma reached Wreck Island and sat on it, shivering and worrying about Robbie, until someone remembered about her and sent a motorboat out to get her. No one complimented her on her feat of daring or referred to her as Miss Jesus, as she later realized she'd been hoping they would. Instead they said what a damn fool she'd been to try such a thing.

"Why didn't you stop me then?" Emma said, doubly annoyed because she knew they were right. (She'd made it, though. She'd completed the walk.)

The Wreck Bay bartender—he was the one chewing her out—said everyone knew she was that sort of a woman. An idea get in her head, no use trying to get it out. He shrugged, went on polishing glasses, and Emma realized that she was not hidden away and invisible here, as she always supposed herself to be in foreign countries, but much discussed.

Emma felt terrible about Robbie. She sat at his bedside, where he lay wrapped in several blankets despite the heat, and held his hand, and actually did say, "Robbie, what have I done to you?" Emma, like most people, rapidly falls into stock postures in times of stress. Only in books do people pause to think of original ways of phrasing their grief and fear. Robbie was a kind and agreeable man whom she loved, and she'd almost killed him.

Robbie was badly chilled. Emma sent for the local doctor to come and look at him. Emma knew this doctor already, having been treated by him for a staph infection on her leg from a coral scrape she'd picked up in the harbour. The doctor—who was from India, and who felt very much in exile on St. Eunice, where there were no other Indians—liked giving people shots. He'd confided to Emma that he gave them to himself, when there was nobody else around. So he gave Robbie a shot, and the whites of Robbie's eyes returned to normal size.

Emma made weak tea for Robbie and coaxed him to eat, going so far as to bake him some cookies. It was an extra effort in the heat. Robbie lay around covered with a sheet, like half a corpse, while Emma grovelled. He accepted her apologies, looking wan and forgiving and pastel as an Easter card, his red hair making his face look whitish green. As soon as he felt better he became more grumpy than usual. He was humiliated by the whole episode; he felt he was aging, almost on the shelf already, although Emma, being twenty-three, didn't understand this at the time. She wondered—though only for an instant—whether she really wanted to marry Robbie after all. But soon Robbie recovered and they flew back to the real world, and love went on as usual, until it stopped.

*　　*　　*

From this episode, she told me, Emma learned that her bubble of invulnerability, although it still worked well enough for her, was not strong enough to extend itself to those around her. This is why she always worries about heart seizures, car accidents, epidemics, faulty firearms, and cigarettes left carelessly on the edges of tables, when she is in love. She knows she will not be the one to die first.

BLUEBEARD'S EGG

Sally stands at the kitchen window, waiting for the sauce she's reducing to come to a simmer, looking out. Past the garage the lot sweeps downwards, into the ravine; it's a wilderness there, of bushes and branches and what Sally thinks of as vines. It was her idea to have a kind of terrace, built of old railroad ties, with wild flowers growing between them, but Edward says he likes it the way it is. There's a playhouse down at the bottom, near the fence; from here she can just see the roof. It has nothing to do with Edward's kids, in their earlier incarnations, before Sally's time; it's more ancient than that, and falling apart. Sally would like it cleared away. She thinks drunks sleep in it, the men who live under the bridges down there, who occasionally wander over the fence (which is broken down, from where they step on it) and up the hill, to emerge squinting like moles into the light of Sally's well-kept back lawn.

Off to the left is Ed, in his windbreaker; it's officially spring, Sally's blue scylla is in flower, but it's chilly for this time of year. Ed's windbreaker is an old one he won't throw out; it still says WILDCATS, relic of some team he was on in high school, an era so prehistoric Sally can barely imagine it; though picturing Ed at high school is not all that difficult. Girls would have had crushes on

131

him, he would have been unconscious of it; things like that don't change. He's puttering around the rock garden now; some of the rocks stick out too far and are in danger of grazing the side of Sally's Peugeot, on its way to the garage, and he's moving them around. He likes doing things like that, puttering, humming to himself. He won't wear work gloves, though she keeps telling him he could squash his fingers.

Watching his bent back with its frayed, poignant lettering, Sally dissolves; which is not infrequent with her. *My darling Edward*, she thinks. *Edward Bear, of little brain. How I love you.* At times like this she feels very protective of him.

Sally knows for a fact that dumb blondes were loved, not because they were blondes, but because they were dumb. It was their helplessness and confusion that were so sexually attractive, once; not their hair. It wasn't false, the rush of tenderness men must have felt for such women. Sally understands it.

For it must be admitted: Sally is in love with Ed because of his stupidity, his monumental and almost energetic stupidity: energetic, because Ed's stupidity is not passive. He's no mere blockhead; you'd have to be working at it to be that stupid. Does it make Sally feel smug, or smarter than he is, or even smarter than she really is herself? No; on the contrary, it makes her humble. It fills her with wonder that the world can contain such marvels as Ed's colossal and endearing thickness. He is just so *stupid*. Every time he gives her another piece of evidence, another tile that she can glue into place in the vast mosaic of his stupidity she's continually piecing together, she wants to hug him, and often does; and he is so stupid he can never figure out what for.

Because Ed is so stupid he doesn't even know he's stupid. He's a child of luck, a third son who, armed with nothing but a certain feeble-minded amiability, manages to make it through the forest with all its witches and traps and pitfalls and end up with the princess, who is Sally, of course. It helps that he's handsome.

On good days she sees his stupidity as innocence, lamblike, shining with the light of (for instance) green daisied meadows in the sun. (When Sally starts thinking this way about Ed, in terms of the calendar art from the service-station washrooms of her childhood, dredging up images of a boy with curly golden hair, his arm thrown around the neck of an Irish setter—a notorious brainless beast, she reminds herself—she knows she is sliding over the edge, into a ghastly kind of sentimentality, and that she must stop at once, or Ed will vanish, to be replaced by a stuffed facsimile, useful for little else but an umbrella stand. Ed is a real person, with a lot more to him than these simplistic renditions allow for; which sometimes worries her.) On bad days though, she sees his stupidity as wilfulness, a stubborn determination to shut things out. His obtuseness is a wall, within which he can go about his business, humming to himself, while Sally, locked outside, must hack her way through the brambles with hardly so much as a transparent raincoat between them and her skin.

Why did she choose him (or, to be precise, as she tries to be with herself and sometimes is even out loud, *hunt him down*), when it's clear to everyone she had other options? To Marylynn, who is her best though most recent friend, she's explained it by saying she was spoiled when young by reading too many Agatha Christie murder mysteries, of the kind in which the clever and witty heroine passes over the equally clever and witty first-lead male, who's helped solve the crime, in order to marry the second-lead male, the stupid one, the one who would have been arrested and condemned and executed if it hadn't been for her cleverness. Maybe this is how she sees Ed: if it weren't for her, his blundering too-many-thumbs kindness would get him into all sorts of quagmires, all sorts of sink-holes he'd never be able to get himself out of, and then he'd be done for.

"Sink-hole" and "quagmire" are not flattering ways of speaking about other women, but this is what is at the back of Sally's mind; specifically, Ed's two previous wives. Sally didn't exactly extricate him from their clutches. She's never even met the first one, who moved to the west coast fourteen years ago and sends Christmas cards, and the second one was middle-aged and already in the act of severing herself from Ed before Sally came along. (For Sally, "middle-aged" means anyone five years older than she is. It has always meant this. She applies it only to women, however. She doesn't think of Ed as middle-aged, although the gap between them is considerably more than five years.)

Ed doesn't know what happened with these marriages, what went wrong. His protestations of ignorance, his refusal to discuss the finer points, is frustrating to Sally, because she would like to hear the whole story. But it's also cause for anxiety: if he doesn't know what happened with the other two, maybe the same thing could be happening with her and he doesn't know about that, either. Stupidity like Ed's can be a health hazard, for other people. What if he wakes up one day and decides that she isn't the true bride after all, but the false one? Then she will be put into a barrel stuck full of nails and rolled downhill, endlessly, while he is sitting in yet another bridal bed, drinking champagne. She remembers the brand name, because she bought it herself. Champagne isn't the sort of finishing touch that would occur to Ed, though he enjoyed it enough at the time.

But outwardly Sally makes a joke of all this. "He doesn't know," she says to Marylynn, laughing a little, and they shake their heads. If it were them, they'd know, all right. Marylynn is in fact divorced, and she can list every single thing that went wrong, item by item. After doing this, she adds that her divorce was one of the best things that ever happened to her. "I was just a nothing before," she says. "It made me pull myself together."

Sally, looking across the kitchen table at Marylynn, has to agree that she is far from being a nothing now. She started out re-doing people's closets, and has worked that up into her own interior-design firm. She does the houses of the newly rich, those who lack ancestral furniture and the confidence to be shabby, and who wish their interiors to reflect a personal taste they do not in reality possess.

"What they want are mausoleums," Marylynn says, "or hotels," and she cheerfully supplies them. "Right down to the ash-trays. Imagine having someone else pick out your ash-trays for you."

By saying this, Marylynn lets Sally know that she's not including her in that category, though Sally did in fact hire her, at the very first, to help with a few details around the house. It was Marylynn who redesigned the wall of closets in the master bedroom and who found Sally's massive Chinese mahogany table, which cost her another seven hundred dollars to have stripped. But it turned out to be perfect, as Marylynn said it would. Now she's dug up a nineteenth-century keyhole desk, which both she and Sally know will be exactly right for the bay-windowed alcove off the living room. "Why do you need it?" Ed said in his puzzled way. "I thought you worked in your study." Sally admitted this, but said they could keep the telephone bills in it, which appeared to satisfy him. She knows exactly what she needs it for: she needs it to sit at, in something flowing, backlit by the morning sunlight, gracefully dashing off notes. She saw a 1940's advertisement for coffee like this once; and the husband was standing behind the chair, leaning over, with a worshipful expression on his face.

Marylynn is the kind of friend Sally does not have to

explain any of this to, because it's assumed between them. Her intelligence is the kind Sally respects.

Marylynn is tall and elegant, and makes anything she is wearing seem fashionable. Her hair is prematurely grey and she leaves it that way. She goes in for loose blouses in cream-coloured silk, and eccentric scarves gathered from interesting shops and odd corners of the world, thrown carelessly around her neck and over one shoulder. (Sally has tried this toss in the mirror, but it doesn't work.) Marylynn has a large collection of unusual shoes; she says they're unusual because her feet are so big, but Sally knows better. Sally, who used to think of herself as pretty enough and now thinks of herself as doing quite well for her age, envies Marylynn her bone structure, which will serve her well when the inevitable happens.

Whenever Marylynn is coming to dinner, as she is to-day—she's bringing the desk, too—Sally takes especial care with her clothes and make-up. Marylynn, she knows, is her real audience for such things, since no changes she effects in herself seem to affect Ed one way or the other, or even to register with him. "You look fine to me" is all he says, no matter how she really looks. (But does she want him to see her more clearly, or not? Most likely not. If he did he would notice the incipient wrinkles, the small pouches of flesh that are not quite there yet, the network forming beneath her eyes. It's better as it is.)

Sally has repeated this remark of Ed's to Marylynn, adding that he said it the day the Jacuzzi overflowed because the smoke alarm went off, because an English muffin she was heating to eat in the bathtub got stuck in the toaster, and she had to spend an hour putting down newspaper and mopping up, and only had half an hour to dress for a dinner they were going to. "Really I looked like the wrath of God," said Sally. These days she finds herself repeating to Marylynn many of the things Ed says: the stupid things. Marylynn is the only one of Sally's friends she has confided in to this extent.

"Ed is cute as a button," Marylynn said. "In fact, he's just like a button: he's so bright and shiny. If he were mine, I'd get him bronzed and keep him on the mantelpiece."

Marylynn is even better than Sally at concocting formulations for Ed's particular brand of stupidity, which can irritate Sally: coming from herself, this sort of comment appears to her indulgent and loving, but from Marylynn it borders on the patronizing. So then she sticks up for Ed, who is by no means stupid about everything. When you narrow it down, there's only one area of life he's hopeless about. The rest of the time he's intelligent enough, some even say brilliant: otherwise, how could he be so successful?

Ed is a heart man, one of the best, and the irony of this is not lost on Sally: who could possibly know less about the workings of hearts, real hearts, the kind symbolized by red satin surrounded by lace and topped by pink bows, than Ed? Hearts with arrows in them. At the same time, the fact that he's a heart man is a large part of his allure. Women corner him on sofas, trap him in bay-windows at cocktail parties, mutter to him in confidential voices at dinner parties. They behave this way right in front of Sally, under her very nose, as if she's invisible, and Ed lets them do it. This would never happen if he were in banking or construction.

As it is, everywhere he goes he is beset by sirens. They want him to fix their hearts. Each of them seems to have a little something wrong—a murmur, a whisper. Or they faint a lot and want him to tell them why. This is always what the conversations are about, according to Ed, and Sally believes it. Once she'd wanted it herself, that mirage. What had she invented for him, in the beginning?

A heavy heart, that beat too hard after meals. And he'd been so sweet, looking at her with those stunned brown eyes of his, as if her heart were the genuine topic, listening to her gravely as if he'd never heard any of this twaddle before, advising her to drink less coffee. And she'd felt such triumph, to have carried off her imposture, pried out of him that miniscule token of concern.

Thinking back on this incident makes her uneasy, now that she's seen her own performance repeated so many times, including the hand placed lightly on the heart, to call attention of course to the breasts. Some of these women have been within inches of getting Ed to put his head down on their chests, right there in Sally's living room. Watching all this out of the corners of her eyes while serving the liqueurs, Sally feels the Aztec rise within her. *Trouble with your heart? Get it removed*, she thinks. *Then you'll have no more problems.*

Sometimes Sally worries that she's a nothing, the way Marylynn was before she got a divorce and a job. But Sally isn't a nothing; therefore, she doesn't need a divorce to stop being one. And she's always had a job of some sort; in fact she has one now. Luckily Ed has no objection; he doesn't have much of an objection to anything she does.

Her job is supposed to be full-time, but in effect it's part-time, because Sally can take a lot of the work away and do it at home, and, as she says, with one arm tied behind her back. When Sally is being ornery, when she's playing the dull wife of a fascinating heart man—she does this with people she can't be bothered with—she says she works in a bank, nothing important. Then she watches their eyes dismiss her. When, on the other hand, she's trying to impress, she says she's in P.R. In reality she runs the in-house organ for a trust company, a medium-sized one. This is a thin magazine, nicely printed, which is supposed to make the employees feel that some of the boys are doing worthwhile things out there and are human beings as well. It's still the boys, though the few women in anything resembling key positions are wheeled out regularly, bloused and suited and smiling brightly, with what they hope will come across as confidence rather than aggression.

This is the latest in a string of such jobs Sally has held over the years: comfortable enough jobs that engage only half of her cogs and wheels, and that end up leading nowhere. Technically she's second-in-command: over her is a man who wasn't working out in management, but who couldn't be fired because his wife was related to the chairman of the board. He goes out for long alcoholic lunches and plays a lot of golf, and Sally runs the show. This man gets the official credit for everything Sally does right, but the senior executives in the company take Sally aside when no one is looking and tell her what a great gal she is and what a whiz she is at holding up her end.

The real pay-off for Sally, though, is that her boss provides her with an endless supply of anecdotes. She dines out on stories about his dim-wittedness and pomposity, his lobotomized suggestions about what the two of them should cook up for the magazine; *the organ*, as she says he always calls it. "He says we need some fresh blood to perk up the organ," Sally says, and the heart men grin at her. "He actually said that?" Talking like this about her boss would be reckless—you never know what might get back to him, with the world as small as it is—if Sally were afraid of losing her job, but she isn't. There's an unspoken agreement between her and this man: they both know that if she goes, he goes, because who else would put up with him? Sally might angle for his job, if she were stupid enough to disregard his family connections, if she coveted the trappings of power. But she's just fine where she is.

Jokingly, she says she's reached her level of incompetence. She says she suffers from fear of success.

Her boss is white-haired, slender, and tanned, and looks like an English gin ad. Despite his vapidity he's outwardly distinguished, she allows him that. In truth she pampers him outrageously, indulges him, covers up for him at every turn, though she stops short of behaving like a secretary: she doesn't bring him coffee. They both have a secretary who does that anyway. The one time he made a pass at her, when he came in from lunch visibly reeling, Sally was kind about it.

Occasionally, though not often, Sally has to travel in connection with her job. She's sent off to places like Edmonton, where they have a branch. She interviews the boys at the middle and senior levels; they have lunch, and the boys talk about ups and downs in oil or the slump in the real-estate market. Then she gets taken on tours of shopping plazas under construction. It's always windy, and grit blows into her face. She comes back to home base and writes a piece on the youthfulness and vitality of the West.

She teases Ed, while she packs, saying she's going off for a rendezvous with a dashing financier or two. Ed isn't threatened; he tells her to enjoy herself, and she hugs him and tells him how much she will miss him. He's so dumb it doesn't occur to him she might not be joking. In point of fact, it would have been quite possible for Sally to have had an affair, or at least a one- or two-night stand, on several of these occasions: she knows when those chalk lines are being drawn, when she's being dared to step over them. But she isn't interested in having an affair with anyone but Ed.

She doesn't eat much on the planes; she doesn't like the food. But on the return trip, she invariably saves the pre-packaged parts of the meal, the cheese in its plastic wrap, the miniature chocolate bar, the bag of pretzels.

She ferrets them away in her purse. She thinks of them as supplies, that she may need if she gets stuck in a strange airport, if they have to change course because of snow or fog, for instance. All kinds of things could happen, although they never have. When she gets home she takes the things from her purse and throws them out.

Outside the window Ed straightens up and wipes his earth-smeared hands down the sides of his pants. He begins to turn, and Sally moves back from the window so he won't see that she's watching. She doesn't like it to be too obvious. She shifts her attention to the sauce: it's in the second stage of a *sauce suprême*, which will make all the difference to the chicken. When Sally was learning this sauce, her cooking instructor quoted one of the great chefs, to the effect that the chicken was merely a canvas. He meant as in painting, but Sally, in an undertone to the woman next to her, turned it around. "Mine's canvas anyway, sauce or no sauce," or words to that effect.

Gourmet cooking was the third night course Sally has taken. At the moment she's on her fifth, which is called *Forms of Narrative Fiction*. It's half reading and half writing assignments—the instructor doesn't believe you can understand an art form without at least trying it yourself—and Sally purports to be enjoying it. She tells her friends she takes night courses to keep her brain from atrophying, and her friends find this amusing: whatever else may become of Sally's brain, they say, they don't see atrophying as an option. Sally knows better, but in any case there's always room for improvement. She may have begun taking the courses in the belief that this would make her more interesting to Ed, but she soon gave up on that idea: she appears to be neither more nor less interesting to Ed now than she was before.

Most of the food for tonight is already made. Sally tries

to be well organized: the overflowing Jacuzzi was an aberration. The cold watercress soup with walnuts is chilling in the refrigerator, the chocolate mousse ditto. Ed, being Ed, prefers meatloaf to sweetbreads with pine nuts, butterscotch pudding made from a package to chestnut purée topped with whipped cream. (Sally burnt her fingers peeling the chestnuts. She couldn't do it the easy way and buy it tinned.) Sally says Ed's preference for this type of food comes from being pre-programmed by hospital cafeterias when he was younger: show him a burned sausage and a scoop of instant mashed potatoes and he salivates. So it's only for company that she can unfurl her *boeuf en daube* and her salmon *en papillote*, spread them forth to be savoured and praised.

What she likes best about these dinners though is setting the table, deciding who will sit where and, when she's feeling mischievous, even what they are likely to say. Then she can sit and listen to them say it. Occasionally she prompts a little.

Tonight will not be very challenging, since it's only the heart men and their wives, and Marylynn, whom Sally hopes will dilute them. The heart men are forbidden to talk shop at Sally's dinner table, but they do it anyway. "Not what you really want to listen to while you're eating," says Sally. "All those tubes and valves." Privately she thinks they're a conceited lot, all except Ed. She can't resist needling them from time to time.

"I mean," she said to one of the leading surgeons, "basically it's just an exalted form of dress-making, don't you think?"

"Come again?" said the surgeon, smiling. The heart men think Sally is one hell of a tease.

"It's really just cutting and sewing, isn't it?" Sally murmured. The surgeon laughed.

"There's more to it than that," Ed said, unexpectedly, solemnly.

"What more, Ed?" said the surgeon. "You could say there's a lot of embroidery, but that's in the billing." He chuckled at himself.

Sally held her breath. She could hear Ed's verbal thought processes lurching into gear. He was delectable.

"Good judgement," Ed said. His earnestness hit the table like a wet fish. The surgeon hastily downed his wine.

Sally smiled. This was supposed to be a reprimand to her, she knew, for not taking things seriously enough. *Oh, come on, Ed*, she could say. But she knows also, most of the time, when to keep her trap shut. She should have a light-up JOKE sign on her forehead, so Ed would be able to tell the difference.

The heart men do well. Most of them appear to be doing better than Ed, but that's only because they have, on the whole, more expensive tastes and fewer wives. Sally can calculate these things and she figures Ed is about par.

These days there's much talk about advanced technologies, which Sally tries to keep up on, since they interest Ed. A few years ago the heart men got themselves a new facility. Ed was so revved up that he told Sally about it, which was unusual for him. A week later Sally said she would drop by the hospital at the end of the day and pick Ed up and take him out for dinner; she didn't feel like cooking, she said. Really she wanted to check out the facility; she likes to check out anything that causes the line on Ed's excitement chart to move above level.

At first Ed said he was tired, that when the day came to an end he didn't want to prolong it. But Sally wheedled and was respectful, and finally Ed took her to see his new gizmo. It was in a cramped, darkened room with an examining table in it. The thing itself looked like a television screen hooked up to some complicated hardware.

Ed said that they could wire a patient up and bounce sound waves off the heart and pick up the echoes, and they would get a picture on the screen, an actual picture, of the heart in motion. It was a thousand times better than an electrocardiogram, he said: they could see the faults, the thickenings and cloggings, much more clearly.

"Colour?" said Sally.

"Black and white," said Ed.

Then Sally was possessed by a desire to see her own heart, in motion, in black and white, on the screen. At the dentist's she always wants to see the X-rays of her teeth, too, solid and glittering in her cloudy head. "Do it," she said, "I want to see how it works," and though this was the kind of thing Ed would ordinarily evade or tell her she was being silly about, he didn't need much persuading. He was fascinated by the thing himself, and he wanted to show it off.

He checked to make sure there was nobody real booked for the room. Then he told Sally to slip out of her clothes, the top half, brassière and all. He gave her a paper gown and turned his back modestly while she slipped it on, as if he didn't see her body every night of the week. He attached electrodes to her, the ankles and one wrist, and turned a switch and fiddled with the dials. Really a technician was supposed to do this, he told her, but he knew how to run the machine himself. He was good with small appliances.

Sally lay prone on the table, feeling strangely naked. "What do I do?" she said.

"Just lie there," said Ed. He came over to her and tore a hole in the paper gown, above her left breast. Then he started running a probe over her skin. It was wet and slippery and cold, and felt like the roller on a roll-on deodorant.

"There," he said, and Sally turned her head. On the screen was a large grey object, like a giant fig, paler in the middle, a dark line running down the centre. The sides moved in and out, two wings fluttered in it, like an uncertain moth's.

"That's it?" said Sally dubiously. Her heart looked so insubstantial, like a bag of gelatin, something that would melt, fade, disintegrate, if you squeezed it even a little.

Ed moved the probe, and they looked at the heart from the bottom, then the top. Then he stopped the frame, then changed it from a positive to a negative image. Sally began to shiver.

"That's wonderful," she said. He seemed so distant, absorbed in his machine, taking the measure of her heart, which was beating over there all by itself, detached from her, exposed and under his control.

Ed unwired her and she put on her clothes again, neutrally, as if he were actually a doctor. Nevertheless this transaction, this whole room, was sexual in a way she didn't quite understand; it was clearly a dangerous place. It was like a massage parlour, only for women. Put a batch of women in there with Ed and they would never want to come out. They'd want to stay in there while he ran his probe over their wet skins and pointed out to them the defects of their beating hearts.

"Thank you," said Sally.

Sally hears the back door open and close. She feels Ed approaching, coming through the passages of the house towards her, like a small wind or a ball of static electricity. The hair stands up on her arms. Sometimes he makes her so happy she thinks she's about to burst; other times she thinks she's about to burst anyway.

He comes into the kitchen, and she pretends not to notice. He puts his arms around her from behind, kisses her on the neck. She leans back, pressing herself into him. What they should do now is go into the bedroom (or even the living room, even the den) and make love, but it wouldn't occur to Ed to make love in the middle of the day. Sally often comes across articles in magazines about how to improve your sex life, which leave her feeling disappointed, or reminiscent: Ed is not Sally's first and only man. But she knows she shouldn't expect too much of Ed. If Ed were more experimental, more interested in variety, he would be a different kind of man altogether: slyer, more devious, more observant, harder to deal with.

As it is, Ed makes love in the same way, time after time, each movement following the others in an exact order. But it seems to satisfy him. Of course it satisfies him: you can always tell when men are satisfied. It's Sally who lies awake, afterwards, watching the pictures unroll across her closed eyes.

Sally steps away from Ed, smiles at him. "How did you make out with the women today?" she says.

"What women?" says Ed absently, going towards the sink. He knows what women.

"The ones out there, hiding in the forsythia," says Sally. "I counted at least ten. They were just waiting for a chance."

She teases him frequently about these troops of women, which follow him around everywhere, which are invisible to Ed but which she can see as plain as day.

"I bet they hang around outside the front door of the hospital," she will say, "just waiting till you come out. I bet they hide in the linen closets and jump out at you from behind, and then pretend to be lost so you'll take them by the short cut. It's the white coat that does it. None of those women can resist the white coats. They've been conditioned by Young Doctor Kildare."

"Don't be silly," says Ed today, with equanimity. Is he blushing, is he embarrassed? Sally examines his face closely, like a geologist with an aerial photograph, looking for telltale signs of mineral treasure: markings, bumps, hollows. Everything about Ed means something, though it's difficult at times to say what.

Now he's washing his hands at the sink, to get the earth off. In a minute he'll wipe them on the dish towel instead of using the hand towel the way he's supposed to. Is that complacency, in the back turned to her? Maybe there really are these hordes of women, even though she's made them up. Maybe they really do behave that way. His shoulders are slightly drawn up: is he shutting her out?

"I know what they want," she goes on. "They want to get into that little dark room of yours and climb up onto your table. They think you're delicious. They'll gobble you up. They'll chew you into tiny pieces. There won't be anything left of you at all, only a stethoscope and a couple of shoelaces."

Once Ed would have laughed at this, but today he doesn't. Maybe she's said it, or something like it, a few times too often. He smiles though, wipes his hands on the dish towel, peers into the fridge. He likes to snack.

"There's some cold roast beef," Sally says, baffled.

Sally takes the sauce off the stove and sets it aside for later: she'll do the last steps just before serving. It's only two-thirty. Ed has disappeared into the cellar, where Sally knows he will be safe for a while. She goes into her study, which used to be one of the kids' bedrooms, and sits down at her desk. The room has never been completely redecorated: there's still a bed in it, and a dressing table with a blue flowered flounce Sally helped pick out, long before the kids went off to university: "flew the coop," as Ed puts it.

Sally doesn't comment on the expression, though she would like to say that it wasn't the first coop they flew. Her house isn't even the real coop, since neither of the kids is hers. She'd hoped for a baby of her own when she married Ed, but she didn't want to force the issue. Ed didn't object to the idea, exactly, but he was neutral about it, and Sally got the feeling he'd had enough babies already. Anyway, the other two wives had babies, and look what happened to them. Since their actual fates have always been vague to Sally, she's free to imagine all kinds of things, from drug addiction to madness. Whatever it was resulted in Sally having to bring up their kids, at least from puberty onwards. The way it was presented by the first wife was that it was Ed's turn now. The second wife was more oblique: she said that the child wanted to spend some time with her father. Sally was left out of both these equations, as if the house wasn't a place she lived in, not really, so she couldn't be expected to have any opinion.

Considering everything, she hasn't done badly. She likes the kids and tries to be a friend to them, since she can hardly pretend to be a mother. She describes the three of them as having an easy relationship. Ed wasn't around much for the kids, but it's him they want approval from, not Sally; it's him they respect. Sally is more like a confederate, helping them get what they want from Ed.

When the kids were younger, Sally used to play Monopoly with them, up at the summer place in Muskoka Ed owned then but has since sold. Ed would play too, on his vacations and on the weekends when he could make it up. These games would all proceed along the same lines. Sally would have an initial run of luck and would buy up everything she had a chance at. She didn't care whether it was classy real estate, like Boardwalk or Park Place, or those dingy little houses on the other side of the tracks; she would even buy train stations, which the kids would pass over, preferring to save their cash reserves for better investments. Ed, on the other hand, would plod along, getting a little here, a little there. Then, when Sally was feeling flush, she would blow her money on next-to-useless luxuries such as the electric light company; and when the kids started to lose, as they invariably did, Sally would lend them money at cheap rates or trade them things of her own, at a loss. Why not? She could afford it.

Ed meanwhile would be hedging his bets, building up blocks of property, sticking houses and hotels on them. He preferred the middle range, respectable streets but not flashy. Sally would land on his spaces and have to shell out hard cash. Ed never offered deals, and never accepted them. He played a lone game, and won more often than not. Then Sally would feel thwarted. She would say she guessed she lacked the killer instinct; or she would say that for herself she didn't care, because after all it was only a game, but he ought to allow the kids to win, once in a while. Ed couldn't grasp the concept of allowing other people to win. He said it would be condescending towards the children, and anyway you couldn't arrange to have a dice game turn out the way you wanted it to, since it was partly a matter of chance. If it was chance, Sally would think, why were the games so similar to one another? At the end, there would be Ed, counting up his paper cash, sorting it out into piles of bills of varying denominations, and Sally, her vast holdings dwindled to a few shoddy blocks on Baltic Avenue, doomed to foreclosure: extravagant, generous, bankrupt.

On these nights, after the kids were asleep, Sally would have two or three more rye-and-gingers than were good for her. Ed would go to bed early—winning made him satisfied and drowsy—and Sally would ramble about the house or read the endings of murder mysteries she had already read once before, and finally she would slip into bed and wake Ed up and stroke him into arousal, seeking comfort.

Sally has almost forgotten these games. Right now the kids are receding, fading like old ink; Ed on the contrary looms larger and larger, the outlines around him darkening. He's constantly developing, like a Polaroid print, new colours emerging, but the result remains the same: Ed is a surface, one she has trouble getting beneath.

"Explore your inner world," said Sally's instructor in *Forms of Narrative Fiction*, a middle-aged woman of scant fame who goes in for astrology and the Tarot pack and writes short stories, which are not published in any of the magazines Sally reads. "Then there's your outer one," Sally said afterwards, to her friends. "For instance, she should really get something done about her hair." She made this trivial and mean remark because she's fed up with her inner world; she doesn't need to explore it. In her inner world is Ed, like a doll within a Russian wooden doll, and in Ed is Ed's inner world, which she can't get at.

She takes a crack at it anyway: Ed's inner world is a forest, which looks something like the bottom part of their ravine lot, but without the fence. He wanders around in there, among the trees, not heading in any special direction. Every once in a while he comes upon a strange-looking plant, a sickly plant choked with weeds and briars. Ed kneels, clears a space around it, does some pruning, a little skilful snipping and cutting, props it up. The plant revives, flushes with health, sends out a grateful red blossom. Ed continues on his way. Or it may be a conked-out squirrel, which he restores with a drop from his flask of magic elixir. At set intervals an angel appears, bringing him food. It's always meatloaf. That's fine with Ed, who hardly notices what he eats, but the angel is getting tired of being an angel. Now Sally begins thinking about the angel: why are its wings frayed and dingy grey around the edges, why is it looking so withered and frantic? This is where all Sally's attempts to explore Ed's inner world end up.

She knows she thinks about Ed too much. She knows she should stop. She knows she shouldn't ask, "Do you still love me?" in the plaintive tone that sets even her own teeth on edge. All it achieves is that Ed shakes his head, as if not understanding why she would ask this, and pats her hand. "Sally, Sally, " he says, and everything proceeds as usual; except for the dread that seeps into things, the most ordinary things, such as rearranging the chairs and changing the burnt-out lightbulbs. But what is it she's afraid of? She has what they call everything: Ed, their wonderful house on a ravine lot, something she's always wanted. (But the hill is jungly, and the house is made of ice. It's held together only by Sally, who sits in the middle of it, working on a puzzle. The puzzle is Ed. If she should ever solve it, if she should ever fit the last cold splinter into place, the house will melt and flow away down the hill, and then . . .) It's a bad habit, fooling around with her head this way. It does no good. She knows that if she could quit she'd be happier. She ought to be able to: she's given up smoking.

She needs to concentrate her attention on other things. This is the real reason for the night courses, which she picks almost at random, to coincide with the evenings Ed isn't in. He has meetings, he's on the boards of charities, he has trouble saying no. She runs the courses past herself, mediaeval history, cooking, anthropology, hoping her mind will snag on something; she's even taken a course in geology, which was fascinating, she told her friends, all that magma. That's just it: everything is fascinating, but nothing enters her. She's always a star pupil, she does well on the exams and impresses the teachers, for which she despises them. She is familiar with her brightness, her techniques; she's surprised other people are still taken in by them.

Forms of Narrative Fiction started out the same way. Sally was full of good ideas, brimming with helpful suggestions. The workshop part of it was anyway just like a committee meeting, and Sally knew how to run those, from behind, without seeming to run them: she'd done it lots of times at work. Bertha, the instructor, told Sally she had a vivid imagination and a lot of untapped creative energy. "No wonder she never gets anywhere, with a name like Bertha," Sally said, while having coffee afterwards with two of the other night-coursers. "It goes with her outfits, though." (Bertha sports the macramé look, with health-food sandals and bulky-knit sweaters and hand-weave skirts that don't do a thing for her square figure, and too many Mexican rings on her hands, which she doesn't wash often enough.) Bertha goes in for assignments, which she calls learning by doing. Sally likes assignments: she likes things that can be completed and then discarded, and for which she gets marks.

The first thing Bertha assigned was The Epic. They read *The Odyssey* (selected passages, in translation, with a plot summary of the rest); then they poked around in James Joyce's *Ulysses*, to see how Joyce had adapted the epic form to the modern-day novel. Bertha had them keep a Toronto notebook, in which they had to pick out various spots around town as the ports of call in *The Odyssey*, and say why they had chosen them. The notebooks were read out loud in class, and it was a scream to see who had chosen what for Hades. (The Mount Pleasant Cemetery, McDonald's, where, if you eat the forbidden food, you never get back to the land of the living, the University Club with its dead ancestral souls, and so forth.) Sally's was the hospital, of course; she had no difficulty with the trench filled with blood, and she put the ghosts in wheelchairs.

After that they did The Ballad, and read gruesome accounts of murders and betrayed love. Bertha played them tapes of wheezy old men singing traditionally, in the Doric mode, and assigned a newspaper scrapbook, in which you had to clip and paste up-to-the-minute equivalents. The *Sun* was the best newspaper for these. The fiction that turned out to go with this kind of plot was the kind Sally liked anyway, and she had no difficulty concocting a five-page murder mystery, complete with revenge.

But now they are on Folk Tales and the Oral Tradition, and Sally is having trouble. This time, Bertha wouldn't let them read anything. Instead she read to them, in a voice, Sally said, that was like a gravel truck and was not conducive to reverie. Since it was the Oral Tradition, they weren't even allowed to take notes; Bertha said the original hearers of these stories couldn't read, so the stories were memorized. "To re-create the atmosphere," said Bertha, "I should turn out the lights. These stories were always told at night." "To make them creepier?" someone offered. "No," said Bertha. "In the days, they worked." She didn't do that, though she did make them sit in a circle.

"You should have seen us," Sally said afterwards to Ed, "sitting in a circle, listening to fairy stories. It was just like kindergarten. Some of them even had their mouths open. I kept expecting her to say, 'If you need to go, put up your hand.'" She was meaning to be funny, to amuse Ed with this account of Bertha's eccentricity and the foolish appearance of the students, most of them middle-aged, sitting in a circle as if they had never grown up at all. She was also intending to belittle the course, just slightly. She always did this with her night courses, so Ed wouldn't get the idea there was anything in her life that was even remotely as important as he was. But Ed didn't seem to need this amusement or this belittlement. He took her information earnestly, gravely, as if Bertha's behaviour was, after all, only the procedure of a specialist. No one knew better than he did that the procedures of specialists often looked bizarre or incomprehensible to onlookers. "She probably has her reasons," was all he would say.

The first stories Bertha read them, for warm-ups ("No memorizing for *her*," said Sally), were about princes who got amnesia and forgot about their true loves and married girls their mothers had picked out for them. Then they had to be rescued, with the aid of magic. The stories didn't say what happened to the women the princes had already married, though Sally wondered about it. Then Bertha read them another story, and this time they were supposed to remember the features that stood out for them and write a five-page transposition, set in the present and cast in the realistic mode. ("In other words," said Bertha, "no real magic.") They couldn't use the Universal Narrator, however: they had done that in their Ballad assignment. This time they had to choose a point of view. It could be the point of view of anyone or anything in the story, but they were limited to one only. The story she was about to read, she said, was a variant of the Bluebeard motif, much earlier than Perrault's sentimental rewriting of it. In Perrault, said Bertha, the girl has to be rescued by her brothers; but in the earlier version things were quite otherwise.

This is what Bertha read, as far as Sally can remember:

There were once three young sisters. One day a beggar with a large basket on his back came to the door and asked for some bread. The eldest sister brought him some, but no sooner had she touched him than she was compelled to jump into his basket, for the beggar was really a wizard in disguise. ("So much for United Appeal," Sally murmured. "She should have said, 'I gave at the office.'")

The wizard carried her away to his house in the forest, which was large and richly furnished. "Here you will be happy with me, my darling," said the wizard, "for you will have everything your heart could desire."

This lasted for a few days. Then the wizard gave the girl an egg and a bunch of keys. "I must go away on a journey," he said, "and I am leaving the house in your charge. Preserve this egg for me, and carry it about with you everywhere; for a great misfortune will follow from its loss. The keys open every room in the house. You may go into each of them and enjoy what you find there, but do not go into the small room at the top of the house, on pain of death." The girl promised, and the wizard disappeared.

At first the girl contented herself with exploring the rooms, which contained many treasures. But finally her curiosity would not let her alone. She sought out the smallest key, and, with beating heart, opened the little door at the top of the house. Inside it was a large basin full of blood, within which were the bodies of many women, which had been cut to pieces; nearby were a chopping block and an axe. In her horror, she let go of the egg, which fell into the basin of blood. In vain did she try to wipe away the stain: every time she succeeded in removing it, back it would come.

The wizard returned, and in a stern voice asked for the egg and the keys. When he saw the egg, he knew at once she had disobeyed him and gone into the forbidden room. "Since you have gone into the room against my will," he said, "you shall go back into it against your own." Despite her pleas he threw her down, dragged her by the hair into the little room, hacked her into pieces and threw her body into the basin with the others.

Then he went for the second girl, who fared no better than her sister. But the third was clever and wily. As soon as the wizard had gone, she set the egg on a shelf, out of harm's way, and then went immediately and opened the forbidden door. Imagine her distress when she saw the cut-up bodies of her two beloved sisters; but she set the parts in order, and they joined together and her sisters stood up and moved, and were living and well. They embraced each other, and the third sister hid the other two in a cupboard.

When the wizard returned he at once asked for the egg. This time it was spotless. "You have passed the test," he said to the third sister. "You shall be my bride." ("And second prize," said Sally, to herself this time, "is *two* weeks in Niagara Falls.") The wizard no longer had any power over her, and had to do whatever she asked. There was more, about how the wizard met his come-uppance and was burned to death, but Sally already knew which features stood out for her.

At first she thought the most imporant thing in the story was the forbidden room. What would she put in the forbidden room, in her present-day realistic version? Certainly not chopped-up women. It wasn't that they were too unrealistic, but they were certainly too sick, as well as being too obvious. She wanted to do something more clever. She thought it might be a good idea to have the curious woman open the door and find nothing there at all, but after mulling it over she set this notion aside. It would leave her with the problem of why the wizard would have a forbidden room in which he kept nothing.

That was the way she was thinking right after she got the assignment, which was a full two weeks ago. So far she's written nothing. The great temptation is to cast herself in the role of the cunning heroine, but again it's too predictable. And Ed certainly isn't the wizard; he's nowhere near sinister enough. If Ed were the wizard, the room would contain a forest, some ailing plants and feeble squirrels, and Ed himself, fixing them up; but then, if it were Ed the room wouldn't even be locked, and there would be no story.

Now, as she sits at her desk, fiddling with her felt-tip pen, it comes to Sally that the intriguing thing about the story, the thing she should fasten on, is the egg. Why an egg? From the night course in Comparative Folklore she took four years ago, she remembers that the egg can be a fertility symbol, or a necessary object in African spells, or something the world hatched out of. Maybe in this story it's a symbol of virginity, and that is why the wizard requires it unbloodied. Women with dirty eggs get murdered, those with clean ones get married.

But this isn't useful either. The concept is so outmoded. Sally doesn't see how she can transpose it into real life without making it ridiculous, unless she sets the story in, for instance, an immigrant Portuguese family, and what would she know about that?

Sally opens the drawer of her desk and hunts around in it for her nail file. As she's doing this, she gets the brilliant idea of writing the story from the point of view of the egg. Other people will do the other things: the clever girl, the wizard, the two blundering sisters, who weren't smart enough to lie, and who will have problems afterwards, because of the thin red lines running all over their bodies, from where their parts joined together. But no one will think of the egg. How does it feel, to be the innocent and passive cause of so much misfortune?

(Ed isn't the Bluebeard: Ed is the egg. Ed Egg, blank and pristine and lovely. Stupid, too. Boiled, probably. Sally smiles fondly.)

But how can there be a story from the egg's point of view, if the egg is so closed and unaware? Sally ponders this, doodling on her pad of lined paper. Then she resumes the search for her nail file. Already it's time to begin getting ready for her dinner party. She can sleep on the

157

problem of the egg and finish the assignment tomorrow, which is Sunday. It's due on Monday, but Sally's mother used to say she was a whiz at getting things done at the last minute.

After painting her nails with *Nuit Magique*, Sally takes a bath, eating her habitual toasted English muffin while she lies in the tub. She begins to dress, dawdling; she has plenty of time. She hears Ed coming up out of the cellar; then she hears him in the bathroom, which he has entered from the hall door. Sally goes in through the other door, still in her slip. Ed is standing at the sink with his shirt off, shaving. On the weekends he leaves it until necessary, or until Sally tells him he's too scratchy.

Sally slides her hands around his waist, nuzzling against his naked back. He has very smooth skin, for a man. Sally smiles to herself: she can't stop thinking of him as an egg.

"Mmm," says Ed. It could be appreciation, or the answer to a question Sally hasn't asked and he hasn't heard, or just an acknowledgement that she's there.

"Don't you ever wonder what I think about?" Sally says. She's said this more than once, in bed or at the dinner table, after dessert. She stands behind him, watching the swaths the razor cuts in the white of his face, looking at her own face reflected in the mirror, just the eyes visible above his naked shoulder. Ed, lathered, is Assyrian, sterner than usual; or a frost-covered Arctic explorer; or demi-human, a white-bearded forest mutant. He scrapes away at himself, methodically destroying the illusion.

"But I already know what you think about," says Ed.

"How?" Sally says, taken aback.

"You're always telling me," Ed says, with what might be resignation or sadness; or maybe this is only a simple statement of fact.

Sally is relieved. If that's all he's going on, she's safe.

*   *   *

Marylynn arrives half an hour early, her pearl-coloured Porsche leading two men in a delivery truck up the driveway. The men install the keyhole desk, while Marylynn supervises: it looks, in the alcove, exactly as Marylynn has said it would, and Sally is delighted. She sits at it to write the cheque. Then she and Marylynn go into the kitchen, where Sally is finishing up her sauce, and Sally pours them each a Kir. She's glad Marylynn is here: it will keep her from dithering, as she tends to do just before people arrive. Though it's only the heart men, she's still a bit nervous. Ed is more likely to notice when things are wrong than when they're exactly right.

Marylynn sits at the kitchen table, one arm draped over the chairback, her chin on the other hand; she's in soft grey, which makes her hair look silver, and Sally feels once again how banal it is to have ordinary dark hair like her own, however well-cut, however shiny. It's the confidence she envies, the negligence. Marylynn doesn't seem to be trying at all, ever.

"Guess what Ed said today?" Sally says.

Marylynn leans further forward. "What?" she says, with the eagerness of one joining in a familiar game.

"He said, 'Some of these femininists go too far,' " Sally reports. " '*Femininists*.' Isn't that sweet?"

Marylynn holds the pause too long, and Sally has a sudden awful thought: maybe Marylynn thinks she's showing off, about Ed. Marylynn has always said she's not ready for another marriage yet; still, Sally should watch herself, not rub her nose in it. But then Marylynn laughs indulgently, and Sally, relieved, joins in.

"Ed is unbelievable," says Marylynn. "You should pin his mittens to his sleeves when he goes out in the morning."

"He shouldn't be let out alone," says Sally.

159

"You should get him a seeing-eye dog," says Marylynn, "to bark at women."

"Why?" says Sally, still laughing but alert now, the cold beginning at the ends of her fingers. Maybe Marylynn knows something she doesn't; maybe the house is beginning to crumble, after all.

"Because he can't see them coming," says Marylynn. "That's what you're always telling me."

She sips her Kir; Sally stirs the sauce. "I bet he thinks I'm a femininist," says Marylynn.

"You?" says Sally. "Never." She would like to add that Ed has given no indication of thinking anything at all about Marylynn, but she doesn't. She doesn't want to take the risk of hurting her feelings.

The wives of the heart men admire Sally's sauce; the heart men talk shop, all except Walter Morly, who is good at by-passes. He's sitting beside Marylynn, and paying far too much attention to her for Sally's comfort. Mrs. Morly is at the other end of the table, not saying much of anything, which Marylynn appears not to notice. She keeps on talking to Walter about St. Lucia, where they've both been.

So after dinner, when Sally has herded them all into the living room for coffee and liqueurs, she takes Marylynn by the elbow. "Ed hasn't seen our desk yet," she says, "not up close. Take him away and give him your lecture on nineteenth-century antiques. Show him all the pigeon-holes. Ed loves pigeon-holes." Ed appears not to get this.

Marylynn knows exactly what Sally is up to. "Don't worry," she says, "I won't rape Dr. Morly; the poor creature would never survive the shock," but she allows herself to be shunted off to the side with Ed.

Sally moves from guest to guest, smiling, making sure

everything is in order. Although she never looks directly, she's always conscious of Ed's presence in the room, any room; she perceives him as a shadow, a shape seen dimly at the edge of her field of vision, recognizable by the outline. She likes to know where he is, that's all. Some people are on their second cup of coffee. She walks towards the alcove: they must have finished with the desk by now.

But they haven't, they're still in there. Marylynn is bending forward, one hand on the veneer. Ed is standing too close to her, and as Sally comes up behind them she sees his left arm, held close to his side, the back of it pressed against Marylynn, her shimmering upper thigh, her ass to be exact. Marylynn does not move away.

It's a split second, and then Ed sees Sally and the hand is gone; there it is, on top of the desk, reaching for a liqueur glass.

"Marylynn needs more Tia Maria," he says. "I just told her that people who drink a little now and again live longer." His voice is even, his face is as level as ever, a flat plain with no signposts.

Marylynn laughs. "I once had a dentist who I swear drilled tiny holes in my teeth, so he could fix them later," she says.

Sally sees Ed's hand outstretched towards her, holding the empty glass. She takes it, smiling, and turns away. There's a roaring sound at the back of her head; blackness appears around the edges of the picture she is seeing, like a television screen going dead. She walks into the kitchen and puts her cheek against the refrigerator and her arms around it, as far as they will go. She remains that way, hugging it; it hums steadily, with a sound like comfort. After a while she lets go of it and touches her hair, and walks back into the living room with the filled glass.

Marylynn is over by the french doors, talking with Walter Morly. Ed is standing by himself, in front of the fireplace, one arm on the mantelpiece, his left hand out of sight in his pocket.

Sally goes to Marylynn, hands her the glass. "Is that enough?" she says.

Marylynn is unchanged. "Thanks, Sally," she says, and goes on listening to Walter, who has dragged out his usual piece of mischief: some day, when they've perfected it, he says, all hearts will be plastic, and this will be a vast improvement on the current model. It's an obscure form of flirtation. Marylynn winks at Sally, to show that she knows he's tedious. Sally, after a pause, winks back.

She looks over at Ed, who is staring off into space, like a robot which has been parked and switched off. Now she isn't sure whether she really saw what she thought she saw. Even if she did, what does it mean? Maybe it's just that Ed, in a wayward intoxicated moment, put his hand on the nearest buttock, and Marylynn refrained from a shriek or a flinch out of good breeding or the desire not to offend him. Things like this have happened to Sally.

Or it could mean something more sinister: a familiarity between them, an understanding. If this is it, Sally has been wrong about Ed, for years, forever. Her version of Ed is not something she's perceived but something that's been perpetrated on her, by Ed himself, for reasons of his own. Possibly Ed is not stupid. Possibly he's enormously clever. She thinks of moment after moment when this cleverness, this cunning, would have shown itself if it were there, but didn't. She has watched him so carefully. She remembers playing Pick Up Sticks, with the kids, Ed's kids, years ago: how if you moved one stick in the tangle, even slightly, everything else moved also.

She won't say anything to him. She can't say anything: she can't afford to be wrong, or to be right either. She goes back into the kitchen and begins to scrape the plates. This is unlike her—usually she sticks right with the party until it's over—and after a while Ed wanders out. He stands silently, watching her. Sally concentrates on the scraping: dollops of *sauce suprême* slide into the plastic bag, shreds of lettuce, rice, congealed and lumpy. What is left of her afternoon.

"What are you doing out here?" Ed asks at last.

"Scraping the plates," Sally says, cheerful, neutral. "I just thought I'd get a head start on tidying up."

"Leave it," says Ed. "The woman can do that in the morning." That's how he refers to Mrs. Rudge, although she's been with them for three years now: *the woman*. And Mrs. Bird before her, as though they are interchangeable. This has never bothered Sally before. "Go on out there and have a good time."

Sally puts down the spatula, wipes her hands on the hand towel, puts her arms around him, holds on tighter than she should. Ed pats her shoulder. "What's up?" he says; then, "Sally, Sally." If she looks up, she will see him shaking his head a little, as if he doesn't know what to do about her. She doesn't look up.

Ed has gone to bed. Sally roams the house, fidgeting with the debris left by the party. She collects empty glasses, picks up peanuts from the rug. After a while she realizes that she's down on her knees, looking under a chair, and she's forgotten what for. She goes upstairs, creams off her make-up, does her teeth, undresses in the darkened bedroom and slides into bed beside Ed, who is breathing deeply as if asleep. *As if*.

Sally lies in bed with her eyes closed. What she sees is her own heart, in black and white, beating with that insubstantial moth-like flutter, a ghostly heart, torn out of her and floating in space, an animated valentine with no colour. It will go on and on forever; she has no control over it. But now she's seeing the egg, which is not small and cold and white and inert but larger than a real egg and golden pink, resting in a nest of brambles, glowing softly as though there's something red and hot inside it. It's almost pulsing; Sally is afraid of it. As she looks it darkens: rose-red, crimson. This is something the story left out, Sally thinks: the egg is alive, and one day it will hatch. But what will come out of it?

SPRING SONG
OF THE FROGS

Women's lips are paler again. They wax and wane, from season to season. They haven't been this pale for years; not for fifteen or twenty years at least. Will can't remember when it was, when he last saw those shades of rich vanilla, of melting orange sherbet, of faded pink satin, on women's mouths. Some time before he started really noticing. All this past winter the lips were dark instead, mulberry, maroon, so that the mouths looked like the mouths of old-fashioned dolls, sharply defined against the china white of the skin. Now the skins are creamier, except on the ones who have ignored whatever wordless decree has gone out and have begun to tan.

This woman, whose name is Robyn, has a mouth the colour of a fingernail, the wan half-moon at the base. Her own fingernails are painted to match: someone has decided that they should no longer look as if they've been dipped in blood. She has on a loose cool dress, cotton in a pink so faint it's like something that's run in the wash, with buttons down the front, the top three undone. By the way she's glanced down once or twice, she's wondering if she's gone too far.

Will smiles at her, looking into her eyes, which are possibly blue; he can't tell in this light. She smiles back. She won't be able to keep staring him in the eye for long.

After she blinks and shifts, she'll have three choices. The menu, on grey paper with offset handwriting, French style, which she's already studied; the view off to the side, towards the door, but it's too early for that; or the wall behind him. Will knows what's on it: a framed poster advertising a surrealist art show of several years back, with a drawing on it, fleshy pink with pinky-grey shadows, which suggests a part of the body, though it's difficult to say which part. Something about to grow hair, become sexual in a disagreeable way. Either she'll react to it or she won't see it all. Instead she'll glance at her own reflection in the glass, checking herself out as if she's a stranger she might consider picking up: a deep look, brief but sincere.

The waitress arrives, a thin girl in a red brushcut, with a purple feather earring dangling from one ear. She stands as though her head is fixed on a hook and the rest of her body is drooping down from it, with no tendons. She's wearing what could be tuxedo pants. The restaurant is in a district of second-hand clothing stores, where foreign-looking women with stumpy legs and black hair pulled back into buns come to shuffle through the racks, and also where girls like this one get their outlandish costumes. The belt is wide red plastic, and could be either twenty-five years old or brand new; the shirt is a man's dress shirt, with pleats, the sleeves rolled to the elbow. The girl's arms, bone-skinny and white, come out of the puffs of cloth like the stems of peonies that have been grown in darkness.

Her thighs will be much the same. Will can remember the thighs in the ancient men's magazines, the ones that were passed around when he was at school, black-and-white photos on cheap paper, with no air-brushing, the plump women posed in motel rooms, the way the garters would sink into the flesh of thighs and rump. Now there's no flesh, the thighs have shrivelled up, they're all muscle and bone. Even the *Playboy* centrefolds look as if they're made of solid gristle. It's supposed to be sexy to show them in leg warmers.

Will asks Robyn if she'd like something to drink.

"A Perrier with a twist," says Robyn, looking up, giving the waitress the same smile she's just given Will.

Will orders a Bloody Mary and wonders if he's made a mistake. Possibly this waitress is a man. He's been here several times before, never without a slight but enjoyable sense of entering forbidden territory. Any place with checked tablecloths gives him this feeling, which is left over from when he was a student and thought he would end up being something other than what he has become. In those days he drew illustrations for the campus newspaper, and designed sets. For a while he kept up the drawing, as a hobby, or that's what his ex-wife called it. Maybe later he'll go back to it, when he has the time. Some days he wanders into the galleries down here, to see what the young kids are up to. The owners approach him with cynical deference, as if all he has to offer, to them or anyone else, is his money. He never buys anything.

The waitress returns with the drinks, and Will, in view of the two slight bumps visible on her ribcage, decides that she really is a woman after all.

"I thought for a minute she was a man," he says to Robyn.

"Really?" Robyn says. She glances at the waitress, now at the next table. "Oh no," she says, as if it's a mistake she herself would never have made. "No. Definitely a woman."

"Some bread?" Will says. The bread here is placed in tiny baskets, suspended over the tables by a sort of rope-and-pulley arrangement. To get to the bread you have to either stand up or lower the basket by unhitching the rope from where it's fastened on the wall; which is awkward, but Will enjoys doing it. Maybe the theory is that your food will appeal to you more if you're allowed to participate in it, or maybe the baskets are just some designer's fiasco. He always has bread here.

"Pardon?" says Robyn, as if *bread* is a word she's never heard before. "Oh. No thanks." She gives a little shudder, as if the thought of it is slightly repulsive. Will is annoyed, but determined to have bread anyway. It's good bread, thick, brown, and warm. He turns to the wall, undoes the rope, and the basket creaks downwards.

"Oh, that's very cute," says Robyn. He catches it then, the look she's giving herself in the glass behind him. Now they are going to have to make their way through the rest of the lunch somehow. Why does he keep on, what's he looking for that's so hard to find? She has generous breasts, that's what impelled him: the hope of generosity.

The waitress comes back and Robyn, pursing her pastel-coloured lips, orders a spinach salad without the dressing. Will is beginning to sweat; he's feeling claustrophobic and is anxious to be gone. He tries to think about running his hand up her leg and around her thigh, which might be full and soft, but it's no good. She wouldn't enjoy it.

* * *

Cynthia is white on white. Her hair is nearly blonde, helped out, Will suspects: her eyebrows and eyelashes are darker. Her skin is so pale it looks powdered. She's not wearing the hospital gown but a white nightgown with ruffles, childish, Victorian, reminiscent of lacey drawers and Kate Greenaway greeting cards. Under the cloth, Will thinks, she must be translucent; you would be able to see her veins and intestines, like a guppy's. She draws the sheet up to her chest, backing away from him, against the headboard of the bed, a position that reminds him of a sickly Rosetti madonna, cringing against the wall while the angel of the Annunciation threatens her with fullness.

Will smiles with what he hopes is affability. "How are

you doing, Cynthia?" he says. There's a basket on the night table, with oranges and an apple; also some flowers.

"Okay," she says. She smiles, a limp smile that denies the message. Her eyes are anxious and cunning. She wants him to believe her and go away.

"Your mum and dad asked me to drop by," Will says. Cynthia is his niece.

"I figured," says Cynthia. Maybe she means that he wouldn't have come otherwise, or maybe she means that they have sent him as a substitute for themselves. She is probably right on both counts. It's a family myth that Will is Cynthia's favourite uncle. Like many myths, it had some basis in truth, once, when—just after his own marriage broke up—he was reaching for a sense of family, and would read Cynthia stories and tickle her under the arms. But that was years ago.

Last night, over the phone, his sister used this past as leverage. "You're the only one who can talk to her. She's cut us off." Her voice was angry rather than despairing.

"Well, I don't know," Will said dubiously. He has no great faith in his powers as a mediator, a confidant, even a strong shoulder. He used to have Cynthia up to the farm, when his own sons were younger and Cynthia was twelve or so. She was tanned then, a tomboy; she liked to wander over the property by herself, picking wild apples. At night she would wolf down the dinners Will would cook for the four of them, five if he had a woman up—plates of noodles Alfredo, roast beef with Yorkshire pudding, fried chicken, steaks, sometimes a goose which he'd bought from the people across the way.

There was nothing wrong with Cynthia then; she wore her hair loose, her skin was golden, and Will felt a disturbing sexual pull towards her which he certainly doesn't feel now. The boys felt it too, and would tease and provoke her, but she stood up to them. She said there was nothing they could do she couldn't do too, and she was almost right. Then they got into their motorcycle-and-car phase, and Cynthia changed. All of a sudden she didn't like getting grease on her hands; she began painting her nails. Will sees this now as the beginning of the end.

"It's an epidemic," his sister said over the phone. "It's some kind of a fad. You know what she actually said? She actually said a lot of the girls at school were doing it. She's so goddamned competitive."

"I'll go in," Will said. "Is there anything I should take? Some cheese maybe?" His sister is married to a man whose eyebrows are so faint they're invisible. Will, who doesn't like him, thinks of him as an albino.

"How about a good slap on the backside," said his sister. "Not that she's got one left."

Then she began to cry, and Will said she shouldn't worry, he was sure it would all turn out fine in the end.

At the moment he doesn't believe it. He looks around the room, searching for a chair. There is one, but Cynthia's sky-blue dressing-gown is across it. Just as well: if he sits down, he'll have to stay longer.

"Just okay?" he says.

"I gained a pound," she says. This is intended to placate him. He'll have to check with the doctor, as his sister wants a full report, and Cynthia, she claims, is not accurate on the subject of her weight.

"That's wonderful," he says. Maybe it's true, since she's so unhappy about it.

"I hardly ate anything," she says, plaintively but also boasting.

"You're trying though," says Will. "That's good." Now that he's here, he wishes to be helpful. "Maybe tomorrow you'll eat more."

"But if I hardly ate anything and I gained a pound," she says, "what's going to happen? I'll get fat."

Will doesn't know what to say. Reason, he knows, doesn't work; it's been tried. It would do no good to tell her she's a wraith, that if she doesn't eat she'll digest herself, that her heart is a muscle like any other muscle and if it isn't fed it will atrophy.

Suddenly Will is hungry. He's conscious of the oranges and the apple, right beside him on the night table, round and brightly coloured and filled with sweet juice. He wants to take something, but would that be depriving her?

"Those look good," he says.

Cynthia is scornful, as if this is some crude ploy of his to coax her to eat. "Have some," she says. "Have it all. As long as I don't have to watch. You can put it in your pocket." She speaks of the fruit as if it were an undifferentiated mass, like cold porridge.

"That's all right," says Will. "I'll leave it here for you."

"Have the flowers then," says Cynthia. This gesture too is contemptuous: he has needs, she doesn't. She is beyond needs.

Will casts around for anything: some hook, some handhold. "You should get better," he says, "so you can come up to the farm. You like it there." To himself he sounds falsely genial, wheedling.

"I'd be in the way," Cynthia says, looking away from him, out the window. Will looks too. There's nothing out there but the windows of another hospital building. "Sometimes I can see them doing operations," she says.

"I'd enjoy it," Will says, not knowing whether he's lying. "I get lonely up there on the weekends." This is true enough, but as soon as he's said it it sounds like whining.

Cynthia looks at him briefly. "You," she says, as if she has a monopoly, and who is he to talk? "Anyway, you don't have to go there if you don't want to. Nobody's making you."

Will feels shabby, like an out-of-work man begging for handouts on the street. He has seen such men and turned away from them, thinking about how embarrassed he would be if he were in their place, shuffling like that. Now he sees that what counts for them is not his feeling of embarrassment but the money. He stands foolishly beside Cynthia's bed, his offering rejected.

Cynthia has a short attention span. She's looking at her hands, spread out on the sheet now. The nails are peach-coloured, newly polished. "I used to be pretty, when I was younger," she says.

Will wants to shake her. She's barely eighteen, she doesn't know a thing about age or time. He could say, "You're pretty now," or he could say, "You'd be pretty if you'd put on some weight," but either one of these would be playing by her rules, so he says neither. Instead he says good-bye, pecks her on the cheek, and leaves, feeling as defeated as she wants him to feel. He hasn't made any difference.

*   *   *

Will parks his silver BMW in the parking space, takes the key out of the ignition, puts it carefully into his pocket. Then he remembers that he should keep the key handy to lock the car from the outside. This is one of the advantages of the BMW: you can never lock yourself out. He drove a Porsche for a while, after his marriage broke up. It made him feel single and ready for anything, but he doesn't feel like that any more. His moustache went about the same time as that car.

The parking space is off to the left of the farmhouse, demarcated by railroad ties and covered with white crushed gravel. It was like that when he bought the place, but that's what he probably would have done anyway. He keeps meaning to plant some flowers, zinnias perhaps, behind the railroad ties, but so far he hasn't got around to it.

He gets out, goes to the trunk for the groceries. Halfway to the house he realizes he's forgotten to lock the car, and goes back to do it. It's not as safe around here as it used to be. Last year he had a break-in, some kids from the town, out joy-riding. They broke plates and spread peanut butter on the walls, drank his liquor and smashed the bottles, and, as far as he could tell, screwed in all the beds. They were caught because they pinched the television set and tried to sell it. Everything was insured, but Will felt humiliated. Now he has bolt locks, and bars on the cellar windows, but anyone could break in if they really wanted to. He's thinking of getting a dog.

The air inside the house smells dead, as if it has heated and then cooled, absorbing the smells of furniture, old wood, paint, dust. He hasn't been here for several weeks. He sets the bags down on the kitchen table, opens a few windows. In the living room there's a vase with wizened daffodils, the water stagnant and foul. He sets the vase out on the patio; he'll empty it later.

Will bought this place after his marriage broke up, so he and the boys would have somewhere they could spend time together in a regular way. Also, his wife made it clear that she'd like some weekends off. The house was renovated by the people who lived here before; just as well, since Will never would have had the time to supervise, though he frequently sketches out plans for his ideal house. Not everything here is the way he would have done it, but he likes the board-and-batten exterior and the big opened-up kitchen. Despite some jumpiness lingering from the break-in, he feels good here, better than he does in his apartment in the city.

His former house is his wife's now; he doesn't like going there. Sometimes there are younger men, referred to by their first names only. Now that the boys are almost grown up, this doesn't bother him as much as it used to: she might as well be having a good time, though the turnover rate is high. When they were married she didn't enjoy anything much, including him, including sex. She never told him what was expected of him, and he never asked.

Will unpacks the groceries, stows away the food. He likes doing this, slotting the eggs into their egg-shaped holes in the refrigerator, filing the spinach in the crisper, stashing the butter in the compartment marked BUTTER, pouring the coffee beans into the jar labelled COFFEE. It makes him feel that some things at least are in their right places. He leaves the steaks on the counter, uncorks the wine, hunts for some candles. Of the pair he finds, one has been chewed by mice. Hardened droppings are scattered about the drawer. Mice are a new development. There must be a hole somewhere. Will is standing with the chewed candle in his hand, pondering remedies, when he hears a car outside.

He looks out the kitchen window. Since the break-in, he's less willing to open the door without knowing who's outside. But it's Diane, in a car he hasn't seen before, a cream-coloured Subaru. She always keeps her cars very clean. For some reason she's chosen to back up the driveway, in memory, perhaps, of the time she got stuck in the snow and he told her it would have been easier to get out if she'd been pointing down.

He puts the candle on the counter and goes into the downstairs bathroom. He smiles at himself, checking to see if there's anything caught between his teeth. He doesn't look bad. Then he goes out to welcome Diane. He realizes he hasn't been sure until now that she would really turn up. It could be he doesn't deserve it.

She slides out of the car, stands up, gives him a hug and a peck on the cheek. She has big sunglasses on, with silly palm trees over the eyebrows. This is the kind of extravagance Will has always liked about her. He hugs her back, but she doesn't want to be held too long. "I brought you something," she says, and searches inside the car.

Will watches her while she's bending over. She has a wide cotton skirt on, pulled tight around the waist; she's lost a lot of weight. He used to think of her as a hefty woman, well-fleshed and athletic, but now she's almost spindly. In his arms she felt frail, diminished.

She straightens and turns, thrusting a bottle of wine at him, and a round of Greek bread, fresh and spongy. Will is reassured. He puts his arm around her waist and hugs her again, trying to make it companionable so she won't feel pressured. "I'm glad to see you," he says.

Diane sits at the kitchen table and they drink wine; Will fools with the steaks, rubbing them with garlic, massaging them with pepper and a pinch or two of dried mustard. She used to help him with the cooking, she knows where everything's kept. But tonight she's acting more like a guest.

"Heard any good jokes lately?" she says. This in itself is a joke, since it was Diane who told the jokes, not Will. Diane was the one Will was with when his marriage stopped creaking and groaning and finally just fell apart. She wasn't the reason though, as he made a point of telling her. He said it could have been anyone; he didn't want her to feel responsible. He's not sure what happened after that, why they stopped seeing one another. It wasn't the sex: with her he was a good lover. He knows she liked him, and she got on well with the boys. But one day she said, "Well, I guess that's that," and Will didn't have the presence of mind to ask her what she meant.

"That's your department," Will says.

"Only because you were so sad then," says Diane. "I was trying to cheer you up. You were dragging around like you had a thyroid deficiency or something." She fiddles with her sunglasses, which are on the table. "Now it's your turn."

"You know I'm no good at it," Will says.

Diane nods. "Bad timing," she says. She stands up,

reaches past Will to the counter. "What's this?" she says, picking up the chewed candle. "Something fall off?"

* * *

They eat at the round oak table they bought together at a country auction, one of the local farmers closing up and selling out. Diane has dug out the white linen table napkins she gave him one year, and has lit both candles, the chewed and the unchewed. "I believe in festivity," she said.

Now there are silences, which they both attempt to fill. Diane says she wants to talk about money. It's the right time in her life for her to become interested in money, and isn't Will an authority? She makes quite a lot, but it's hard for her to save. She wants Will to explain inflation.

Will doesn't want to talk about money, but he does it anyway, to please her. Pleasing her is what he would like to do, but she doesn't seem too pleased. Her face is thinner and more lined, which makes her look more elegant but less accessible. She's less talkative than she used to be, as well. He remembers her voice as louder, more insistent; she would tease him, pull him up short. He found it amusing and it took his mind off himself. He thinks women in general are becoming more silent: it goes with their new pale lips. They're turning back to secrecy, concealment. It's as if they're afraid of something, but Will can't imagine what.

Half of Diane's steak lies on her plate, untouched. "So tell me about gold," she says.

"You're not hungry?" Will asks her.

"I was ravenous," she says. "But I'm full." Her hair has changed too. It's longer, with light streaks. Altogether she is more artful.

"I like being with you," Will says. "I always did."

176

"But not quite enough," Diane says, and then, to make it light, "you should put an ad in the paper, Will. The personals, *NOW* magazine. 'Nice man, executive, with good income, no encumbrances, desires to meet . . .' "

"I guess I'm not very good at relationships," Will says. In his head, he's trying to complete Diane's ad. Desires to meet what? A woman who would not look at herself in the glass of the picture behind him. A woman who would like what he cooks.

"Bullshit," Diane says, with a return to her old belligerence. "What makes you think you're that much worse at it than anyone else?"

Will looks at her throat, where it's visible at the V-neck of her blouse. He hasn't seen an overnight case, but maybe it's in the car. He said no strings attached.

"There's a full moon," he says. "We should go out onto the patio."

"Not quite," says Diane, squinting up through the glass. "And it's freezing out there, I bet."

Will goes upstairs for a plaid blanket from the boys' room to wrap around her. What he has in mind is a couple of brandies on the patio, and then they will see. As he's coming back down the stairs, he hears her in the bathroom: it sounds as if she's throwing up. Will pours the brandies, carries them outside. He wonders if he should go in, knock on the bathroom door. What if it's food poisoning? He knows he should feel compassion; instead he feels betrayed by her.

But when she comes out to stand beside him, she seems all right, and Will decides not to ask her about it. He wraps the blanket around her and keeps his arm there, and Diane leans against him.

"We could sit down," he says, in case she doesn't like the position.

"Hey," she says, "you got me flowers." She's spotted

the withered daffodils. "Always so thoughtful. I bet they smell nice, too."

"I wanted you to hear the frogs," Will says. "We're just at the end of the frog season." The frogs live in the pond, down beyond the slope of the lawn. Or maybe they're toads, he's never been sure. For Will they've come to mean spring and the beginning of summer: possibilities, newness. Their silvery voices are filling the air around them now, like crickets but more prolonged, sweeter.

"What a man," Diane says. "For some it's nightingales, for some it's frogs. Next I get a box of chocolate-covered slugs, right?"

Will would like to kiss her, but the timing is wrong. She's shivering a little; against his arm she feels angular, awkward, as if she's withholding her body from him, though not quite. They stand there looking at the moon, which is cold and lopsided, and listening to the trilling of the frogs. This doesn't have the effect on Will he has hoped it would. The voices coming from the darkness below the curve of the hill sound thin and ill. There aren't as many frogs as there used to be, either.

SCARLET IBIS

Some years ago now, Christine went with Don to Trinidad. They took Lilian, their youngest child, who was four then. The others, who were in school, stayed with their grandmother.

Christine and Don sat beside the hotel pool in the damp heat, drinking rum punch and eating strange-tasting hamburgers. Lilian wanted to be in the pool all the time—she could already swim a little—but Christine didn't think it was a good idea, because of the sun. Christine rubbed sun block on her nose, and on the noses of Lilian and Don. She felt that her legs were too white and that people were looking at her and finding her faintly ridiculous, because of her pinky-white skin and the large hat she wore. More than likely, the young black waiters who brought the rum punch and the hamburgers, who walked easily through the sun without paying any attention to it, who joked among themselves but were solemn when they set down the glasses and plates, had put her in a category; one that included fat, although she was not fat exactly. She suggested to Don that perhaps he was tipping too much. Don said he felt tired.

"You felt tired before," Christine said. "That's why we came, remember? So you could get some rest."

Don took afternoon naps, sprawled on his back on one

of the twin beds in the room—Lilian had a fold-out cot—his mouth slightly open, the skin of his face pushed by gravity back down towards his ears, so that he looked tauter, thinner, and more aquiline in this position than he did when awake. Deader, thought Christine, taking a closer look. People lying on their backs in coffins usually—in her limited experience—seemed to have lost weight. This image, of Don encoffined, was one that had been drifting through her mind too often for comfort lately.

It was hopeless expecting Lilian to have an afternoon nap too, so Christine took her down to the pool or tried to keep her quiet by drawing with her, using Magic Markers. At that age Lilian drew nothing but women or girls, wearing very fancy dresses, full-skirted, with a lot of decoration. They were always smiling, with red, curvy mouths, and had abnormally long thick eyelashes. They did not stand on any ground—Lilian was not yet putting the ground into her pictures—but floated on the page as if it were a pond they were spread out on, arms outstretched, feet at the opposite sides of their skirts, their elaborate hair billowing around their heads. Sometimes Lilian put in some birds or the sun, which gave these women the appearance of giant airborne balloons, as if the wind had caught them under their skirts and carried them off, light as feathers, away from everything. Yet, if she were asked, Lilian would say these women were walking.

After a few days of all this, when they ought to have adjusted to the heat, Christine felt they should get out of the hotel and do something. She did not want to go shopping by herself, although Don suggested it; she felt that nothing she tried on helped her look any better, or, to be more precise, that it didn't much matter how she looked. She tried to think of some other distraction, mostly for the sake of Don. Don was not noticeably more rested, although he had a sunburn—which, instead of giving him a glow of health, made him seem angry—and he'd started drumming his fingers on tabletops again. He said he was having trouble sleeping: bad dreams, which he could not remember. Also the air-conditioning was clogging up his nose. He had been under a lot of pressure lately, he said.

Christine didn't need to be told. She could feel the pressure he was under, like a clenched mass of something, tissue, congealed blood, at the back of her own head. She thought of Don as being encased in a sort of metal carapace, like the shell of a crab, that was slowly tightening on him, on all parts of him at once, so that something was sure to burst, like a thumb closed slowly in a car door. The metal skin was his entire body, and Christine didn't know how to unlock it for him and let him out. She felt as if all her ministrations—the cold washcloths for his headaches, the trips to the drugstore for this or that bottle of pills, the hours of tiptoeing around, intercepting the phone, keeping Lilian quiet, above all the mere act of witnessing him, which was so draining—were noticed by him hardly at all: moths beating on the outside of a lit window, behind which someone important was thinking about something of major significance that had nothing to do with moths. This vacation, for instance, had been her idea, but Don was only getting redder and redder.

Unfortunately, it was not carnival season. There were restaurants, but Lilian hated sitting still in them, and one thing Don did not need was more food and especially more drink. Christine wished Don had a sport, but considering the way he was, he would probably overdo it and break something.

"I had an uncle who took up hooking rugs," she'd said to him one evening after dinner. "When he retired. He got them in kits. He said he found it very restful." The aunt that went with that uncle used to say, "I said for better or for worse, but I never said for lunch."

"Oh, for God's sake, Christine," was all Don had to

say to that. He'd never thought much of her relatives. His view was that Christine was still on the raw side of being raw material. Christine did not look forward to the time, twenty years away at least, when he would be home all day, pacing, drumming his fingers, wanting whatever it was that she could never identify and never provide.

In the morning, while the other two were beginning breakfast, Christine went bravely to the hotel's reception desk. There was a thin, elegant brown girl behind it, in lime green, Rasta beads, and *Vogue* make-up, coiled like spaghetti around the phone. Christine, feeling hot and porous, asked if there was any material on things to do. The girl, sliding her eyes over and past Christine as if she were a minor architectural feature, selected and fanned an assortment of brochures, continuing to laugh lightly into the phone.

Christine took the brochures into the ladies' room to preview them. Not the beach, she decided, because of the sun. Not the boutiques, not the night clubs, not the memories of Old Spain.

She examined her face, added lipstick to her lips, which were getting thin and pinched together. She really needed to do something about herself, before it was too late. She made her way back to the breakfast table. Lilian was saying that the pancakes weren't the same as the ones at home. Don said she had to eat them because she had ordered them, and if she was old enough to order for herself she was old enough to know that they cost money and couldn't be wasted like that. Christine wondered silently if it was a bad pattern, making a child eat everything on her plate, whether she liked the food or not: perhaps Lilian would become fat, later on.

Don was having bacon and eggs. Christine had asked Don to order yoghurt and fresh fruit for her, but there was nothing at her place.

"They didn't have it," Don said.

"Did you order anything else?" said Christine, who was now hungry.

"How was I supposed to know what you want?" said Don.

"We're going to see the Scarlet Ibis," Christine announced brightly to Lilian. She would ask them to bring back the menu, so she could order.

"What?" said Don. Christine handed him the brochure, which showed some red birds with long curved bills sitting in a tree; there was another picture of one close up, in profile, one demented-looking eye staring out from its red feathers like a target.

"They're very rare," said Christine, looking around for a waiter. "It's a preservation."

"You mean a preserve," said Don, reading the brochure. "In a swamp? Probably crawling with mosquitoes."

"I don't want to go," said Lilian, pushing scraps of a pancake around in a pool of watery syrup. This was her other complaint, that it wasn't the right kind of syrup.

"Imitation maple flavouring," Don said, reading the label.

"You don't even know what it is," said Christine. "We'll take some fly dope. Anyway, they wouldn't let tourists go there if there were that many mosquitoes. It's a *mangrove* swamp; that isn't the same as our kind."

"I'm going to get a paper," said Don. He stood up and walked away. His legs, coming out of the bottoms of his Bermuda shorts, were still very white, with an overglaze of pink down the backs. His body, once muscular, was losing tone, sliding down towards his waist and buttocks. He was beginning to slope. From the back, he had the lax, demoralized look of a man who has been confined in an institution, though from the front he was brisk enough.

Watching him go, Christine felt the sickness in the pit of her stomach that was becoming familiar to her these days. Maybe the pressure he was under was her. Maybe she was a weight. Maybe he wanted her to lift up, blow away somewhere, like a kite, the children hanging on behind her in a long string. She didn't know when she had first noticed this feeling; probably after it had been there some time, like a knocking on the front door when you're asleep. There had been a shifting of forces, unseen, unheard, underground, the sliding against each other of giant stones; some tremendous damage had occurred between them, but who could tell when?

"Eat your pancakes," she said to Lilian, "or your father will be annoyed." He would be annoyed anyway: she annoyed him. Even when they made love, which was not frequently any more, it was perfunctory, as if he were listening for something else, a phone call, a footfall. He was like a man scratching himself. She was like his hand.

Christine had a scenario she ran through often, the way she used to run through scenarios of courtship, back in high school: flirtation, pursuit, joyful acquiescence. This was an adult scenario, however. One evening she would say to Don as he was getting up from the table after dinner, "Stay there." He would be so surprised by her tone of voice that he would stay.

"I just want you to sit there and look at me," she would say.

He would not say, "For God's sake, Christine." He would know this was serious.

"I'm not asking much from you," she would say, lying.

"What's going on?" he would say.

"I want you to see what I really look like," she would say. "I'm tired of being invisible." Maybe he would, maybe he wouldn't. Maybe he would say he was coming on with a headache. Maybe she would find herself walking on nothing, because maybe there was nothing there. So far she hadn't even come close to beginning, to giving the initial command: "Stay," as if he were a trained dog. But that was what she wanted him to do, wasn't it? "Come back" was more like it. He hadn't always been under pressure.

Once Lilian was old enough, Christine thought, she could go back to work full time. She could brush up her typing and shorthand, find something. That would be good for her; she wouldn't concentrate so much on Don, she would have a reason to look better, she would either find new scenarios or act out the one that was preoccupying her. Maybe she was making things up, about Don. It might be a form of laziness.

*   *   *

Christine's preparations for the afternoon were careful. She bought some mosquito repellant at a drugstore, and a chocolate bar. She took two scarves, one for herself, one for Lilian, in case it was sunny. The big hat would blow off, she thought, as they were going to be in a boat. After a short argument with one of the waiters, who said she could only have drinks by the glass, she succeeded in buying three cans of Pepsi, not chilled. All these things she packed into her bag; Lilian's bag, actually, which was striped in orange and yellow and blue and had a picture of Mickey Mouse on it. They'd used it for the toys Lilian brought with her on the plane.

After lunch they took a taxi, first through the hot streets of the town, where the sidewalks were too narrow or nonexistent and the people crowded onto the road and there was a lot of honking, then out through the cane fields, the road becoming bumpier, the driver increasing speed. He drove with the car radio on, the left-hand window open, and his elbow out, a pink jockey cap tipped back on his head. Christine had shown him the brochure and asked him if he knew where the swamp was; he'd grinned at her and said everybody knew. He said he could take them, but it was too far to go out and back so he would wait there for them. Christine knew it meant extra money, but did not argue.

They passed a man riding a donkey, and two cows wandering around by the roadside, anchored by ropes around their necks which were tied to dragging stones. Christine pointed these out to Lilian. The little houses among the tall cane were made of cement blocks, painted light green or pink or light blue; they were built up on open-work foundations, almost as if they were on stilts. The women who sat on the steps turned their heads, unsmiling, to watch their taxi as it went by.

Lilian asked Christine if she had any gum. Christine didn't. Lilian began chewing on her nails, which she'd taken up since Don had been under pressure. Christine told her to stop. Then Lilian said she wanted to go for a swim. Don looked out the window. "How long did you say?" he asked. It was a reproach, not a question.

Christine hadn't said how long because she didn't know; she didn't know because she'd forgotten to ask. Finally they turned off the main road onto a smaller, muddier one, and parked beside some other cars in a rutted space that had once been part of a field.

"I meet you here," said the driver. He got out of the car, stretched, turned up the car radio. There were other drivers hanging around, some of them in cars, others sitting on the ground drinking from a bottle they were passing around, one asleep.

Christine took Lilian's hand. She didn't want to appear stupid by having to ask where they were supposed to go next. She didn't see anything that looked like a ticket office.

"It must be that shack," Don said, so they walked towards it, a long shed with a tin roof; on the other side of it was a steep bank and the beginning of the water. There were wooden steps leading down to a wharf, which was the same brown as the water itself. Several boats were tied up to it, all of similar design: long and thin, almost like barges, with rows of bench-like seats. Each boat had a small outboard motor at the back. The names painted on the boats looked East Indian.

Christine took the scarves out of her bag and tied one on her own head and one on Lilian's. Although it was beginning to cloud over, the sun was still very bright, and she knew about rays coming through overcast, especially in the tropics. She put sun block on their noses, and thought that the chocolate bar had been a silly idea. Soon it would be a brown puddle at the bottom of her bag, which luckily was waterproof. Don paced behind them as Christine knelt.

An odd smell was coming up from the water: a swamp smell, but with something else mixed in. Christine wondered about sewage disposal. She was glad she'd made Lilian go to the bathroom before they'd left.

There didn't seem to be anyone in charge, anyone to buy the tickets from, although there were several people beside the shed, waiting, probably: two plumpish, middle-aged men in T-shirts and baseball caps turned around backwards, an athletic couple in shorts with outside pockets, who were loaded down with cameras and binoculars, a trim grey-haired woman in a tailored pink summer suit that must have been far too hot. There was another woman off to the side, a somewhat large woman in a floral print dress. She'd spread a Mexican-looking shawl on the weedy grass near the shed and was sitting down on it, drinking a pint carton of orange juice through a straw. The others looked wilted and dispirited, but not this woman. For her, waiting seemed to be an activity, not something imposed: she gazed around her, at the bank, the brown water, the line of sullen mangrove trees beyond, as if she were enjoying every minute.

This woman seemed the easiest to approach, so Christine went over to her. "Are we in the right place?" she said. "For the birds."

The woman smiled at her and said they were. She had

a broad face, with high, almost Slavic cheekbones and round red cheeks like those of an old-fashioned wooden doll, except that they were not painted on. Her taffy-coloured hair was done in waves and rolls, and reminded Christine of the pictures on the Toni home-permanent boxes of several decades before.

"We will leave soon," said the woman. "Have you seen these birds before? They come back only at sunset. The rest of the time they are away, fishing." She smiled again, and Christine thought to herself that it was a pity she hadn't had bands put on to even out her teeth when she was young.

This was the woman's second visit to the Scarlet Ibis preserve, she told Christine. The first was three years ago, when she stopped over here on her way to South America with her husband and children. This time her husband and children had stayed back at the hotel: they hadn't seen a swimming pool for such a long time. She and her husband were Mennonite missionaries, she said. She herself didn't seem embarrassed by this, but Christine blushed a little. She had been raised Anglican, but the only vestige of that was the kind of Christmas cards she favoured: prints of mediaeval or Renaissance old masters. Religious people of any serious kind made her nervous: they were like men in raincoats who might or might not be flashers. You would be going along with them in the ordinary way, and then there could be a swift movement and you would look down to find the coat wide open and nothing on under it but some pant legs held up by rubber bands. This had happened to Christine in a train station once.

"How many children do you have?" she said, to change the subject. Mennonite would explain the wide hips: they liked women who could have a lot of children.

The woman's crooked-toothed smile did not falter. "Four," she said, "but one of them is dead."

"Oh," said Christine. It wasn't clear whether the four

included the one dead, or whether that was extra. She knew better than to say, "That's too bad." Such a comment was sure to produce something about the will of God, and she didn't want to deal with that. She looked to make sure Lilian was still there, over by Don. Much of the time Lilian was a given, but there were moments at which she was threatened, unknown to herself, with sudden disappearance. "That's my little girl, over there," Christine said, feeling immediately that this was a callous comment; but the woman continued to smile, in a way that Christine now found eerie.

A small brown man in a Hawaiian-patterned shirt came around from behind the shed and went quickly down the steps to the wharf. He climbed into one of the boats and lowered the outboard motor into the water.

"Now maybe we'll get some action," Don said. He had come up behind her, but he was talking more to himself than to her. Christine sometimes wondered whether he talked in the same way when she wasn't there at all.

A second man, East Indian, like the first, and also in a hula-dancer shirt, was standing at the top of the steps, and they understood they were to go over. He took their money and gave each of them a business card in return; on one side of it was a coloured picture of an ibis, on the other a name and a phone number. They went single file down the steps and the first man handed them into the boat. When they were all seated—Don, Christine, Lilian, and the pink-suited woman in a crowded row, the two baseball-cap men in front of them, the Mennonite woman and the couple with the cameras at the very front—the second man cast off and hopped lightly into the bow. After a few tries the first man got the motor started, and they putt-putted slowly towards an opening in the trees, leaving a wispy trail of smoke behind them.

It was cloudier now, and not so hot. Christine talked with the pink-suited woman, who had blonde hair elegantly done up in a French roll. She was from Vienna, she said; her husband was here on business. This was the first time she had been on this side of the Atlantic Ocean. The beaches were beautiful, much finer than those of the Mediterranean. Christine complimented her on her good English, and the woman smiled and told her what a beautiful little girl she had, and Christine said Lilian would get conceited, a word that the woman had not yet added to her vocabulary. Lilian was quiet; she had caught sight of the woman's bracelet, which was silver and lavishly engraved. The woman showed it to her. Christine began to enjoy herself, despite the fact that the two men in front of her were talking too loudly. They were drinking beer, from cans they'd brought with them in a paper bag. She opened a Pepsi and shared some with Lilian. Don didn't want any.

They were in a channnel now; she looked at the trees on either side, which were all the same, dark-leaved, rising up out of the water, on masses of spindly roots. She didn't know how long they'd been going.

It began to rain, not a downpour but heavily enough, large cold drops. The Viennese woman said, "It's raining," her eyes open in a parody of surprise, holding out her hand and looking up at the sky like someone in a child's picture book. This was for the benefit of Lilian. "We will get wet," she said. She took a white embroidered handkerchief out of her purse and spread it on the top of her head. Lilian was enchanted with the handkerchief and asked Christine if she could have one, too. Don said they should have known, since it always rained in the afternoons here.

The men in baseball caps hunched their shoulders, and one of them said to the Indian in the bow, "Hey, we're getting wet!"

The Indian's timid but closed expression did not change; with apparent reluctance he pulled a rolled-up sheet of

190

plastic out from somewhere under the front seat and handed it to the men. They spent some time unrolling it and getting it straightened out, and then everyone helped to hold the plastic overhead like a roof, while the boat glided on at its unvarying pace, through the mangroves and the steam or mist that was now rising around them.

"Isn't this an adventure?" Christine said, aiming it at Lilian. Lilian was biting her nails. The rain pattered down. Don said he wished he'd brought a paper. The men in baseball caps began to sing, sounding oddly like boys at a summer camp who had gone to sleep one day and awakened thirty years later, unaware of the sinister changes that had taken place in them, the growth and recession of hair and flesh, the exchange of their once-clear voices for the murky ones that were now singing off-key, out of time:

> "They say that in the army,
> the girls are rather fine,
> They promise Betty Grable,
> they give you Frankenstein . . ."

They had not yet run out of beer. One of them finished a can and tossed it overboard, and it bobbed beside the boat for a moment before falling behind, a bright red dot in the borderless expanse of dull green and dull grey. Christine felt virtuous: she'd put her Pepsi can carefully into her bag, for disposal later.

Then the rain stopped, and after some debate about whether it was going to start again or not, the two baseball-cap men began to roll up the plastic sheet. While they were doing this there was a jarring thud. The boat rocked violently, and the one man who was standing up almost pitched overboard, then sat down with a jerk.

"What the hell?" he said.

The Indian at the back reversed the motor.

"We hit something," said the Viennese woman. She clasped her hands, another classic gesture.

"Obviously," Don said in an undertone. Christine smiled at Lilian, who was looking anxious. The boat started forward again.

"Probably a mangrove root," said the man with the cameras, turning half round. "They grow out under the water." He was the kind who would know.

"Or an alligator," said one of the men in baseball caps. The other man laughed.

"He's joking, darling," Christine said to Lilian.

"But we are sinking," said the Viennese woman, pointing with one outstretched hand, one dramatic finger.

Then they all saw what they had not noticed before. There was a hole in the boat, near the front, right above the platform of loose boards that served as a floor. It was the size of a small fist. Whatever they'd hit had punched right through the wood, as if it were cardboard. Water was pouring through.

"This tub must be completely rotten," Don muttered, directly to Christine this time. This was a role she was sometimes given when they were among people Don didn't know: the listener. "They get like that in the tropics."

"Hey," said one of the men in baseball caps. "You up front. There's a hole in the goddamned boat."

The Indian glanced over his shoulder at the hole. He shrugged, looked away, began fishing in the breast pocket of his sports shirt for a cigarette.

"Hey. Turn this thing around," said the man with the camera.

"Couldn't we get it fixed, and then start again?" said Christine, intending to conciliate. She glanced at the Mennonite woman, hoping for support, but the woman's broad flowered back was towards her.

"If we go back," the Indian said patiently—he could understand English after all—"you miss the birds. It will be too dark."

"Yeah, but if we go forward we sink."

"You will not sink," said the Indian. He had found a cigarette, already half-smoked, and was lighting it.

"He's done it before," said the largest baseball cap. "Every week he gets a hole in the goddamned boat. Nothing to it."

The brown water continued to come in. The boat went forward.

"Right," Don said, loudly, to everyone this time. "He thinks if we don't see the birds, we won't pay him."

That made sense to Christine. For the Indians, it was a lot of money. They probably couldn't afford the gas if they lost the fares. "If you go back, we'll pay you anyway," she called to the Indian. Ordinarily she would have made this suggestion to Don, but she was getting frightened.

Either the Indian didn't hear her or he didn't trust them, or it wasn't his idea of a fair bargain. He didn't smile or reply.

For a few minutes they all sat there, waiting for the problem to be solved. The trees went past. Finally Don said, "We'd better bail. At this rate we'll be in serious trouble in about half an hour."

"I should not have come," said the Viennese woman, in a tone of tragic despair.

"What with?" said the man with the cameras. The men in baseball caps had turned to look at Don, as if he were worthy of attention.

"Mummy, are we going to sink?" said Lilian.

"Of course not, darling," said Christine. "Daddy won't let us."

"Anything there is," said the largest baseball-cap man. He poured the rest of his beer over the side. "You got a jack-knife?" he said.

Don didn't, but the man with the cameras did. They watched while he cut the top out of the can, knelt down, moved a loose platform board so he could get at the water, scooped, dumped brown water over the side. Then the other men started taking the tops off their own beer cans, including the full ones, which they emptied out. Christine produced the Pepsi can from her bag. The Mennonite woman had her pint juice carton.

"No mosquitoes, at any rate," Don said, almost cheerfully.

They'd lost a lot of time, and the water was almost up to the floor platform. It seemed to Christine that the boat was becoming heavier, moving more slowly through the water, that the water itself was thicker. They could not empty much water at a time with such small containers, but maybe, with so many of them doing it, it would work.

"This really *is* an adventure," she said to Lilian, who was white-faced and forlorn. "Isn't this fun?"

The Viennese woman was not bailing; she had no container. She was making visible efforts to calm herself. She had taken out a tangerine, which she was peeling, over the embroidered handkerchief which she'd spread out on her lap. Now she produced a beautiful little pen-knife with a mother-of-pearl handle. To Lilian she said, "You are hungry? Look, I will cut in pieces, one piece for you, then one for me, *ja*?" The knife was not really needed, of course. It was to distract Lilian, and Christine was grateful.

There was an audible rhythm in the boat: scrape, dump; scrape, dump. The men in baseball caps, rowdy earlier, were not at all drunk now. Don appeared to be enjoying himself, for the first time on the trip.

But despite their efforts, the level of the water was rising.

"This is ridiculous," Christine said to Don. She stopped bailing with her Pepsi can. She was discouraged and also frightened. She told herself that the Indians wouldn't keep going if they thought there was any real danger, but she wasn't convinced. Maybe they didn't care if everybody drowned; maybe they thought it was Karma. Through the hole the brown water poured, with a steady flow, like a cut vein. It was up to the level of the loose floor boards now.

Then the Mennonite woman stood up. Balancing herself, she removed her shoes, placing them carefully side by side under the seat. Christine had once watched a man do this in a subway station; he'd put the shoes under the bench where she was sitting, and a few minutes later had thrown himself in front of the oncoming train. The two shoes had remained on the neat yellow-tiled floor, like bones on a plate after a meal. It flashed through Christine's head that maybe the woman had become unhinged and was going to leap overboard; this was plausible, because of the dead child. The woman's perpetual smile was a fraud then, as Christine's would have been in her place.

But the woman did not jump over the side of the boat. Instead she bent over and moved the platform boards. Then she turned around and lowered her large flowered rump onto the hole. Her face was towards Christine now; she continued to smile, gazing over the side of the boat at the mangroves and their monotonous roots and leaves as if they were the most interesting scenery she had seen in a long time. The water was above her ankles; her skirt was wet. Did she look a little smug, a little clever or self-consciously heroic? Possibly, thought Christine, though from that round face it was hard to tell.

"Hey," said one of the men in baseball caps, "now you're cooking with gas!" The Indian in the bow looked at the woman; his white teeth appeared briefly.

The others continued to bail, and after a moment Christine began to scoop and pour with the Pepsi can again. Despite herself, the woman impressed her. The water probably wasn't that cold but it was certainly filthy, and who could tell what might be on the other side of the hole? Were they far enough south for piranhas? Yet there was the Mennonite woman plugging the hole with her bottom, serene as a brooding hen, and no doubt unaware of the fact that she was more than a little ridiculous. Christine could imagine the kinds of remarks the men in baseball caps would make about the woman afterwards. "Saved by a big butt." "Hey, never knew it had more than one use." "Finger in the dike had nothing on her." That was the part that would have stopped Christine from doing such a thing, even if she'd managed to think of it.

Now they reached the long aisle of mangroves and emerged into the open; they were in a central space, like a lake, with the dark mangroves walling it around. There was a chicken-wire fence strung across it, to keep any boats from going too close to the Scarlet Ibis' roosting area: that was what the sign said, nailed to a post that was sticking at an angle out of the water. The Indian cut the motor and they drifted towards the fence; the other Indian caught hold of the fence, held on, and the boat stopped, rocking a little. Apart from the ripples they'd caused, the water was dead flat calm; the trees doubled in it appeared black, and the sun, which was just above the western rim of the real trees, was a red disk in the hazy grey sky. The light coming from it was orangy-red and tinted the water. For a few minutes nothing happened. The man with the cameras looked at his watch. Lilian was restless, squirming on the seat. She wanted to draw; she wanted to swim in the pool. If Christine had known the whole thing would take so long she wouldn't have brought her.

"They coming," said the Indian in the bow.

"Birds ahoy," said one of the men in baseball caps, and pointed, and then there were the birds all right, flying through the reddish light, right on cue, first singly, then in flocks of four or five, so bright, so fluorescent that they were like painted flames. They settled into the trees, screaming hoarsely. It was only the screams that revealed them as real birds.

The others had their binoculars up. Even the Viennese woman had a little pair of opera glasses. "Would you look at that," said one of the men. "Wish I'd brought my movie camera."

Don and Christine were without technology. So was the Mennonite woman. "You could watch them forever," she said, to nobody in particular. Christine, afraid that she would go on to say something embarrassing, pretended not to hear her. *Forever* was loaded.

She took Lilian's hand. "See those red birds?" she said. "You might never see one of those again in your entire life." But she knew that for Lilian these birds were no more special than anything else. She was too young for them. She said, "Oh," which was what she would have said if they had been pterodactyls or angels with wings as red as blood. Magicians, Christine knew from Lilian's last birthday party, were a failure with small children, who didn't see any reason why rabbits shouldn't come out of hats.

Don took hold of Christine's hand, a thing he had not done for some time; but Christine, watching the birds, noticed this only afterwards. She felt she was looking at a picture, of exotic flowers or of red fruit growing on trees, evenly spaced, like the fruit in the gardens of mediaeval paintings, solid, clear-edged, in primary colours. On the other side of the fence was another world, not real but at the same time more real than the one on this side, the men and women in their flimsy clothes and aging bodies, the decrepit boat. Her own body seemed fragile and empty, like blown glass.

The Mennonite woman had her face turned up to the sunset; her body was cut off at the neck by shadow, so that her head appeared to be floating in the air. For the first time she looked sad; but when she felt Christine watching her she smiled again, as if to reassure her, her face luminous and pink and round as a plum. Christine felt the two hands holding her own, mooring her, one on either side.

Weight returned to her body. The light was fading, the air chillier. Soon they would have to return in the increasing darkness, in a boat so rotten a misplaced foot would go through it. The water would be black, not brown; it would be full of roots.

"Shouldn't we go back?" she said to Don.

Lilian said, "Mummy, I'm hungry," and Christine remembered the chocolate bar and rummaged in her bag. It was down at the bottom, limp as a slab of bacon but not liquid. She brought it out and peeled off the silver paper, and gave a square to Lilian and one to Don, and ate one herself. The light was pink and dark at the same time, and it was difficult to see what she was doing.

When she told about this later, after they were safely home, Christine put in the swamp and the awful boat, and the men singing and the suspicious smell of the water. She put in Don's irritability, but only on days when he wasn't particularly irritable. (By then, there was less pressure; these things went in phases, Christine decided. She was glad she had never said anything, forced any issues.) She put in how good Lilian had been even though she hadn't wanted to go. She put in the hole in the boat, her own panic, which she made amusing, and the ridiculous bailing with the cans, and the Indians' indifference to their fate. She put in the Mennonite woman sitting on the hole like a big fat hen, making this funny, but admiring also, since the woman's solution to the problem had been so simple and obvious that no one else had thought of it. She left out the dead child.

She put in the rather hilarious trip back to the wharf,

with the Indian standing up in the bow, beaming his heavy-duty flashlight at the endless, boring mangroves, and the two men in the baseball caps getting into a mickey and singing dirty songs.

She ended with the birds, which were worth every minute of it, she said. She presented them as a form of entertainment, like the Grand Canyon: something that really ought to be seen, if you liked birds, and if you should happen to be in that part of the world.

THE SALT GARDEN

Alma turns up the heat, stirs the clear water in the red enamel pot, adds more salt, stirs, adds. She's making a supersaturated solution: re-making it. She made it already, at lunchtime, with Carol, but she didn't remember that you had to boil the water and she just used hot water from the tap. Nothing happened, though Alma had promised that a salt tree would form on the thread they hung down into the water, suspending it from a spoon laid crossways on the top of the glass.

"It takes time," Alma said. "It'll be here when you come home," and Carol went trustingly back to school, while Alma tried to figure out what she'd done wrong.

This experiment thing is new. Alma isn't sure where Carol picked it up. Surely not from school: she's only in grade two. But they're doing everything younger and younger. It upsets Alma to see them trying on her high heels and putting lipstick on their little mouths, even though she knows it's just a game. They wiggle their hips, imitating something they've seen on television. Maybe the experiments come from television too.

Alma has racked her brains, as she always does when Carol expresses interest in anything, searching for information she ought to possess but usually doesn't. These days, Alma encourages anything that will involve the two

201

of them in an activity that will block out questions about the way they're living; about the whereabouts of Mort, for instance. She's tried trips to the zoo, sewing dolls' dresses, movies on Saturdays. They all work, but only for a short time.

When the experiments came up, she remembered about putting vinegar into baking soda, to make it fizz; that was a success. Then other things started coming back to her. Now she can recall having been given a small chemistry set as a child, at the age of ten or so it must have been, by her father, who had theories in advance of his time. He thought girls should be brought up more like boys, possibly because he had no sons: Alma is an only child. Also he wanted her to do better than he himself had done. He had a job beneath his capabilities, in the post office, and he felt thwarted by that. He didn't want Alma to feel thwarted: that was how he'd attempted to warn Alma away from an early marriage, from leaving university to put Mort through architectural school by working as a secretary for a food-packaging company. "You'll wake up one day and you'll feel thwarted," he told her. Alma sometimes wonders whether this word describes what she feels, but usually decides that it doesn't.

Long before that period, though, he'd tried to interest Alma in chess and mathematics and stamp collecting, among other things. Not much of this rubbed off on Alma, at least not to her knowledge; at the predictable age she became disappointingly obsessed with make-up and clothes, and her algebra marks took a downturn. But she does retain a clear image of the chemistry set, with its miniature test tubes and the wire holder for them, the candle for heating them, and the tiny corked bottles, so appealingly like doll's-house glassware, with the mysterious substances in them: crystals, powders, solutions, potions. Some of these things had undoubtedly been poisonous; probably you could not buy such chemistry sets for children now. Alma is glad not to have missed out on it, because it was alchemy, after all, and that was how the instruction book presented it: magic. *Astonish your friends. Turn water to milk. Turn water to blood.* She remembers terminology, too, though the meanings have grown hazy with time. *Precipitate. Sublimation.*

There was a section on how to do tricks with ordinary household objects, such as how to make a hard-boiled egg go into a milk bottle, back in the days when there were milk bottles. (Alma thinks about them and sees the cream floating on the top, tastes the cardboard tops she used to beg to be allowed to lick off, smells the horse droppings from the wagons: she's getting old.) How to turn milk sour in an instant. How to make invisible writing with lemon juice. How to stop cut apples from turning brown. It's from this part of the instruction book (the best section, because who could resist the thought of mysterious powers hidden in the ordinary things around you?) that she's called back the supersaturated solution and the thread: *How to make a magical salt garden.* It was one of her favourites.

Alma's mother had complained about the way Alma was using up the salt, but her father said it was a cheap price to pay for the development of Alma's scientific curiosity. He thought Alma was learning about the spaces between molecules, but it was no such thing, as Alma and her mother both silently knew. Her mother was Irish, in dark contrast to her father's clipped and cheerfully bitter Englishness; she read tea-leaves for the neighbour women, which only they regarded as a harmless amusement. Maybe it's from her that Alma has inherited her bad days, her stretches of fatalism. Her mother didn't agree with her father's theories about Alma, and emptied out her experiments whenever possible. For her mother, Alma's fiddling in the kitchen was merely an excuse to avoid work, but Alma wasn't thinking even of that. She just liked the snowfall in miniature, the enclosed, protected world in the glass, the crystals forming on the thread, like the pictures of the Snow Queen's palace in the Hans Christian Andersen book at school. She can't remember ever having astonished any of her friends with tricks from the instruction book. Astonishing herself was enough.

The water in the pot is boiling again; it's still clear. Alma adds more salt, stirs while it dissolves, adds more. When salt gathers at the bottom of the pot, swirling instead of vanishing, she turns off the heat. She puts another spoon into the glass before pouring the hot water into it: otherwise the glass might break. She knows about this from having broken several of her mother's drinking glasses in this way.

She picks up the spoon with the thread tied to it and begins to lower the thread into the glass. While she is doing this, there is a sudden white flash, and the kitchen is blotted out with light. Her hand goes blank, then appears before her again, black, like an after-image on the retina. The outline of the window remains, framing her hand, which is still suspended above the glass. Then the window itself crumples inward, in fragments, like the candy-crystal of a shatter-proof windshield. The wall will be next, curving in towards her like the side of an inflating balloon. In an instant Alma will realize that the enormous sound has come and gone and burst her eardrums so that she is deaf, and then a wind will blow her away.

Alma closes her eyes. She can go on with this, or she can try to stop, hold herself upright, get the kitchen back. This isn't an unfamiliar experience. It's happened to her now on the average of once a week, for three months or more; but though she can predict the frequency she never knows when. It can be at any moment, when she's run the bathtub full of water and is about to step in, when she's sliding her arms into the sleeves of her coat, when she's making love, with Mort or Theo, it could be either of them and it has been. It's always when she's thinking about something else.

It isn't speculation: it's more like a hallucination. She's never had hallucinations before, except a long time ago when she was a student and dropped acid a couple of times. Everyone was doing it then, and she hadn't taken much. There had been moving lights and geometric patterns, which she'd watched in a detached way. Afterwards she'd wondered what all the talk about cosmic profundity had been about, though she hadn't wanted to say anything. People were very competitive about the meaningfulness of their drug trips in those days.

But none of it had been like this. It's occurred to her that maybe these things are acid flashes, though why should she be getting them now, fifteen years later, with none in between? At first she was so badly frightened that she'd considered going to see someone about it: a doctor, a psychiatrist. Maybe she's borderline epileptic. Maybe she's becoming schizophrenic or otherwise going mad. But there don't seem to be any other symptoms: just the flash and the sound, and being blown through the air, and the moment when she hits and falls into darkness.

The first time, she ended up lying on the floor. She'd been with Mort then, having dinner in a restaurant, during one of their interminable conversations about how things could be arranged better. Mort loves the word *arrange*, which is not one of Alma's favourites. Alma is a romantic: if you love someone, what needs arranging? And if you don't, why put in the effort? Mort, on the other hand, has been reading books about Japan; also he thinks they should draw up a marriage contract. On that occasion, Alma pointed out that they were already married. She wasn't sure where Japan fitted in: if he wanted her to scrub his back, that was all right, but she didn't want to be Wife Number One, not if it implied a lot of other numbers, either in sequence or simultaneously.

Mort has a girl friend, or that's how Alma refers to her. Terminology is becoming difficult these days: *mistress* is no longer suitable, conjuring up as it does peach-coloured negligées trimmed in fur, and mules, which nobody wears any more; nobody, that is, like Mort's girl friend, who is a squarely built young woman with a blunt-cut pageboy and freckles. And *lover* doesn't seem to go with the emotions Mort appears to feel towards this woman, whose name is Fran. Fran isn't the name of a mistress or a lover; more of a wife, but Alma is the wife. Maybe it's the name that's confusing Mort. Maybe that's why he feels, not passion or tenderness or devotion towards this woman, but a mixture of anxiety, guilt, and resentment, or this is what he tells Alma. He sneaks out on Fran to see Alma and calls Alma from telephone booths, and Fran doesn't know about it, which is the reverse of the way things used to be. Alma feels sorry for Fran, which is probably a defence.

It's not Fran that Alma objects to, as such. It's the rationalization of Fran. It's Mort proclaiming that there's a justifiable and even moral reason for doing what he does, that it falls into subsections, that men are polygamous by nature and so forth. That's what Alma can't stand. She herself does what she does because it's what she does, but she doesn't preach about it.

The dinner was more difficult for Alma than she'd anticipated, and because of this she had an extra drink. She stood up to go to the bathroom, and then it happened. She came to covered with wine and part of the tablecloth. Mort told her she'd fainted. He didn't say so, but she knew he put it down to hysteria, brought on by her problems with him, which to this day neither of them has precisely defined but which he thinks of as her problems, not his. She also knew that he thought she did it on purpose, to draw attention to herself, to collect sympathy and concern from him, to get him to listen to her. He was irritated. "If you were feeling dizzy," he said, "you should have gone outside."

Theo, on the other hand, was flattered when she passed out in his arms. He put it down to an excess of sexual passion, brought on by his technique, although again he didn't say so. He was quite pleased with her, and rubbed her hands and brought her a glass of water.

Theo is Alma's lover: no doubt about the terminology there. She met him at a party. He introduced himself by asking if she'd like another drink. (Mort, on the other hand, introduced himself by asking if she knew that if you cut the whiskers off cats they would no longer be able to walk along fences, which should have been a warning of some kind to Alma, but was not.) She was in a tangle with Mort, and Theo appeared to be in a similar sort of tangle with his wife, so they seemed to each other comparatively simple. That was before they had begun to accumulate history, and before Theo had moved out of his house. At that time they had been clutchers, specialists in hallways and vestibules, kissing among the hung-up coats and the rows of puddling rubbers.

Theo is a dentist, though not Alma's dentist. If he were her dentist, Alma doubts that she ever would have ended up having what she still doesn't think of as an affair with him. She feels that the inside of her mouth, and especially the insides of her teeth, are intimate in an anti-sexual way; surely a man would be put off by such evidences of bodily imperfection, of rot. (Alma doesn't have bad teeth; still, even a look inside with that little mirror, even the terminology, *orifice, cavity, mandible, molar . . .)*

Dentistry, for Theo, is hardly a vocation. He hadn't felt called by teeth; he's told her he picked dentistry because he didn't know what else to do; he had good fine-motor coordination, and it was a living, to put it mildly.

"You could have been a gigolo," Alma said to him on that occasion. "You would have got extra in tips." Theo, who does not have a rambunctious sense of humour and is fastidious about clean underwear, was on the verge of being shocked, which Alma enjoyed. She likes making him feel more sexual than he is, which in turn makes him more sexual. She indulges him.

So, when she found herself lying on Theo's broadloom, with Theo bending over her, gratified and solicitous, saying, "Sorry, was I too rough?" she did nothing to correct his impression.

"It was like a nuclear explosion," she said, and he thought she was using a simile. Theo and Mort have one thing in common: they've both elected themselves as the cause of these little manifestations of hers. That, or female body chemistry: another good reason why women shouldn't be allowed to be airplane pilots, a sentiment Alma once caught Theo expressing.

The content of Alma's hallucinations doesn't surprise her. She suspects that other people are having similar or perhaps identical experiences, just as, during the Middle Ages, many people saw (for instance) the Virgin Mary, or witnessed miracles: flows of blood that stopped at the touch of a bone, pictures that spoke, statues that bled. As for now, you could get hundreds of people to swear they've been on spaceships and talked with extraterrestrial beings. These kinds of delusions go in waves, Alma thinks, in epidemics. Her lightshows, her blackouts, are no doubt as common as measles, only people aren't admitting to them. Most likely they're doing what she should do, trotting off to their doctors and getting themselves renewable prescriptions for Valium or some other pill that will smooth out the brain. They don't want anyone to think they're unstable, because although most would agree that what she's afraid of is something it's right to be afraid of, there's a consensus about how much. Too much fear is not normal.

Mort, for instance, thinks everyone should sign petitions and go on marches. He signs petitions himself, and brings them for Alma to sign, on occasions when he's visiting her legitimately. If she signed them during one of his sneak trips, Fran would know and put two and two together, and by now not even Alma wants that. She likes Mort better now that she sees less of him. Let Fran do his laundry, for a change. The marches he goes to with Fran, however, as they are more like social occasions. It's for this reason that Alma herself doesn't attend the marches: she doesn't want to make things awkward for Fran, who is touchy enough already on the subject of Alma. There are certain things, like parent-teacher conferences, that Mort is allowed to attend with Alma, and other things that he isn't. Mort is sheepish about these restrictions, since one of his avowed reasons for leaving Alma was that he felt too tied down.

Alma agrees with Mort about the marches and petitions, out loud that is. It's reasonable to suppose that if only everyone in the world would sign the petitions and go on the marches, the catastrophe itself would not occur. Now is the time to stand up and be counted, to throw your body in front of the juggernaut, as Mort himself does in the form of donations to peace groups and letters to politicians, for which he receives tax receipts and neatly typed form letters in response. Alma knows that Mort's way makes sense, or as much sense as anything, but she has never been a truly sensible person. This was one of her father's chief complaints about her. She could never bring herself to squeeze in her two hands the birds that flew into their plate-glass window and injured themselves, as her father taught her to do, in order to collapse their lungs. Instead she wanted to keep them in boxes filled with cotton wool and feed them with an eyedropper, thus causing them—according to her father—to die a lingering and painful death. So he would collapse their lungs himself, and Alma would refuse to look, and grieve afterwards.

Marrying Mort was not sensible. Getting involved with Theo was not sensible, Alma's clothes are not and never have been sensible, especially the shoes. Alma knows that if a fire ever broke out in her house, the place would burn to the ground before she could make up her mind about what to do, even though she's in full possession of all the possibilities (extinguisher, fire department's number, wet cloth to put over the nose). So, in the face of Mort's hearty optimism, Alma shrugs inwardly. She tries hard to believe, but she's an infidel and not proud of it. The sad truth is that there are probably more people in the world like her than like Mort. Anyway, there's a lot of money tied up in those bombs. She doesn't interfere with him or say anything negative, however. The petitions are as constructive a hobby as any, and the marches keep him active and happy. He's a muscular man with a reddish face, who's inclined to overweight and who needs to work off energy to avoid the chance of a heart attack, or that's what the doctor says. It's all a good enough way to pass the time.

Theo, on the other hand, deals with the question by not dealing with it at all. He lives his life as if it isn't there, a talent for obliviousness that Alma envies. He just goes on filling teeth, filling teeth, as if all the tiny adjustments he's making to people's mouths are still going to matter in ten years, or five, or even two. Maybe, Alma thinks in her more cynical moments, they can use his

dental records for identification when they're sorting out
the corpses, if there are any left to sort; if sorting will be
a priority, which she very much doubts. Alma has tried
to talk about it, once or twice, but Theo has said he
doesn't see any percentage in negative thinking. It will
happen or it won't, and if it doesn't the main worry will
be the economy. Theo makes investments. Theo is planning his retirement. Theo has tunnel vision and Alma
doesn't. She has no faith in people's ability to pull themselves out of this hole, and no sand to stick her head into.
The thing is there, standing in one corner of whatever
room she happens to be in, like a stranger whose face you
know you could see clearly if you were only to turn your
head. Alma doesn't turn her head. She doesn't want to
look. She goes about her business, most of the time; except for these minor lapses.

Sometimes she tells herself that this isn't the first time
people have thought they were coming to the end of the
world. It's happened before, during the Black Death for
instance, which Alma remembers as having been one of
the high points of second-year university. The world hadn't
come to an end, of course, but believing it was going to
had much the same effect.

Some of them decided it was their fault and went around
flagellating themselves, or each other, or anyone else handy.
Or they prayed a lot, which was easier then because you
had some idea of who you were supposed to be talking
to. Alma doesn't think this is a dependable habit of mind
any more, since there's an even chance that the button
will be pushed by some American religious maniac who
wants to play God and help Revelations along, someone
who really believes that he and a few others will be raised
up incorruptible afterwards, and therefore everyone else
can rot. Mort says this is a mistake unlikely to be made
by the Russians, who've done away with the afterlife and
have to be serious about this one. Mort says the Russians

are better chess players, which isn't much consolation to Alma. Her father's attempts to teach her chess had not been too successful, as Alma had a way of endowing the pieces with personalities and crying when her Queen got killed.

Or you could wall yourself up, throw the corpses outside, carry around oranges stuck with cloves. Dig shelters. Issue instructional handbooks.

Or you could steal things from the empty houses, strip the necklaces from the bodies.

Or you could do what Mort was doing. Or you could do what Theo was doing. Or you could do what Alma was doing.

Alma thinks of herself as doing nothing. She goes to bed at night, she gets up in the morning, she takes care of Carol, they eat, they talk, sometimes they laugh, she sees Mort, she sees Theo, she looks for a better job, though not in a way that convinces her. She thinks about going back to school and finishing her degree: Mort says he will pay, they've both agreed he owes her that, though when it comes right down to it she isn't sure she wants to. She has emotions: she loves people, she feels anger, she is happy, she gets depressed. But somehow she can't treat these emotions with as much solemnity as she once did. Never before has her life felt so effortless, as if all responsibility has been lifted from her. She floats. There's a commercial on television, for milk she thinks, that shows a man riding at the top of a wave on a surfboard: moving, yet suspended, as if there is no time. This is how Alma feels: removed from time. Time presupposes a future. Sometimes she experiences this state as apathy, other times as exhilaration. She can do what she likes. But what does she like?

She remembers something else they did during the Black Death: they indulged themselves. They pigged out on their winter supplies, they stole food and gorged, they danced in the streets, they copulated indiscriminately with whoever was available. Is this where she's heading, on top of her wave?

Alma rests the spoon on the two edges of the glass. Now the water is cooling and the salt is coming out of solution. It forms small transparent islands on the surface that thicken as the crystals build up, then break and drift down through the water, like snow. She can see a faint white fuzz of salt gathering on the thread. She kneels so that her eyes are level with the glass, rests her chin and hands on the table, watches. It's still magic. By the time Carol comes home from school, there will be a whole winter in the glass. The thread will be like a tree after a sleet storm. She can't believe how beautiful this is.

After a while she gets up and walks through her house, through the whitish living room which Mort considers Japanese in the less-is-more tradition but which has always reminded her of a paint-by-numbers page only a quarter filled in, past the naked-wood end wall, up the staircase from which Mort removed the banisters. He also took out too many walls, omitted too many doors; maybe that's what went wrong with the marriage. The house is in Cabbagetown, one of the larger ones. Mort, who specializes in renovations, did it over and likes to bring people there to display it to them. He views it, still, as the equivalent of an advertising brochure. Alma, who is getting tired of going to the door in her second-best dressing gown with her hair in a towel and finding four men in suits standing outside it, headed by Mort, is thinking about getting the locks changed. But that would be too definitive. Mort still thinks of the house as his, and he thinks of her as part of the house. Anyway, with the slump in house-building that's going on, and considering who pays the bills, she ought to be glad to do her bit to help out; which Mort has narrowly avoided saying.

She reaches the white-on-white bathroom, turns on the taps, fills the tub with water which she colours blue with a capful of German bath gel, climbs in, sighs. She has some friends who go to isolation tanks and float in total darkness, for hours on end, claiming that this is relaxing and also brings you in touch with your deepest self. Alma has decided to give this experience a pass. Nevertheless, the bathtub is where she feels safest (she's never passed out in the bathtub) and at the same time most vulnerable (what if she were to pass out in the bathtub? She might drown).

When Mort still lived with her and Carol was younger, she used to lock herself into the bathroom, chiefly because it had a door that closed, and do what she called "spending time with herself," which amounted to daydreaming. She's retained the habit.

At one period, long ago it seems now, though it's really just a couple of months, Alma indulged from time to time in a relatively pleasant fantasy. In this fantasy she and Carol were living on a farm, on the Bruce Peninsula. She'd gone on a vacation there once, with Mort, back before Carol was born, when the marriage was still behaving as though it worked. They'd driven up the Bruce and crossed over onto Manitoulin Island in Lake Huron. She'd noticed the farms then, how meagre they were, how marginal, how many rocks had been pulled out of the fields and piled into cairns and rows. It was one of these farms she chose for her fantasy, on the theory that nobody else would want it.

She and Carol heard about the coming strike on the radio, as they were doing the dishes in the farm kitchen after lunch. (Improbable in itself, she now realizes: it would be too fast for that, too fast to reach a radio show.) Luckily, they raised all their own vegetables, so they had lots around. Initially Alma was vague about what these would be. She'd included celery, erroneously, she knows now: you could never grow celery in soil like that.

Alma's fantasies are big on details. She roughs them in first, then goes back over them, putting in the buttons and zippers. For this one she needed to make a purchase of appropriate seeds, and to ask for advice from the man in the hardware store. "Celery?" he said. (A balding, fatherly small-town retailer, wearing braces on his pants, a ring of sweat under each arm of his white shirt. Still, the friendliness was tricky. Probably he had contempt for her. Probably he told stories about her to his cronies in the beer parlour, a single woman with a child, living by herself out there on that farm. The cronies would cruise by on her sideroad in their big second-hand cars, staring at her house. She would think twice about going outside in shorts, bending over to pull out weeds. If she got raped, everyone would know who did it but none of them would tell. This man would not be the one but he would say after a few beers that she had it coming. This is a facet of rural life Alma must consider seriously before taking it up.)

"Celery?" he said. "Up here? Lady, you must be joking." So Alma did away with the celery, which wouldn't have kept well anyway.

But there were beets and carrots and potatoes, things that could be stored. They'd dug a large root cellar into the side of a hill; it was entered by a door that slanted and that somehow had several feet of dirt stuck onto the outside of it. But the root cellar was much more than a root cellar: it had several rooms, for instance, and electric lights (with power coming from where? It was details like this that when closely examined helped to cause the eventual collapse of the fantasy, though for the electricity Alma filled in with a small generator worked by runoff from the pond).

Anyway, when they heard the news on the radio, she and Carol did not panic. They walked, they did not run, sedately to the root cellar, where they went inside and shut the door behind them. They did not forget the radio, which was a transistor, though of course it was no use after the initial strike, in which all the stations were presumably vaporized. On the shelves built neatly into one wall were rows and rows of bottled water. There they stayed, eating carrots and playing cards and reading entertaining books, until it was safe to come out, into a world in which the worst had already happened so no longer needed to be feared.

This fantasy is no longer functional. For one thing, it could not be maintained for very long in the concrete detail Alma finds necessary before practical questions with no answers began to intrude (ventilation?). In addition, Alma had only an approximate idea of how long they would have to stay in there before the danger would be over. And then there was the problem of refugees, marauders, who would somehow find out about the potatoes and carrots and come with (guns? sticks?). Since it was only her and Carol, the weapons were hardly needed. Alma began to equip herself with a rifle, then rifles, to fend off these raiders, but she was always outnumbered and outgunned.

The major flaw, however, was that even when things worked and escape and survival were possible, Alma found that she couldn't just go off like that and leave other people behind. She wanted to include Mort, even though he'd behaved badly and they weren't exactly together, and if she let him come she could hardly neglect Theo. But

Theo could not come, of course, without his wife and children, and then there was Mort's girl friend Fran, whom it would not be fair to exclude.

This arrangement worked for a while, without the quarrelling Alma would have expected. The prospect of imminent death is sobering, and Alma basked for a time in the gratitude her generosity inspired. She had intimate chats with the two other women about their respective men, and found out several things she didn't know; the three of them were on the verge of becoming really good friends. In the evenings they sat around the kitchen table which had appeared in the root cellar, peeling carrots together in a companionable way and reminiscing about what it had been like when they all lived in the city and didn't know each other, except obliquely through the men. Mort and Theo sat at the other end, drinking the Scotch they'd brought with them, mixed with bottled water. The children got on surprisingly well together.

But the root cellar was too small really, and there was no way to enlarge it without opening the door. Then there was the question of who would sleep with whom and at what times. Concealment was hardly possible in such a confined space, and there were three women but only two men. This was all too close to real life for Alma, but without the benefit of separate dwellings.

After the wife and the girl friend started to insist on having their parents and aunts and uncles included (and why had Alma left hers out?), the fantasy became overpopulated and, very quickly, uninhabitable. Alma could not choose, that was her difficulty. It's been her difficulty all her life. She can't draw the line. Who is she to decide, to judge people like that, to say who must die and who is to be given a chance at life?

The hill of the root cellar, honeycombed with tunnels,

too thoroughly mined, fell in upon itself, and all perished.

When Alma has dried herself off and is rubbing body lotion on herself, the telephone rings.

"Hi, what are you up to?" the voice says.

"Who is this?" Alma says, then realizes that it's Mort. She's embarrassed not to have recognized his voice. "Oh, it's you," she says. "Hi. Are you in a phone booth?"

"I thought I might drop by," says Mort, conspiratorially. "That is, if you'll be there."

"With or without a committee?" Alma says.

"Without," says Mort. What this means is clear enough. "I thought we could make some decisions." He means to be gently persuasive, but comes through as slightly badgering.

Alma doesn't say that he doesn't need her to help him make decisions, since he seems to make them swiftly enough on his own. "What kind of decisions?" she says warily. "I thought we were having a moratorium on decisions. That was your last decision."

"I miss you," Mort says, letting the words float, his voice shifting to a minor key that is supposed to indicate yearning.

"I miss you too," says Alma, hedging her bets. "But this afternoon I promised Carol I'd buy her a pink gym suit. How about tonight?"

"Tonight isn't an option," says Mort.

"You mean you aren't allowed out to play?" says Alma.

"Don't be snarky," Mort says a little stiffly.

"Sorry," says Alma, who isn't. "Carol wants you to come on Sunday to watch 'Fraggle Rock' with her."

"I want to see you alone," Mort says. But he books himself in for Sunday anyway, saying he'll double-check it and call her back. Alma says good-bye and hangs up,

with a sense of relief that is very different from the feelings she's had about saying good-bye to Mort on the telephone in the past; which were, sequentially, love and
desire, transaction of daily business, frustration because
things weren't being said that ought to be, despair and
grief, anger and a sense of being fucked over. She continues on with the body lotion, with special attention to the
knees and elbows. That's where it shows up first, when
you start to look like a four-legged chicken. Despite the
approach of the end of the world, Alma likes to keep in
shape.

She decides to take the streetcar. She has a car and
knows how to drive, she can drive perfectly well, but
lately she's been doing it less and less. Right now she
prefers modes of transportation that do not require any
conscious decisions on her part. She'd rather be pulled
along, on a track if possible, and let someone else do the
steering.

The streetcar stop is outside a health-food store, the
window of which is filled with displays of dried apricots
and carob-covered raisins, magical foods that will preserve you from death. Alma too has had her macrobiotic
phase: she knows what elements of superstitious hope
the consumption of such talismans involves. It would
have been just as effective to have strung the raisins on
a thread and worn them around her neck, to ward off
vampires. On the brick wall of the store, between the
window and the door, someone has written in spray paint:
JESUS HATES YOU.

The streetcar comes and Alma gets on. She's going to
the subway station, where she will get off and swiftly
buy a pink gym suit and two pairs of summer socks for
Carol and go down the stairs and get onto a subway train
going north, using the transfer she's just stuck into her

219

purse. You aren't supposed to use transfers for stopovers but Alma feels reckless.

The car is a little crowded. She stands near the back door, looking out the window, thinking about nothing in particular. It's a sunny day, one of the first, and warm; things are too bright.

All at once some people near the back door begin to shout: *Stop! Stop!* Alma doesn't hear them at first, or she hears them at the level of non-comprehension: she knows there is noise, but she thinks it's just some teenagers fooling around, being too loud, the way they do. The streetcar conductor must think this too, because he keeps on going, at a fast clip, spinning along, while more and more people are shouting and then screaming, *Stop! Stop! Stop!* Then Alma begins to shout too, for she sees what is wrong: there's a girl's arm caught in the back door, and the girl herself is outside, being dragged along it must be; Alma can't see her but she knows she's there.

Alma finds herself jumping up and down, like a frustrated child, and screaming "*Stop! Stop!*" with the rest of them, and still the man drives on, oblivious. Alma wants someone to throw something or hit him, why is no one moving? They're packed in too close, and the ones at the front don't know, can't see. This goes on for hours which are really minutes, and finally he slows down and stops. He gets out, walks around to the back.

Luckily there's an ambulance right beside them, so the girl is put into it. Alma can't see her face or how badly injured she is, though she cranes her neck, but she can hear the noises she's making: not crying, not whimpering, something more animal and abandoned, more terrified. The most frightening thing must have been not the pain but the sense that no one could see or hear her.

Now that the streetcar has stopped and the crisis is over, people around Alma begin muttering to one another. The driver should be removed, they say. He should lose his licence, or whatever it is they have. He should be arrested. But he comes back and pushes something at the front and the doors open. They will all have to get off the streetcar, he says. He sounds angry, as if the girl caught in the door and the shouting have been someone else's fault.

They aren't far from the subway stop and the store where Alma intends to do her furtive shopping: Alma can walk. At the next stoplight she looks back. The driver is standing beside the streetcar, hands in his pockets, talking with a policeman. The ambulance is gone. Alma notices that her heart is pounding. This is how it is in riots, she thinks, or fires: someone begins to shout and then you're in the middle of it, without knowing what is happening. It goes too fast, and you shut out the cries for help. If people had shouted "help" instead of "stop," would the driver have heard them sooner? But the people did shout, and he did stop, eventually.

Alma can't find a pink gym suit in Carol's size, so she buys a mauve one instead. There will be repercussions about that. She makes it onto the subway train, using her spurious transfer, and begins her short journey through the darkness she can see outside the window, watching her own face floating on the glass that seals it out. She sits with her hands clasped around the package on her lap, and begins looking at the hands of the people across from her. She's found herself doing this quite often lately: noticing what the hands are like, how they are almost luminous, even the hands of old people, knobby hands with blue veins and mottles. These symptoms of age don't frighten her as a foretaste of her own future, the way they once did; they no longer revolt her. Male or female, it doesn't matter; the hands she's looking at right now belong to a middle-aged woman of no distinction, they're lumpy and blunt, with chipped orange nail polish, they're clutching a brown leather purse.

Sometimes she has to restrain an impulse to get up, cross the aisle, sit down, take hold of these alien hands. It would be misunderstood. She can remember feeling this way once, a long time ago, when she was on a plane, going to join Mort at a conference in Montreal. They were planning to take a mini-vacation together after it. Alma was excited by the prospect of the hotel room, the aroma of luxury and illicit sex that would surround them. She looked forward to being able to use the bath towels and drop them on the floor without having to think about who was going to wash them. But the plane had started to lurch around in the air, and Alma was frightened. When it took a dip, like an elevator going down, she'd actually grabbed the hand of the man sitting next to her; not that it would make any difference whose hand you were holding if there really was a crash. Still, it made her feel safer. Then, of course, he'd tried to pick her up. He was fairly nice in the end: he sold real estate, he said.

Sometimes she studies Theo's hands, finger by finger, nail by nail. She rubs them over her body, puts the fingers in her mouth, curling her tongue around them. He thinks it's merely eroticism. He thinks he's the only person whose hands she thinks about in this way.

Theo lives in a two-bedroom apartment in a high-rise not far from his office. Or at least Alma thinks he lives there. Though it makes her feel, not unpleasantly, a little like a call girl, it's where she meets him, because he doesn't like coming to her house. He still considers it Mort's territory. He doesn't think of Alma as Mort's territory, only the house, just as his own house, where his wife lives with their three children, is still his territory. That's how he speaks of it: "my house." He goes there on weekends, just as Mort goes to Alma's house. Alma suspects he and his wife sneak into bed, just as she and Mort do, feeling like students in a fifties dorm, swearing each other to secrecy. They tell themselves that it would never do for Fran to find out. Alma hasn't been explicit about Theo to Mort, though she's hinted that there's someone. That made him perk up. "I guess I have no right to complain," he said.

"I guess you don't," said Alma. It's ridiculous the way the five of them carry on, but it would seem just as ridiculous to Alma not to go to bed with Mort. After all, he is her husband. It's something she's always done. Also, the current arrangement has done wonders for their sex life. Being a forbidden fruit suits her. She's never been one before.

But if Theo is still sleeping with his wife, Alma doesn't want to know about it. He has every right, in a way, but she would be jealous. Oddly enough, she doesn't much care any more what goes on between Mort and Fran. Mort is thoroughly hers already; she knows every hair on his body, every wrinkle, every rhythm. She can relax into him with scarcely a thought, and she doesn't have to make much conscious effort to please him. It's Theo who's the unexplored territory, it's with Theo that she has to stay alert, go carefully, not allow herself to be lulled into a false sense of security: Theo, who at first glance appears so much gentler, more considerate, more tentative. For Alma, he's a swamp to Mort's forest: she steps lightly, ready to draw back. Yet it's his body—shorter, slighter, more sinewy than Mort's—she's possessive about. She doesn't want another woman touching it, especially one who's had more time to know it than she's had. The last time she saw Theo (here, in this apartment building, the impersonal white lobby of which she's now entering), he said he wanted to show her some recent snapshots of his family. Alma excused herself and went into the bathroom. She didn't want to see a picture of Theo's wife, but also she felt that even to look would be a violation of both of them; the use, by Theo, of two women to cancel each other out. It's occurred to her that she is to Theo's wife as Mort's girl friend is to her: the usurper, in a way, but also the one to be pitied because of what is not being admitted.

She knows that the present balance of power can't last. Sooner or later, pressures will be brought to bear. The men will not be allowed to drift back and forth between their women, their houses. Barriers will be erected, signs will go up: STAY PUT OR GET OUT. Rightly so; but none of these pressures will come from Alma. She likes things the way they are. She's decided that she prefers having two men rather than one: it keeps things even. She loves both of them, she wants both of them; which means, some days, that she loves neither and wants neither. It makes her less anxious and less vulnerable, and suggests multiple futures. Theo may go back to his wife, or wish to move in with Alma. (Recently he asked her an ominous question—"What do you want?"—which Alma dodged.) Mort may want to return, or he may decide to start over with Fran. Or Alma could lose both of them and be left alone with Carol. This thought, which would once have given rise to panic and depression not unconnected with questions of money, doesn't worry her much at the moment. She wants it to go on the way it is forever.

Alma steps into the elevator and is carried up. Weightlessness encloses her. It's a luxury; her whole life is a luxury. Theo, opening the door for her, is a luxury, especially his skin, which is smooth and well-fed and darker than hers, which comes of his being part Greek, a generation or two back, and which smells of brisk sweetish chemicals. Theo amazes her, she loves him so much she can barely see him. Love burns her out; it burns out Theo's features so that all she can see in the dimmed apartment is an outline, shining. She's not on the wave, she's in it, warm and fluid. This is what she wants. They don't get as far as the bedroom, but collapse onto the living-room rug, where Theo makes love to her as if he's running for a train he's never going to catch.

Time passes, and Theo's details reappear, a mole here, a freckle there. Alma strokes the back of his neck, lifting her hand to look surreptitiously at her watch: she has to be back in time for Carol. She must not forget the gym suit, cast aside in its plastic bag at the door, along with her purse and shoes.

"That was magnificent," says Alma. It's true.

Theo smiles, kisses the inside of her wrist, holds it for a few seconds as if listening for the pulse, picks up her half-slip from the floor, hands it to her with tenderness and deference, as if presenting her with a bouquet of flowers. As if she's a lady on a chocolate box. As if she's dying, and only he knows it and wants to keep it from her.

"I hope," he says pleasantly, "that when this is all over we won't be enemies."

Alma freezes, the half-slip half on. Then air goes into her, a silent gasp, a scream in reverse, because she's noticed at once: he didn't say "if," he said "when." Inside his head there's a schedule. All this time during which she's been denying time, he's been checking off the days, doing a little countdown. He believes in predestination. He believes in doom. She should have known that, being such a neat person, he would not be able to stand anarchy forever. They must leave the water, then, and emerge onto dry land. She will need more clothes, because it will be colder there.

"Don't be silly," Alma says, pulling imitation satin up to her waist like a bedsheet. "Why would we?"

"It happens," says Theo.

"Have I ever done or said anything to make you feel it would happen to us?" Alma says. Maybe he's going back to his wife. Maybe he isn't, but has decided anyway that she will not do, not on a daily basis, not for the rest of his life. He still believes there will be one. So does she, or why would she be this upset?

"No," says Theo, scratching his leg, "but it's the kind of thing that happens." He stops scratching, looks at her, that look she used to consider sincere. "I just want you to know I like you too well for that."

Like. That finishes it, or does it? As often with Theo, she's unsure of what is being said. Is he expressing devotion, or has it ended already, without her having been aware of it? She's become used to thinking that in a relationship like theirs everything is given and nothing is demanded, but perhaps it's the other way around. Nothing is given. Nothing is even *a given.* Alma feels suddenly too visible, too blatant. Perhaps she should return to Mort and become once more unseen.

"I like you too," she says. She finishes dressing, while he continues to lie on the floor, gazing at her fondly, like someone waving to a departing ship, who nevertheless looks forward to the moment when he can go and have his dinner. He doesn't care what she's going to do next.

"Day after tomorrow?" he says, and Alma, who wants to have been wrong, smiles back.

"Beg and plead," she says.

"I'm not good at it," he says. "You know how I feel."

Once, Alma would not even have paused at this; she would have been secure in the belief that he felt the same way she did. Now she decides that it's a matter of polite form with him to pretend she understands him. Or maybe it's an excuse, come to think of it, so he will never have to come right out on the table and affirm anything or explain himself.

"Same time?" she says.

The last of her buttons is done up. She'll pick up her shoes at the door. She kneels, leans over to kiss him good-bye. Then there is an obliterating flash of light, and Alma slides to the floor.

When she comes to, she's lying on Theo's bed. Theo is dressed (in case he had to call an ambulance, she thinks), and sitting beside her, holding her hand. This time he isn't pleased. "I think you have low blood pressure," he says, being unable to ascribe it to sexual excitement. "You should have it checked out."

"I thought maybe it was the real thing, this time," Alma whispers. She's relieved; she's so relieved the bed feels weightless beneath her, as if she's floating on water.

Theo misunderstands her. "You're telling me it's over?" he says, with resignation or eagerness, she can't tell.

"It's not over," Alma says. She closes her eyes; in a minute, she'll feel less dizzy, she'll get up, she'll talk, she'll walk. Right now the salt drifts down behind her eyes, falling like snow, down through the ocean, past the dead coral, gathering on the branches of the salt tree that rises from the white crystal dunes below it. Scattered on the underwater sand are the bones of many small fish. It is so beautiful. Nothing can kill it. After everything is over, she thinks, there will still be salt.

IN SEARCH OF THE
RATTLESNAKE PLANTAIN

We start in from the shore, through the place where there are a lot of birches. The woods are open, the ground covered with a mat of leaves, dry on the top, pressed down into a damp substratum beneath, threaded through (I know, though I don't look, I have looked before, I have a history of looking) with filaments, strands, roots, and skeins of leaf mould laid through it like fuses, branched like the spreading arteries of watercolour blue in certain kinds of cheese.

Against the dun colour of the fallen leaves, which recedes before us, the birches stand out, or lie. Birches have only a set time to live, and die while standing. Then the tops rot and fall down, or catch and dangle—widow-makers, the loggers used to call them—and the lopped trunks remain upright, hard fungi with undersides like dewed velvet sprouting from them. This patch of woods, with its long vistas and silent pillars, always gives me the same feeling: not fright, not sadness; a muted feeling. The light diffuses here, as through a window high up, in a vault.

"Should have brought a bag," says my mother, who is behind me. We go in single file, my father first, of course, though without his axe, Joanne second so he can explain things to her. I come next and my mother last. In this forest you have to be close to a person to hear what they say. The trees, or more probably the leaves, blot up sound.

"We can come back," I say. Both of us are referring to the birch bark, curls of which lie all around us. They ought to be gathered and used for starting the fire in the wood stove. With dead birches, the skin outlasts the centre, which is the opposite from the way we do it. There is no moment of death for anything, really; only a slow fade, like a candle or an icicle. With anything, the driest parts melt last.

"Should have used your brain," says my father, who has somehow heard her. They have the ability to hear one another, even at a distance, even through obstacles, even though they're in their seventies. My father raised his head without turning his voice, and continues to stomp forward, over the dun leaves and the pieces of Greek temple that litter the ground. I watch his feet, and Joanne's, ahead of me. Really I watch the ground: I'm looking for puffballs. I too have brought no bag, but I can take off my top shirt and make a bundle with it, if I find any.

"Never had one," says my mother cheerfully. "A ball of fluff. Just a little button at the top of my spine, to keep my head from falling off." She rustles along behind me. "Where's he going?" she says.

What we're doing is looking for a bog. Joanne, who writes nature articles, is doing a piece on bogs, and my father knows where there is one. A kettle bog: no way in for the water, and no way out. Joanne has her camera, around her neck on one of those wide embroidered straps like a yodeler's braces, and her binoculars, and her waterproof jacket that folds up into its own pocket and straps around the waist. She is always so well equipped.

She brought her portable one-person kayak up for this visit, assembled it, and whips around over the water in it like a Jesus bug, which is what they used to call those whirligig water beetles you find sheltering in the calm places behind logs, in bays, on stormy days, black and shiny like Joanne's curious eyes.

Yesterday Joanne stepped the wrong way into her kayak and rolled, binoculars and all. Luckily not the camera. We dried her out as well as we could; the binoculars are more or less all right. I knew then that this is the reason I am not as well equipped as Joanne: I am afraid of loss. You shouldn't have a kayak or binoculars or anything else, unless you're prepared to let it sink.

Joanne, who is bright and lives by herself and by her wits, is ready for anything despite her equipment. "They're only binoculars," she said, laughing, as she squelched ashore. She knew the address of the place where she would take them to get them dried out professionally, if all else failed. Also she had a spare pair of hiking boots. She's the kind of woman who can have conversations with strangers on trains, with impunity. They never turn out to be loonies, like the ones I pick, and if they were she would ditch them soon enough. "Shape up or ship out" is a phrase I learned from Joanne.

Up ahead my father stops, looks down, stoops, and pokes. Joanne stoops too but she doesn't uncork the lens of her camera. My father scuffles impatiently among the dried leaves.

"What's he got there?" says my mother, who has caught up with me.

"Nothing," says my father, who has heard her. "No dice. I don't know what's happened to them. They must be disappearing."

My father has a list in his head of things that are disappearing: leopard frogs, certain species of wild orchid, loons, possibly. These are just the things around here. The list for the rest of the world is longer, and lengthening all the time. Tigers, for instance, and whooping cranes. Whales. Redwoods. Strains of wild maize. One species of plant a day. I have lived with this list all my life, and it makes me uncertain about the solidity of the universe. I clutch at things, to stop them, keep them here. If those had been my binoculars, there would have been a fuss.

But right now, right at this moment, I can't remember which thing it is that must be disappearing, or why we are looking for it in the first place.

We're looking for it because this isn't the whole story. The reason I can't remember isn't creeping senility: I could remember perfectly well at the time. But that was *at the time*, and this is a year later. In the meantime, the winter, which is always the meantime, the time during which things happen that you have to know about but would rather skip, my father had a stroke.

He was driving his car, heading north. The stroke happened as he turned from a feeder lane onto an eight-lane highway. The stroke paralyzed his left side, his left hand dragged the wheel over, and the car went across all four lanes of the westbound half of the highway and slid into the guard rail on the other side. My mother was in the car with him.

"The death seat," she said. "It's a miracle we weren't mashed to a pulp."

"That's right," I say. My mother can't drive. "What did you do?"

This is all going on over long-distance telephone, across the Atlantic, the day after the stroke. I am in a phone booth in an English village, and it's drizzling. There's a sack of potatoes in the phone booth too. They don't belong to me. Someone must be storing them in here.

My mother's voice fades in and out, as mine must, for her. I have already said, "Why didn't you call me as soon as it happened?" and she has already said, "No point in upsetting you." I am still a child, from whom the serious, grown-up things must be concealed.

"I didn't want to get out of the car," my mother said. "I didn't want to leave him. He didn't know what had happened. Luckily a nice young man stopped and asked if we were having any trouble, and drove on and called the ambulance."

She was shaken up; how could she not be? But she didn't want me to fly back. Everything was under control, and if I were to fly back it would be a sign that everything was not under control. My father was in the hospital, under control too. The stroke was what they called a transient one. "He can talk again," said my mother. "They say he has a good chance of getting most of it back."

"Most of what?" I said.

"Most of what he lost," said my mother.

After a while I got a letter from my father. It was written in the hospital, where they were doing tests on him. During the brain scan, he overheard one doctor say to another, "Well, there's nothing in there, anyway." My father reported this with some glee. He likes it when people say things they haven't intended to say.

We are past the stand of dying birch, heading inland, where the undergrowth is denser. The bog is somewhere back in there, says my father.

"He doesn't remember," says my mother in a low voice to me. "He's lost."

"I never get lost," says my father, charging ahead now through the saplings. We aren't on a path of any sort, and the trees close in and begin to resemble one another, as they have a habit of doing, away from human markings. But lost people go around in circles, and we are going in a straight line. I remember now what is disappearing, what it is we're supposed to be looking for. It's the rattlesnake plantain, which is a short plant with a bunch of leaves at the base and knobs up the stem. I think it's a variety of orchid. It used to be thick around here, my father has said. What could be causing it to disappear? He doesn't want one of these plants for anything; if he found a rattlesnake plantain, all he would do is look at it. But it would be reassuring, something else that is still with us. So I keep my eyes on the ground.

We find the bog, more or less where it was supposed to be, according to my father. But it's different; it's grown over. You can hardly tell it's a bog, apart from the water that oozes up through the sphagnum moss underfoot. A bog should have edges of moss and sedge that quake when you walk on them, and a dark pool in the centre, of water brown with peat juice. It should remind you of the word *tarn*. This bog has soaked up its water, covered it over and grown trees on it, balsam six feet high by now. We look for pitcher plants, in vain.

This bog is not photogenic. It is mature. Joanne takes a few pictures, with her top-of-the-line camera and never-fail close-up lens. She focusses on the ground, the moss; she takes a footprint filling with water. We stand around, slapping mosquitoes, while she does it. We all know that these aren't the pictures she'll end up using. But she is a good guest.

There are no rattlesnake plantains here. The rattlesnake plantain does not grow in bogs.

It's summer again and I'm back home. The Atlantic lies behind me, like a sheet of zinc, like a time warp. As usual in this house I get more tired than I should; or not tired, sleepy. I read murder mysteries I've read before and go to sleep early, never knowing what year I'll wake up in. Will it be twenty years ago, or twenty years from now? Is it before I got married, is my child—ten and visiting a friend—grown up and gone? There's a chip in the plaster of the room where I sleep, shaped like a pig's head in profile. It's always been there, and each time I come back here I look for it, to steady myself against the current of time that is flowing past and over me, faster and faster. These visits of mine blur together.

This one though is different. Something has been changed, something has stopped. My father, who recovered almost completely from the stroke, who takes five kinds of pills to keep from having another one, who squeezes a woollen ball in his left hand, who however is not paying as much attention to his garden as he used to—my father is ill. I've been here four days and he's been ill the whole time. He lies on the living room sofa in his dressing gown and does not eat or even drink. He sips water, but nothing more.

There have been whispered consultations with my mother, in the kitchen. Is it the pills, is it a virus of some kind? Has he had another stroke, a tiny one, when no one was looking? He's stopped talking much. There's something wrong with his voice, you have to listen very carefully or you can't catch what he's saying.

My mother, who has always handled things, doesn't seem to know what to do. I tell her I'm afraid he'll get dehydrated. I go down to the cellar, where the other phone is, and telephone the doctor, who is hard to reach. I don't want my father to hear me doing this: he will be annoyed, he'll say there's nothing wrong with him, he'll rebel.

I go back upstairs and take his temperature, using the thermometer I used to check my fertility when I was trying to get pregnant. He opens his mouth passively to let me do this; he seems uninterested in the results. His face, a little one-sided from the stroke, appears to have shrunk and fallen in upon itself. His eyes, under his white eyebrows, are almost invisible. The temperature is too high.

"You have a temperature," I tell him. He doesn't seem surprised. I bring a bowl of ice cubes to him, because he says he can't swallow. The ice cubes are something I remember from my childbirth classes, or could it be my husband's ulcer operation? All crisis is one crisis, an improvisation. You seize what is at hand.

"Did he eat the ice cubes?" says my mother, in the kitchen. He doesn't hear her, as he would have once. He doesn't say no.

Later, after dinner, when I am re-reading a bad Agatha Christie dating from the war, my mother comes into my room.

"He says he's going to drive up north," she tells me. "He says there are some trees he has to finish cutting."

"It's the temperature," I say. "He's hallucinating."

"I hope so," says my mother. "He can't drive up there." Maybe she's afraid it isn't the temperature, that this is permanent.

I go with her to their bedroom, where my father is packing. He's put on his clothes, shorts and a white short-sleeved shirt, and shoes and socks. I can't imagine how he got all of this on, because he can hardly stand up. He's in the centre of the room, holding his folded pyjamas as if unsure what to do with them. On the chair is an open rucksack, beside it a package of flashlight batteries.

"You can't drive at night," I say. "It's dark out."

He turns his head from side to side, like a turtle, as if to hear me better. He looks baffled.

"I don't know what's holding you up," he says to my mother. "We have to get up there." Now that he has a temperature, his voice is stronger. I know what it is: he doesn't like the place he finds himself in, he wants to be somewhere else. He wants out, he wants to drive, away from all this illness.

"You should wait till tomorrow," I say.

He sets down the pyjamas and starts looking through his pockets.

"The car keys," he says to my mother.

"Did you give him an aspirin?" I ask her.

"He can't swallow," she says. Her face is white; suddenly she too looks old.

My father has found something in his pocket. It's a folded-up piece of paper. Laboriously he unfolds it, peers at it. It looks like an old grocery list. "The rattlesnake plantain is making a comeback," he says to me. I understand that, from somewhere in there, from underneath the fever, he's trying to send out some good news. He knows things have gone wrong, but it's only part of a cycle. This was a bad summer for wood mice, he told me earlier. He didn't mean that there were a lot of them, but that there were hardly any. The adjective was from the point of view of the mice.

"Don't worry," I say to my mother. "He won't go."

If the worst comes to the worst, I think, I can back my car across the bottom of the driveway. I remember myself, at the age of six, after I'd had my tonsils out. I heard soldiers, marching. My father is afraid.

"I'll help you take off your shoes," my mother says. My father sits down at the edge of the bed, as if tired, as if defeated. My mother kneels. Mutely he holds out a foot.

We're making our way back. My father and mother are off in the woods somewhere, trudging through the undergrowth, young balsam and hazelnut and moose maple, but Joanne and I (why? how did we get separated from them?) are going along the shore, on the theory that, if you're on an island, all you have to do is go along the shore and sooner or later you'll hit the point you started out from. Anyway, this is a short cut, or so we have told each other.

Now there's a steep bank, and a shallow bay where a lot of driftwood has collected—old logs, big around as a hug, their ends sawn off clean. These logs are from the time when they used to do the logging in the winter, cross to the islands by the frozen lakes, cut the trees and drag them to the ice with a team of horses, and float them in the spring to the chute and the mill in log booms, the logs corralled in a floating fence of other logs chained together. The logs in this bay were once escapees. Now they lie like basking whales, lolling in the warmed inshore water, Jesus bugs sheltering behind them, as they turn gradually back to earth. Moss grows on them, and sundew, raising its round leaves like little greenish moons, the sticky hairs standing out from them in rays of light.

Along these sodden and sprouting logs Joanne and I walk, holding on to the shoreside branches for balance. They do the logging differently now; they use chain saws, and trucks to carry the logs out, over gravel roads bulldozed in a week. They don't touch the shoreline though, they leave enough for the eye; but the forest up here is becoming more and more like a curtain, a backdrop behind which is emptiness, or a shambles. The landscape is being hollowed out. From this kind of logging, islands are safer.

Joanne steps on the next log, chocolate brown and hoary with lichen. It rolls in slow motion, and throws her. There goes her second pair of hiking boots, and her pants up to the knees, but luckily not the camera.

"You can't never trust nobody," says Joanne, who is laughing. She wades the rest of the way, to where the shore slopes down and she can squelch up onto dry land.

I pick a different log, make a safe crossing, and follow. Despite our short cut, my parents get back first.

In the morning, the ambulance comes for my father. He's lucid again, that's the term. It makes me think of *lucent:* light comes out of him again, he is no longer opaque. In his husky, obscure voice he even jokes with the ambulance attendants, who are young and reassuring, as they strap him in.

"In case I get violent," he says.

The ambulance doesn't mean a turn for the worse. The doctor has said to take him to Emergency, because there are no beds available in the regular wards. It's summer, and the highway accidents are coming in, and one wing of the hospital is closed, incredibly, for the holidays. But whatever is or is not wrong with him, at least they'll give him an intravenous, to replace the lost fluids.

"He's turning into a raisin," says my mother. She has a list of everything he's failed to eat and drink over the past five days.

I drive my mother to the hospital in my car, and we are there in time to see my father arrive in the ambulance. They unload him, still on the wheeled stretcher, and he is made to disappear through swinging doors, into a space that excludes us.

My mother and I sit on the leatherette chairs, waiting for someone to tell us what is supposed to happen next. There's nothing to read except a couple of outdated copies of *Scottish Life.* I look at a picture of wool-dying. A policeman comes in, talks with a nurse, goes out again.

My mother does not read *Scottish Life.* She sits bolt upright, on the alert, her head swivelling like a periscope. "There don't seem to be any mashed-up people coming in," she says after a while.

"It's the daytime," I say. "I think they come in more at

night." I can't tell whether she's disappointed or comforted by this absence. She watches the swinging doors, as if my father will come stomping out through them at any minute, cured and fully dressed, jingling his car keys in his hand and ready to go.

"What do you suppose he's up to in there?" she says.

THE SUNRISE

❧

Yvonne follows men. She does this discreetly and at a distance, at first; usually she spots them on the subway, where she has the leisure to sit down and look about her, but sometimes she will pass one on the street and turn and walk along behind him, hurrying a little to keep up. Occasionally she rides the subway or goes walking just for this purpose, but more often the sighting is accidental. Once she's made it, though, she postpones whatever she's doing and makes a detour. This has caused her to miss appointments, which bothers her because she's punctual as a rule.

On the subway, Yvonne takes care not to stare too hard: she doesn't want to frighten anyone. When the man gets off the train, Yvonne gets off too and walks to the exit with him, several yards behind. At this point she will either follow him home to see where he lives and lie in wait for him some other day, when she's made up her mind about him, or she'll speak to him once they're out on the street. Two or three times a man has realized he's being shadowed. One actually began to run. Another turned to confront her, back against a nearby drugstore window, as if cornered. One headed for a crowd and lost her in it. These, she thinks, are the ones with guilty consciences.

When the time is right, Yvonne quickens her pace,

comes up beside the man, and touches him on the arm. She always says the same thing:

"Excuse me. You're going to find this strange, but I'd like to draw you. Please don't mistake this for a sexual advance."

Then there's an interval, during which they say *What?* and Yvonne explains. There's no charge, she says, and no strings. She just wants to draw them. They don't have to take their clothes off if they don't want to; the head and shoulders will do nicely. She really is a professional artist. She is not mad.

If they've listened to her initial appeal at all, and most do, it's very hard for them to say no. What does she want from them, after all? Only a small amount of their time, so that they can let her have access to something only they can give. They've been singled out as unique, told they are not interchangeable. No one knows better than Yvonne how seductive this is. Most of them say yes.

Yvonne isn't interested in men who are handsome in the ordinary way: she's not drawing toothpaste ads. Besides, men with capped-looking teeth and regular features, men even remotely like Greek gods, are conscious of the surface they present and of its effect. They display themselves as if their faces are pictures already, finished, varnished, impermeable. Yvonne wants instead whatever it is that's behind the face and sees out through it. She chooses men who look as if things have happened to them, things they didn't like very much, men who show signs of the forces acting upon them, who have been chipped a little, rained on, frayed, like shells on the beach. A jaw slightly undershot, a nose too large or long, eyes of different sizes, asymmetry and counterpoise, these are the qualities that attract her. Men of this kind are not likely to be vain in any standard way. Instead they know that they must depend on something other than appearance to make an impact; but the mere act of being drawn

242

throws them back upon their own unreliable bodies, their imperfect flesh. They watch her as she draws, puzzled, distrustful, yet at the same time vulnerable and oddly confiding. Something of theirs is in her hands.

Once Yvonne gets the men into her studio she is very delicate with them, very tactful. With them in mind she has purchased a second-hand armchair with a footstool to match: solid, comforting, wine velvet, not her usual taste. She sits them in it beside the large window, and turns them so that the light catches on their bones. She brings them a cup of tea or coffee, to put them at ease, and tells them how much she appreciates what they are doing for her. Her gratitude is real: she's about to eat their souls, not the whole soul of course, but even a small amount is not to be taken lightly. Sometimes she puts on a tape, something classical and not too noisy.

If she thinks they're relaxed enough she asks them to take off their shirts. She finds collar-bones very expressive, or rather the slight hollow at the V, the base of the throat; the wish-bone, which gives luck only when broken. The pulse there says something different from the pulse at wrist or temple. This is the place where, in historical movies set in mediaeval times, the arrow goes in.

When Yvonne has arranged her materials and started to draw, she goes quickly: for the sake of the men, she doesn't like to stretch things out. Having been subjected to it herself in her student days, when people posed for each other, she knows how excruciating it is to sit still and let yourself be looked at. The sound of the pencil travelling over the paper raises the small hairs on the skin, as if the pencil is not a pencil at all but a hand being passed over the body, half an inch from the surface. Not surprisingly, some of the men connect this sensation—which can be erotic—with Yvonne, and ask to take her out or see her again or even sleep with her.

Here Yvonne becomes fastidious. She asks if the man

is married, and if he is, she asks if he's happy. She has no wish to get involved with an unhappily married man; she doesn't want to breathe anyone else's black smoke. But if he's happy, why would he want to sleep with her? If he isn't married, she thinks there must be some good reason why not. Mostly, when these invitations are issued, Yvonne refuses, gently and continuing to smile. She discounts protestations of love, passion, and undying friendship, praise of her beauty and talent, claims on her charity, whining, and bluster; she's heard these before. For Yvonne, only the simplest-minded rationale will do. "Because I want to" is about all she'll accept.

Yvonne's studio is right downtown, near the waterfront, in an area of nineteenth-century factories and warehouses, some of which are still used in the original way, some of which have been taken over by people like her. In these streets there are drunks, derelicts, people who live in cardboard boxes; which doesn't bother Yvonne, since she hardly ever goes there at night. On the way to her studio in the mornings she has often passed a man who looks like Beethoven. He has the same domed forehead, overgrown brow bones, gloomy meditative scowl. His hair is grey and long and matted, and he wears a crumbling jeans suit and sneakers tied on with pieces of parcel string, even in winter, and carries a plastic-wrapped bundle that Yvonne thinks must contain everything he owns. He talks to himself and never looks at her. Yvonne would very much like to draw him, but he's far too crazy. She has a well-developed sense of self-protection, which must be why she hasn't landed in serious trouble with any of the men she picks up. This man alarms her, not because she thinks he's dangerous, but because he's a little too much like what she could become.

*   *   *

Nobody knows how old Yvonne is. She looks thirty and dresses as if she were twenty, though sometimes she looks forty and dresses as if she were fifty. Her age depends on the light, and what she wears depends on how she feels, which depends on how old she looks that day, which depends on the light. It's a delicate interaction. She wears her bronze-coloured hair cut short at the back and falling slantwise across her forehead, like Peter Pan's. Sometimes she rigs herself out in black leather pants and rides a very small motorcycle; on the other hand, sometimes she pins on a hat with a little veil, sticks a beauty mark on her cheek with an eyebrow pencil, and slings a second-hand silver fox with three tails around her neck.

She sometimes explains her age by saying she's old enough to remember garter belts when they were just ordinary articles of women's clothing. You wore them when you were young, before you were forced to put on girdles and become rubberized, like mothers. Yvonne remembers the advent of panty-hose, the death of the seamed stocking, whereas for younger women these events are only mythology.

She has another way of dating herself, which she uses less often. Once, when she was young but adult, she had a show of her paintings closed down by the police. It was charged with being obscene. She was one of the first artists in Toronto that this happened to. Just before that, no gallery would even have dared to mount the show, and shortly afterwards, when chains and blood and body parts in supermarket trays had become chic, it would have been considered tame. All Yvonne did at the time was to stick the penises onto men's bodies more or less the way they really were, and erect into the bargain. "I don't see what the big deal was," she can say, still ingenuously. "I was only painting hard-ons. Isn't that what every man wants? The police were just jealous." She goes on to add that she can't make out why, if a penis is a good thing, calling someone a penis-brain is an insult. She has this conversation only with people she knows very well or else has just met. The shocking thing about Yvonne, when she intends to be shocking, is the contrast between certain elements of her vocabulary and the rest of it, which, like her manner, is reserved and even secretive.

For a while she became a sort of celebrity, but that was because she was too inexperienced to know better. People made her into a cause, and even collected money for her, which was nice of them but got in the way, she now feels, of her reputation as a serious artist. It became boring to be referred to as "the penis lady." There was one advantage though: people bought her paintings, though not for ultra-top prices, especially after magic realism came back in. By this time she has money put away: she knows too much about the lives of artists to spend it all and have nothing to fall back on when the wind shifts and the crunch comes, though she sometimes worries that she'll be one of those old women found dead in a pile of empty cat-food cans with a million dollars stashed in her sock. She hasn't had a show now for several years; she calls it "lying low." The truth is she hasn't been producing much except her drawings of men. She has quite a few of them by now, but she isn't sure what she's going to do with them. Whatever she's looking for she hasn't yet found.

At the time of her revolutionary penises, she was more interested in bodies than she is now. Renoir was her hero, and she still admires him as a colourist, but she now finds his great lolloping nudes vapid and meaningless. Recently she's become obsessed with Holbein. A print of his portrait of Georg Gisze hangs in her bathroom, where she can see it while lying in the tub. Georg looks out at her, wearing a black fur coat and a wonderful pink silk shirt, each vein in his hands, each fingernail perfectly rendered, with a suggestion of darkness in his eyes, a wet shine on his lip, the symbols of his spiritual life around him. On his desk stands a vase, signifying the emptiness and vanity of mortal existence, with one carnation in it, signifying the Holy Ghost, or possibly betrothal. Earlier in her life Yvonne used to dismiss this kind of thing as the Rosemary for Remembrance school of flower arranging: everything had to mean something else. The thing about painting penises was that no one ever mistook them for phallic symbols, or indeed for symbols at all. But now she thinks it would be so handy if there were still some language of images like this, commonly known and understood. She would like to be able to put carnations between the fingers of the men she draws, but it's far too late for that. Surely Impressionism was a mistake, with its flesh that was merely flesh, however beautiful, its flowers that were merely flowers. (But what does she mean by "merely"? Isn't that enough, for a flower to be itself? If Yvonne knew the answer . . .)

*   *   *

Yvonne likes to work in the late mornings, when the light is at its best in her studio. After that she sometimes has lunch, with various people she knows. She arranges these lunches from pay phones. She doesn't have a phone herself; when she did have one, she felt she was always at its mercy, whether it was ringing or not; mostly when it was not.

She doles out these lunches to herself like pills, at intervals, when she thinks she needs them. People living alone, she believes, get squirrelly if they go too long without human contact. Yvonne has had to learn how to take care of herself; she didn't always know. She's like a plant—not a sickly one, everybody comments on how healthy she always is—but a rare one, which can flourish and even live only under certain conditions. A transplant. She would like to write down instructions for herself and hand them over to someone else to be carried out, but despite several attempts on her part this hasn't proved to be possible.

She prefers small restaurants with tablecloths; the tablecloth gives her something to hold on to. She sits opposite whoever it is that day, her lárge green eyes looking out from behind the hair that keeps falling down over her forehead, her chin tilted so that the left side of her head is forward. She's convinced that she can hear better with her left ear than with her right, a belief that has nothing to do with deafness.

Her friends enjoy having lunch with Yvonne, though probably they wouldn't enjoy it as much if they did it more often. They would find themselves running out of things to say. As it is, Yvonne is a good listener: she's always so interested in everything. (There's no deception here: she *is* interested in everything, in a way.) She likes to catch up on what people are doing. Nobody gets around to catching up on what she is doing, because she gives the impression of being so serene, so perfectly balanced, that their minds are at rest about her. Whatever she's doing is so obviously the right thing. When they do ask, she has a repertoire of anecdotes about herself which are amusing but not very informative. When she runs out of these, she tells jokes. She writes down the punch lines and keeps them on filing cards in her purse so she won't forget them.

She eats out alone, but not often. When she does, it's usually at sushi bars, where she can sit with her back to the rest of the room and watch the hands of the chefs as they deftly caress and stroke her food. As she eats, she can almost feel their fingers in her mouth.

*   *   *

Yvonne lives on the top floor of a large house in an older but newly stylish part of the city. She has two big rooms, a bathroom, a kitchenette concealed by louvred folding doors which she keeps closed most of the time, and a walk-out deck on which there are several planters made from barrels sawed in two. These once contained rosebushes, not Yvonne's. This floor used to be the attic, and although Yvonne has to go through the rest of the house to get to it, there's a door at the bottom of her stairs that she can lock if she wants to.

The house is owned by a youngish couple named Al and Judy, who both work for the town planning department of City Hall and are full of talk and projects. They intend to expand their own living area into Yvonne's floor when their mortgage is paid off; it will be a study for Al. Meanwhile, they are delighted to have a tenant like Yvonne. These arrangements are so fragile, so open to incompatibility and other forms of disaster, so easily destroyed by stereo sets and mud on the rugs. But Yvonne is a gem, says Judy: they never hear a peep out of her. She's almost too quiet for Al, who would rather hear the footsteps when someone comes up behind him. He refers to Yvonne as "The Shadow," but only when he's had a hard day at work and a couple of drinks.

Anyway, the advantages far outweigh the disadvantages. Al and Judy have a year-old baby named Kimberly, who is at day-care in the mornings and Judy's office in the afternoons, but if they want to go out in the evenings and Yvonne is in, they have no hesitation about leaving Kimberly in her charge. They don't ask her to put Kimberly to bed herself, however. They have never said she's just like one of the family; they don't make that mistake. Sometimes Yvonne comes down and sits in the kitchen while Kimberly is being fed, and Judy thinks she can spot a wistful expression in Yvonne's eyes.

At night when they're lying in bed or in the morning when they're getting dressed, Al and Judy sometimes talk about Yvonne. Each has a different version of her, based on the fact that she never has men over, or even women. Judy thinks she has no sex life at all; she's given it up, for a reason which is probably tragic. Al thinks she does have a sex life, but carries it on elsewhere. A woman who looks like Yvonne—he's not specific—has to be getting it somehow. Judy says he's a dirty old man, and pokes him in the midriff.

"Who knows what evil lurks in the hearts of men?" Al says. "Yvonne knows."

*   *   *

As for Yvonne, the situation suits her, for now. She finds it comforting to hear the sounds of family life going on beneath her, especially in the evenings, and when she goes away Judy waters her plants. She doesn't have many of these. In fact, she doesn't have much of anything, in Judy's opinion: an architectural drawing board, a rug and some cushions and a low table, a couple of framed prints, and, in the bedroom, two futons, one on top of the other. Judy speculated at first that the second was for when some man slept over, but none ever does. Yvonne's place is always very tidy, but to Judy it looks precarious. It's too portable, she feels, as if the whole establishment could be folded up in a minute and transported and unfolded almost anywhere else. Judy tells Al that she wouldn't be surprised one morning to find that Yvonne had simply vanished. Al tells her not to be silly: Yvonne is responsible, she'd never go without giving notice. Judy says she's talking about a feeling, not about what she thinks objectively is really going to happen. Al is always so literal.

Al and Judy have two cats, which are very curious about Yvonne. They climb up to her deck and meow at the french doors to be let in. If she leaves her door ajar, they are up her stairs like a shot. Yvonne has no objection to them, except when they jump on her head while she's resting. Sometimes she will pick up one of them and hold it so that its paws are on either side of her neck and she can feel its heart beating against her. The cats find this position uncomfortable.

*   *   *

Once in a while Yvonne disappears for days, maybe even a week at a time. Al and Judy don't worry about her, since she says when she'll be back and she's always there at the time stated. She never tells them where she's going, but she leaves a sealed envelope with them which she claims contains instructions for how she could be reached in case of an emergency. She doesn't say what would constitute an emergency. Judy sticks the envelope carefully behind the wall telephone in the kitchen; she doesn't know it's empty.

Al and Judy have incorporated these absences of Yvonne's into the romances they have built up about her. In Al's, she's off to meet a lover, whose identity must remain secret, either because he's married or for reasons of state, or both. He imagines this lover as much richer and more important than he is. For Judy, Yvonne is visiting the child or children Judy is convinced she has. The father is a brute, and more strong-willed than Yvonne, who anyone can see is the kind of woman who couldn't stand up to either physical violence or a long court battle. This is the only thing that can excuse, for Judy, Yvonne's abandonment of her children. Yvonne is allowed to see them only at infrequent intervals. Judy pictures her meeting them in restaurants, in parks, the constraint, the anguish of separation. She spoons applesauce into the wet pink oyster-like mouth of Kimberly and bursts into tears.

"Don't be silly," says Al. "She's just off having a roll in the hay. It'll do her a world of good." Al thinks Yvonne has been looking too pale.

"You think sex with a man is the big solution to everything, don't you?" says Judy, wiping her eyes with the sleeve of her sweater.

Al pats her. "Not the only one," he says, "but it's better than a slap with a wet noodle, eh?"

Sometimes it *is* a slap with a wet noodle, thinks Judy, who has been over-tired recently and feels too many demands are being made upon her. But she smiles up at Al with fondness and appreciation. She knows she's lucky. The standard against which she measures her luck is Yvonne.

Thus the existence of Yvonne and her slightly weird behaviour lead to maritial communication and eventual concord. If she knew this, Yvonne would be both pleased and a little scornful; but deep down underneath she would not give a piss.

*   *   *

When everything has been smooth and without painful incident for some time, when the tide has gone out too far, when Yvonne has been wandering along the street, looking with curiosity but no great interest at the lighting fixtures, the coral-encrusted bottles and the bridesmaids' dresses, the waterlogged shoes and the antique candle-holders held up by winged nymphs and the gasping fish that the receding waters have left glistening and exposed in all their detail, when she's gone into the Donut Centre and sat down at the counter and seen the doughnuts under glass beneath her elbows, their tentacles drawn in, breathing lightly, every grain of sugar distinct, she knows that up on the hills, in the large suburban yards, the snakes and moles are coming out of their burrows and the earth is trembling imperceptibly beneath the feet of the old men in cardigans and tweed caps raking their lawns. She gets up and goes out, no faster than usual and not forgetting to leave a tip. She's considerate of waitresses because she never wants to be one again.

She heads for home, trying not to hurry. Behind her, visible over her shoulder if she would only turn her head, and approaching with horrifying but silent speed, is a towering wall of black water. It catches the light of the sun, there are glints of movement, of life caught up in it and doomed, near its translucent crest.

Yvonne climbs the stairs to her apartment, almost running, the two cats bounding up behind her, and hits the bed just as the blackness breaks over her head with a force that tears the pillow out of her hands and blinds and deafens her. Confusion sweeps over and around her, but underneath the surface terror she is not too frightened. She's done this before, she has some trust in the water, she knows that all she has to do is draw her knees up and close everything, ears, eyes, mouth, hands. All she has to do is hold on. Some would advocate that she let go instead, ride with the current, but she's tried it. Collision with other floating objects does her no good. The cats jump on her head, walk on her, purr in her ear; she can hear them in the distance, like flute music on a hillside, up on the shore.

Yvonne can think of no reason for these episodes. There's no trigger for them, no early warning. They're just something that happens to her, like a sneeze. She thinks of them as chemical.

* * *

Today Yvonne is having lunch with a man whose collarbone she admires, or did admire when it was available to her. Right now it isn't, because Yvonne is no longer sleeping with this man. She stopped because of the impossibility of the situation. For Yvonne, situations become impossible quickly. She doesn't like situations.

This is a man with whom Yvonne was once in love. There are several such men in Yvonne's life; she makes a distinction between them and the men she draws. She never draws men she's in love with; she thinks it's because she lacks the necessary distance from them. She sees them, not as form or line or colour or even expression, but as concentrations of the light. (That's her version of it when she's in love; when she isn't, she remembers them as rarified blurs, like something you've spilled on a tablecloth and are trying to wash out. She has occasionally made the mistake of trying to explain all this to the men concerned.) She's no stranger to addiction, having once passed far too many chemical travelogues through her body, and she knows its dangers. As far as she's concerned love is just another form of it.

She can't stand too much of this sort of thing, so her affairs with such men don't last long. She doesn't begin them with any illusions about permanence, or even about temporary domestic arrangements; the days are gone when she could believe that if only she could climb into bed with a man and pull the covers over both their heads, they would be safe.

However, she often likes these men and thinks that something is due them, and so she continues to see them afterwards, which is easy because her separations from them are never unpleasant, not any more. Life is too short.

Yvonne sits across from the man, at a table in a small restaurant, holding on to the tablecloth with one hand, below the table where he can't see it. She's listening to him with her customary interest, head tilted. She misses him intensely; or rather, she misses, not him, but the sensations he used to be able to arouse in her. The light has gone out of him and now she can see him clearly. She finds this objectivity of hers, this clarity, almost more depressing than she can bear, not because there is anything hideous or repellant about this man but because he has now returned to the ordinary level, the level of things she can see, in all their amazing and complex particularity, but cannot touch.

He's come to the end of what he's been saying, which had to do with politics. Now it's time for Yvonne to tell him a joke.

"Why is pubic hair curly?" she says.

"Why?" he says; as usual, he attempts to conceal the shock he feels at hearing her say words like *pubic*. Nice men are more difficult for Yvonne than pigs. If a man is piggish enough, she's glad to see him go.

"So you won't poke your eyes out," says Yvonne, clutching the tablecloth.

Instead of laughing he smiles at her, a little sadly. "I don't know how you do it," he says. "Nothing ever bothers you."

Yvonne pauses. Maybe he's referring to the fact that, in their withdrawal from each other, there were no frantic phone calls from her, no broken dishes, no accusations, no tears. She's tried all these in the past and found them lacking. But maybe he wanted those things, as proof of something, of love perhaps; maybe he's disappointed by her failure to provide them.

"Things bother me," says Yvonne.

"You have so much energy," he goes on, as if he hasn't heard her. "Where do you get it from? What's your secret?"

Yvonne looks down at her plate, on which there is half an apple and walnut and watercress salad and a crust of bread. To touch his hand, which is there in plain view, on the tablecloth a mere six inches away from her wine glass, would be to put herself at risk again, and she is already at risk. Once she delighted in being at risk; but once she did everything too much.

She looks up at him and smiles. "My secret is that I get up every morning to watch the sunrise," she says. This *is* her secret, though it's not the only one; it's only the one that's on offer today. She watches him to see if he's bought it, and he has. This is enough in character for him, it's what he thinks she's really like. He's satisfied that she's all right, that there will be no trouble, which is what he wanted to know. He orders another cup of coffee and asks for the bill. When it comes, Yvonne pays half.

They walk out into the March air, warmer than usual this year, a fact on which they both comment. Yvonne avoids shaking hands with him. It occurs to her that he is the last man she will ever have the energy to love. It's so much work. He waves good-bye to her and gets onto a streetcar and is borne away, towards a set of distant stoplights, along tracks that converge as they recede.

*　　*　　*

Near the streetcar stop there's a small flower shop where you can buy one flower at a time, if one flower is all you want. It's all Yvonne ever wants. Today they have tulips, for the first time this year, and Yvonne chooses a red one, the inside of the cup an acrylic orange. She will take this tulip back to her room and set it in a white bud vase in the sunlight and drink its blood until it dies.

Yvonne carries the tulip in one hand, wrapped in its cone of paper, held stiffly out in front of her as if it's dripping. Walking along past the store windows, into which she peers with her usual eagerness, her usual sense that maybe, today, she will discover behind them something that will truly be worth seeing, she feels as if her feet are not on cement at all but on ice. The blade of the skate floats, she knows, on a thin film of water, which it melts by pressure and which freezes behind it. This is the freedom of the present tense, this sliding edge.

*　　*　　*

Yvonne is drawing another man. As a rule, she draws only men who fall well within the norm: they dress more or less conventionally, they turn out, when asked, to have jobs recognized and respected by society, they're within ten years of her own age, shooting either way. This one is different.

She began to follow him about three blocks past the flower shop, trotting along behind him—he has long legs—with her tulip held up in front of her like a child's flag. He's young, maybe twenty-three, and on the street he was carrying a black leather portfolio, which is now leaning against the wall by her door. His pants were black leather too, and his jacket, under which he was wearing a hot-pink shirt. His head is shaved up the back and sides, leaving a plume on top, dyed fake-fur orang-outang orange, and he has two gold earrings in his left ear. The leather portfolio means that he's an artist or a designer of some sort; she suspects he's a spray-painter, the kind that goes around at night and writes things on brick walls, things like *crunchy granola sucks* and *Save Soviet Jews! Win Big Prizes!* If he ever draws at all, it's with pink and green fluorescent felt pens. She'd bet ten dollars he can't draw fingers. Yvonne's own renderings of fingers are very good.

In the past she's avoided anything that looked like another artist, but there's something about him, the sullenness, the stylistic belligerence, the aggressive pastiness and deliberate potato-sprouting-in-the-cellar lack of health. When she caught sight of him, Yvonne felt a shock of recognition, as if this was what she'd been looking for, though she doesn't yet know why. She ran him to earth outside a submarine shop and said her piece. She expected a rejection, rude at that, but here he is, in her studio, wearing nothing at the moment but his pink shirt, one bloodless leg thrown over the arm of the wine velvet chair. In his hand is the tulip, which clashes violently with the shirt and the chair and his hair, which all clash with each other. He's like a welding-shop accident, a motorcycle driven full tilt into a cement wall. The look he's focussing on her is pure defiance, but defiance of what?

She doesn't know why he agreed to come with her. All he said was, "Sure, why not?" with a look she read as meaning that she totally failed to impress him.

Yvonne draws, her pencil moving lightly over his body. She knows she has to go quickly or he will get restless, he will escape her. She can put the tulip in later, when she paints him. Already she's decided to paint him; he will be her first real painting for years. The tulip will become a poppy; it's almost the right colour anyway.

She's only down to the collar-bone, half visible under the open shirt, when he says, "That's enough," and pulls himself out of the chair and comes over and stands behind her. He puts his hands on her waist and presses himself against her: no preliminaries here, which would suit Yvonne fine—she likes these things to be fast—except that she's uneasy about him. None of her usual mollifications, coffee, music, gratefulness, have worked on him: he's maintained a consistent level of surliness. He's beyond her. She thinks of Al and Judy's cat, the black one, and the time it got its foot caught in the cord of her Venetian blind. It was so enraged she had to throw a towel over it to get it untangled.

"That's *art*," he says, looking over her shoulder.

Yvonne mistakes this for a compliment, until he says, "Art sucks." There's a hiss in the last word.

Yvonne gasps: there is such hatred in his voice. Maybe if she just stands there nothing will happen. He turns away from her and goes to the corner near the door: he wants to show her what he's got in his portfolio. What he does are collages. The settings are all outdoors: woods, meadows, rocks, seashores. Onto them he has pasted women, meticulously cut from magazines, splayed open-legged torsoes with the hands and feet removed, sometimes the heads, over-painted with nail polish in various shades of purple and red, shiny and wet-looking against the paper.

Yet as a lover he is slow and meditative, abstracted,

somnambulent almost, as if the motions he's going through are only a kind of afterthought, like a dog groaning in a dream. The violence is all on the cardboard; it's only art, after all. Maybe everything is only art, Yvonne thinks, picking her sky-blue shirt up off the floor, buttoning it. She wonders how many times in the future she will find herself doing up these particular buttons.

When he's gone out, she locks the door behind him and sits in the red velvet chair. It's herself she's in danger from. She decides to go away for a week. When she comes back she will buy a canvas the size of a doorway and begin again. Though if art sucks and everything is only art, what has she done with her life?

* * *

In her medicine cabinet Yvonne keeps several bottles of pills, which she has collected from doctors on one pretext or another over the years. There was no need to do this, to go through the rigmarole of prescriptions, since anything you want is available on the street and Yvonne knows who from; yet the prescriptions gave her a kind of sanction. Even the actual pieces of paper, with their illegible Arabic-textured scrawls, reassured her, much as a charm would if she believed in them.

At one time she knew exactly how many pills to take, of which kinds, at which precisely timed intervals, to keep from either throwing up or passing out before the right dose had been reached. She knew what she would say ahead of time to fend off those who might otherwise come looking for her, where she would go, which doors she would lock, where and in what position she would lie down; even, and not least importantly, what she would wear. She wanted her body to look well and not be too troublesome to those who would eventually have to deal with it. Clothed corpses are so much less disturbing than naked ones.

But lately she's been forgetting much of this arcane

259

knowledge. She should throw the pills out: they've become obsolete. She's replaced them with something much simpler, more direct, faster, more failure-proof, and, she's been told, less painful. A bathtub full of warm water, her own bathtub in the bathroom she uses every day, and an ordinary razor blade, for which no prescriptions are necessary. The recommendation is that the lights be turned out, to avoid panic: if you can't see the spreading red, you hardly know it's there. A stinging at the wrists, like a minor insect. She pictures herself wearing a flannel nightgown, printed with small pink flowers, that buttons up to the neck. She has not yet bought this.

She keeps a razor blade in her paintbox; it could be for slicing paper. In fact she does slice paper with it, and when it gets dull she replaces it. One side of the blade is taped, since she has no desire to cut her fingers by accident.

Yvonne hardly ever thinks about this razor blade and what it's really doing in her paintbox. She is not obsessed with death, her own or anybody else's. She doesn't approve of suicide; she finds it morally distasteful. She takes care crossing the street, watches what she puts into her mouth, saves her money.

But the razor blade is there all the time, underneath everything. Yvonne needs it there. What it means is that she can control her death; and if she can't do that, what control can she ever possibly achieve over her life?

Perhaps the razor blade is only a kind of *memento mori*, after all. Perhaps it's only a pictorial flirtation. Perhaps it's only a dutiful symbol, like the carnation on the desk of Holbein's young man. He isn't looking at the carnation anyway, he's looking out of the picture, so earnestly, so intently, so sweetly. He's looking at Yvonne, and he can see in the dark.

*   *   *

The days are getting longer, and Yvonne's alarm clock goes off earlier and earlier. In the summers she takes to having afternoon naps, to make up for the sleep she loses to these dawn rituals. She hasn't missed the sunrise for years; she depends on it. It's almost as if she believes that if she isn't there to see it there will be no sunrise at all.

And yet she knows that her dependence is not on something that can be grasped, held in the hand, kept, but only on an accident of the language, because *sunrise* should not be a noun. The sunrise is not a thing, but only an effect of the light caused by the positions of two astronomical bodies in relation to each other. The sun does not really rise at all, it's the earth that turns. The sunrise is a fraud.

Today there's no overcast. Yvonne, standing out on her deck in her too-thin Japanese robe, holds on to the wooden railing to keep from lifting her arms as the sun floats up above the horizon, like a shimmering white blimp, an enormous kite whose string she almost holds in her hand. Light, chilly and thin but light, reaches her from it. She breathes it in.

UNEARTHING SUITE

My parents have something to tell me: something apart from the ordinary course of conversation. I can guess this from the way they sit down first, both on the same chair, my mother on the arm, and turn their heads a little to one side, regarding me with their ultra-blue eyes.

As they have grown older their eyes have become lighter and lighter and more and more bright, as if time is leeching them of darkness, experience clarifying them until they have reached the transparency of stream water. Possibly this is an illusion caused by the whitening of their hair. In any case their eyes are now round and shiny, like the glass-bead eyes of stuffed animals. Not for the first time it occurs to me that I could not have been born, like other people, but must have been hatched out of an egg. My parents' occasional dismay over me was not like the dismay of other parents. It was less dismay than perplexity, the bewilderment of two birds who have found a human child in their nest and have no idea what to do with it.

My father takes a black leather folder from the desk. They both have an air of suppressed excitement, like children waiting for a grown-up friend to open a present they have wrapped; which will contain a joke.

"We went down and bought our urns today," my father says.

"You what?" I say, shocked. There is nothing wrong with my parents. They are in perfect health. I on the other hand have a cold.

"It's best to be prepared," my mother says. "We looked at plots but they're so expensive."

"They take up too much space," says my father, who has always been conscious of the uses to which the earth is wrongly in his opinion put. Conversation around the dinner table when I was growing up concerned itself more than once with how many weeks it would take a pair of fruit flies breeding unchecked to cover the earth to a depth of thirty-two feet. Not many, as I recall. He feels much the same about corpses.

"They give you a little niche too," says my mother.

"It's in here," says my father, indicating the folder as if I am supposed to remember about all this and deal with it at the right time. I am appalled: surely they aren't leaving something, finally, up to me?

"We wanted to be sprinkled," says my mother. "But they told us it's now illegal."

"That's ridiculous," I say. "Why can't you be sprinkled if you want to?"

"The funeral-parlour lobby," says my father, who has been known to be cynical about government decisions. My mother concedes that things might get a bit dusty if everyone were to be sprinkled.

"I'll sprinkle you," I say bravely. "Don't worry about a thing."

This is a rash decision and I've made it on the spur of the moment, as I make all my rash decisions. But I fully intend to carry it out; even though it will mean action, a thing I avoid when possible. Under pretense of a pious visit I will steal my parents from their niche, substituting sand if necessary, and smuggle them away. The ashes part doesn't bother me; in fact I approve of it. Much better than waiting, like the Christians, for God to grow them once more instantaneously from the bone outward, sealed meanwhile rouged and waxed and wired, veins filled with formaldehyde, in cement and bronze vaults, a prey to mould and anaerobic bacteria. If God wants to make my parents again the molecules will do just as well to start with, same as before. It is not a question of matter, which turns over completely every seven years anyway, but of form.

We sit for a minute, considering implications. We are way beyond funerals and mourning, or possibly we have by-passed them. I am thinking about the chase, and being arrested, and how I will foil the authorities: already I am concocting fictions. My father is thinking about fertilizer, in the same tone in which other people think about union with the Infinite. My mother is thinking about the wind.

*   *   *

Photographs have never done justice to my mother. This is because they stop time; to really reflect her they would have to show her as a blur. When I think of her she is often on skis. Her only discoverable ambition as a child was to be able to fly, and much of her subsequent life has been spent in various attempts to take off. Stories of her youth involve scenes in trees and on barn roofs, break-neck dashes on frothy-mouthed runaway horses, speed-skating races, and, when she was older, climbs out of windows onto forbidden fire escapes, done more for the height and adventure than for the end result, an after-hours college date with some young man or other who had been knocked over by her, perhaps literally. For my mother, despite her daunting athleticism and lack of interest in frilly skirts, was much sought after. Possibly

265

men saw her as a challenge: it would be an accomplishment to get her to pause long enough to pay even a fleeting amount of attention to them.

My father first saw her sliding down a banister—I imagine, in the 1920s, that she would have done this side-saddle—and resolved then and there to marry her; though it took him a while to track her down, stalking her from tree to tree, crouching behind bushes, butterfly net at the ready. This is a metaphor but not unjustified.

One of their neighbours recently took me to task about her.

"Your poor mother," she said. "Married to your father."

"What?" I said.

"I see her dragging her groceries back from the supermarket," she said. (True enough, my mother does this. She has a little cart with which she whizzes along the sidewalk, hair wisping out from her head, scarf streaming, exhausting anyone foolhardy enough to make the trip with her; by that I mean myself.) "Your father won't even drive her."

When I told her this story, my mother laughed.

My father said the unfortunate woman obviously didn't know that there was more to him than met the eye.

In recent years my mother has taken up a new winter exercise. Twice a week she goes dancing on figure skates: waltzes, tangos, fox trots. On Tuesday and Thursday mornings she can be observed whirring around the local arena to the tune of "A Bicycle Built For Two" played over the scratchy sound system, speed undiminished, in mittens which do not match her skirt, keeping perfect time.

* * *

My father did what he did because it allows him to do what he does. There he goes now, in among the trees, battered grey felt hat—with or without a couple of trout

266

flies stuck in the band, depending on what year we're talking about—on his head to keep things from falling into his hair, things that are invisible to others but which he knows all too well are lurking up there among the innocent-looking leaves, one or two or a clutch of children of any age tagging along after him, his own or his grandchildren or children attracted at random, as a parade attracts followers, as the sun attracts meteors, their eyes getting larger and larger as wonder after wonder is revealed to them: a sacred white larva that will pupate and fly only after seven years, a miraculous beetle that eats wood, a two-sexed worm, a fungus that crawls. No freak show can hold a candle to my father expounding Nature.

He leaves no stone unturned; but having turned it, to see what may be underneath—and at this point no squeals or expressions of disgust are permitted, on pain of his disfavour—he puts everything carefully back: the grub into its hollow, the woodborer beneath its rotting bark, the worm into its burrow, unless needed of course for fishing. He is not a sentimentalist.

Now he spreads a tarpaulin beneath a likely-looking tree, striped maple let us say, and taps the tree trunk with the pole of his axe. Heaven rewards him with a shower of green caterpillars, which he gathers tenderly in, to carry home with him and feed on leafy branches of the appropriate kind stuck into quart jars of water. These he will forget to replace, and soon the caterpillars will go crawling over our walls and ceiling in search of fodder, to drop as if on cue into the soup. My mother is used to this by now and thinks nothing of it.

Meanwhile the children follow him to the next tree: he is better than magicians, since he explains everything. This is indeed one of his purposes: to explain everything, when possible. He wants to see, he wants to know, only to see and know. I'm aware that it is this mentality, this curiosity, which is responsible for the hydrogen bomb and the imminent demise of civilization and that we would all be better off if we were still at the stone-worshipping stage. Though surely it is not this affable inquisitiveness that should be blamed.

Look, my father has unearthed a marvel: a slug perhaps, a snake, a spider complete with her sack of eggs? Something educational at any rate. You can't see it from here: only the backs of the children's heads as they peer down into his cupped hands.

* * *

My parents do not have houses, like other people. Instead they have earths. These look like houses but are not thought of as houses, exactly. Instead they are more like stopping places, seasonal dens, watering holes on some caravan route which my nomadic parents are always following, or about to follow, or have just come back from following. Much of my mother's time is spent packing and unpacking.

Unlocking the door of one of their earths—and unlike foxes they get rid of the bones, not by burial but by burning, the right thing to do unless you want skunks—I am greeted first by darkness, then by a profusion of objects heaped apparently at random but actually following some arcane scheme of order: stacks of lumber, cans of paint-brush cleaner with paintbrushes soaking in them, some of these dry and stiff or glued to the insides of the cans by the sticky residue left by evaporation, boxes of four-inch spikes, six-quart baskets filled with an assortment of screws, hinges, staples, and roofing-nails, rolls of roofing, axes, saws, brace-and-bits, levels, peevees, spoke-shaves, rasps, drills, post-hole diggers, shovels, mattocks, and crowbars. (Not all of these things are in the same place at the same time: this is a collective memory.) I know what each of these tools is for and may even at some time have used it, which may go part way towards explaining my adult slothfulness. The smell is the smell of my childhood: wood, canvas, tar, kerosene, soil.

This is my father's section of the house. In my mother's, things are arranged, on hooks and shelves, in inviolable order: cups, pots, plates, pans. This is not because my mother makes a fetish of housekeeping but because she doesn't want to waste time on it. All her favourite recipes begin with the word *quick*. Less is more, as far as she is concerned, and this means everything in its place. She has never been interested, luckily, in the house beautiful, but she does insist on the house convenient.

Her space is filled. She does not wish it altered. We used to give her cooking pots for Christmas until we realized that she would much rather have something else.

My father likes projects. My mother likes projects to be finished. Thus you see her, in heavy work gloves, carting cement blocks, one by one, or stacks of wood, from one location to another, dragging underbrush which my father has slashed, hauling buckets of gravel and dumping them out, all in aid of my father's constructionism.

Right now they are digging a large hole in the ground. This will eventually be another earth. My mother has already moved a load of cement blocks to the site, for lining it with; in the mornings she goes to see what animal tracks she can find on the fresh sand, and perhaps to rescue any toads and mice that may have tumbled in.

Although he is never finished, my father does finish things. Last summer a back step suddenly appeared on our log house up north. For twenty years my mother and I had been leaping into space whenever we wanted to reach the clothesline, using biceps and good luck to get ourselves back up and in. Now we descend normally. And there is a sink in the kitchen, so that dirty dishwater no longer has to be carried down the hill in an enamel pail, slopping over onto one's legs, and buried in the garden. It now goes down a drainhole in the approved manner.

My mother has added her completing touch: a small printed sign Scotch-taped to the counter, which reads:

PUT NO FAT DOWN SINK.

A jar of dried bacteria stands nearby: one teaspoonful is poured down at intervals, so the stray tea leaves will be devoured. This prevents clogging.

Meanwhile my father is hard at work, erecting cedar logs into vertical walls for the new outhouse, which will contain a chemical toilet, unlike the old one. He is also building a fireplace out of selected pink granite boulders which my mother steps over and around as she sweeps the leaves off the floor.

Where will it all end? I cannot say. As a child I wrote small books which I began with the words *The End*. I needed to know the end was guaranteed.

My own house is divided in two: a room full of paper, constantly in flux, where process, organicism, and fermentation rule and dustballs breed; and another room, formal in design, rigid in content, which is spotlessly clean and to which nothing is ever added.

* * *

As for me, I will die no doubt of inertia. Though witness to my parents' exhausting vitality, I spent my childhood learning to equate goodness with immobility. Sitting in the bottoms of canoes that would tip if you lurched, crouching in tents that would leak if you touched them in rainstorms, used for ballast in motorboats stacked precariously high with lumber, I was told not to move, and I did not. I was thought of as being well-behaved.

At intervals my father would bundle the family and the necessary provisions into the current car—*Studebaker* is a name I remember—and make a pilgrimage of one kind or another, a thousand miles here, a thousand miles there. Sometimes we were in search of saw-flies; at other times, of grandparents. We would drive as long as possible along the almost empty post-war highways, through the melancholy small towns of Quebec or northern Ontario, sometimes down into the States, where there were more roadside billboards. Long after the minor-key sunsets late at night, when even the White Rose gasoline stations were closed, we would look for a motel; in those days, a string of homemade cottages beside a sign that read FOLDED WINGS, or, more somberly, VALHALLA, the tiny clapboard office festooned with Christmas-tree lights. Ever since then, *vacancy* has been a magic word for me: it means there is room. If we did not find a vacancy my father would simply pull over to the side of the road in some likely-looking spot and put up a tent. There were few campgrounds, no motorcycle gangs; there was more emptiness than there is now. Tents were not so portable then; they were heavy and canvas, and sleeping bags were dank and filled with kapok. Everything was grey or khaki.

During these trips my father would drive as fast as he could, hurling the car forward it seemed by strength of will, pursued by all the unpulled weeds in his gardens, all the caterpillars uncollected in his forests, all the nails that needed to be hammered in, all the loads of dirt that had to be shifted from one place to another. I, meanwhile, would lie on a carefully stowed pile of baggage in the back seat, wedged into a small place beneath the roof. I could see out of the window, and I would watch the landscape, which consisted of many dark trees and of the telephone poles and their curves of wire, which looked as if they were moving up and down. Perhaps it was then that I began the translation of the world into words. It was something you could do without moving.

Sometimes, when we were stationary, I held the ends of logs while my father sawed them, or pulled out designated weeds, but most of the time I lived a life of contemplation. In so far as was possible I sneaked off into the woods to read books and evade tasks, taking with me supplies filched from my mother's tin of cooking raisins and stash of crackers. In theory I can do almost anything; certainly I have been told how. In practice I do as little as possible. I pretend to myself that I would be quite happy in a hermit's cave, living on gruel, if someone else would make the gruel. Gruel, like so many other things, is beyond me.

* * *

What is my mother's secret? For of course she must have one. No one can have a life so apparently cheerful, so seemingly lacking in avalanches and swamps, without having also a secret. By *secret* I mean the price she had to pay. What was the trade-off, what did she sign over to the Devil, for this limpid tranquillity?

She maintains that she once had a quick temper, but no one knows where it has gone. When she was forced to take piano lessons as part of a young lady's battery of accomplishments, she memorized the pieces and played them by rote while reading novels concealed on her lap. "More *feeling*," her teacher would say to her. Pictures of her at four show a shy-looking ringleted child bedecked in the lacey lampshade dresses inflicted on girls before the First World War, but in fact she was inquisitive, inventive, always getting into trouble. One of her first memories is of sliding down a red clay bank in her delicate white post-Victorian pantaloons. She remembers the punishment, true, but she remembers better the lovely feeling of the mud.

Her marriage was an escape from its alternatives. Instead of becoming the wife of some local small-town professional and settling down, in skirts and proper surroundings, to do charity work for the church as would have befitted her status, she married my father and took off down the St. John's river in a canoe, never having slept in a tent before; except once, just before the wedding,

272

when she and her sisters spent a weekend practising. My father knew how to light fires in the rain and what to do about rapids, which alarmed my mother's friends. Some of them thought of her as having been kidnapped and dragged off to the wilderness, where she was imprisoned and forced to contend with no electricity, no indoor plumbing, and hordes of ravening bears. She on the other hand must have felt that she had been rescued from a fate worse than death: antimacassars on the chairs.

Even when we lived in real houses it was something like camping out. There was an improvisational quality to my mother's cooking, as if the ingredients were not bought but scavenged: what we ate depended on what was at hand. She made things out of other things and never threw anything out. Although she did not like dirt, she could never take housecleaning seriously as an end in itself. She polished the hardwood floors by dragging her children over them on an old flannelette blanket. This sounds like fun until I reflect: they were too poor for floor polishers, maids, or babysitters.

After my birth she developed warts, all over both her hands. Her explanation was the ammonia: there were no disposable diapers then. In those days babies wore knitted woollen sweaters, woollen booties, woollen bonnets, and woollen soakers, in which they must have steamed like puddings. My parents did not own a wringer washer; my mother washed everything by hand. During this period she did not get out much to play. In the photographs, she is always posed with a sled or a carriage and one or two suspicious-looking infants. She is never alone.

Possibly she got the warts from being grounded; or, more particularly, from me. It's a burden, this responsibility for the warts of one's mother, but since I missed out on the usual guilts this one will have to do. The warts point towards my mother's secret but do not reveal it. In any case they went away.

My mother lived for two years in the red-light district of Montreal without knowing what it was. She was informed only afterwards, by an older woman who told her she ought not to have done it. "I don't know why not," said my mother. That is her secret.

*　　*　　*

My father studies history. He has been told by Poles that he knows more Polish history than most Poles, by Greeks that he knows more Greek history than most Greeks, by Spaniards that he knows more Spanish history than most Spaniards. Taking the sum total of worldwide *per capita* knowledge into consideration this is probably so. He alone, among my acquaintances, successfully predicted the war in Afghanistan, on the basis of past examples. Who else indeed was paying any attention?

It is his theory that both Hiroshima and the discovery of America were entomological events (the clue is the silkworm) and that fleas have been responsible for more massacres and population depletions than have religions (the clue is the bubonic plague). His overview is dire, though supported, he would hasten to point out, by the facts. Wastefulness, stupidity, arrogance, greed, and brutishness unroll themselves in Technicolor panorama across our dinner table as my father genially carves the roast.

Should civilization as we know it destroy itself, he informs us, ladling the gravy—as is likely, he adds—it will never be able to rebuild itself in its present form, since all available surface metals have long since been exhausted and the extraction of deeper ones is dependent upon metal technologies, which, as you will remember, will have been demolished. There can never be another iron age, another bronze age; we will be stuck—if there is any *we*, which he doubts—with stone and bone, no good for aeroplanes and computers.

He has scant interest in surviving into the twenty-first century. He knows it will be awful. Any person of sense will agree with him (and lest you make the mistake of thinking him merely quaint, let me remind you that many do).

My mother, however, pouring out the tea and forgetting as usual who takes milk, says she wants to live as long as possible. She wants to see what happens.

My father finds this naïve of her, but lets it pass and goes on to discuss the situation in Poland. He recalls to our memories (paying his listeners the compliment, always, of pretending he is merely reminding them of something they have of course already known, long and well) the Second World War Polish cavalry charge against the German tanks: foolishness and bravery. But foolish. But brave. He helps himself to more mashed potato, shaking his head in wonder. Then, changing the subject, he delivers himself of one of those intricate and reprehensible puns he's so fond of.

How to reconcile his grim vision of life on earth with his undoubted enjoyment of it? Neither is a pose. Both are real. I can't remember—though my father could, without question, ferreting among his books to locate the exact reference—which saint it was who, when asked what he would do if the end of the world were due tomorrow, said he would continue to cultivate his garden. The proper study of mankind may be man, but the proper activity is digging.

* * *

My parents have three gardens: one in the city, which produces raspberries, eggplants, irises, and beans; another halfway up, which specializes in peas, potatoes, squash, onions, beets, carrots, broccoli, and cauliflower; and the one up north, small but lovingly cherished, developed from sand, compost, and rations of sheep and horse manure carefully doled out, which yields cabbages, spinach, lettuce, long-lasting rhubarb, and Swiss chard, cool-weather crops.

All spring and summer my parents ricochet from garden to garden, mulching, watering, pulling up the polyphiloprogenitive weeds, "until," my mother says, "I'm bent over like a coat hanger." In the fall they harvest, usually much more than they can possibly eat. They preserve, store, chill, and freeze. They give away the surplus, to friends and family, and to the occasional stranger whom my father has selected as worthy. These are sometimes women who work in bookstores and have demonstrated their discernment and intelligence by recognizing the titles of books my father asks for. On these he will occasionally bestow a cabbage of superior size and delightfulness, a choice clutch of tomatoes, or, if it is fall and he has been chopping and sawing, an elegant piece of wood.

In the winter my parents dutifully chew their way through the end products of their summer's labour, since it would be a shame to waste anything. In the spring, fortified with ever newer and more fertile and rust-resistant varieties from the Stokes Seed Catalogue, they begin again.

My back aches merely thinking about them as I creep out to some sinful junk-food outlet or phone up Pizza Pizza. But in truth the point of all this gardening is not vitaminization or self-sufficiency or the production of food, though these count for something. Gardening is not a rational act. What matters is the immersion of the hands in the earth, that ancient ceremony of which the Pope kissing the tarmac is merely a pallid vestigial remnant.

In the spring, at the end of the day, you should smell like dirt.

* * *

Here is a fit subject for meditation: the dock. I myself use it, naturally, to lie down on. From it I can see the

276

outlines of the shore, which function for me like a memory. At night I sit on it, in a darkness which is like no other, watching stars if there are any. At dusk there are bats; in the mornings, ducks. Underneath it there are leeches, minnows, and the occasional crayfish. This dock, like Nature, is permanently crumbling away and is always the same.

It is built on cribs of logs weighted down by granite boulders, which are much easier to move around underwater than they are on land. For this venture my father immersed himself in the lake, which he otherwise prefers to stay out of. No wonder; even on good days, at the height of summer, it is not what you would call warm. Scars go purple in it, toes go white, lips go blue. The lake is one of those countless pot-holes left by the retreating glaciers, which had previously scraped off all the topsoil and pushed it south. What remained is bedrock, and when you dip yourself into this lake you know that if you stay in it long enough or even very long at all you will soon get down to the essentials.

My father looks at this dock (his eyes narrowing in calculation, his fingers itching) and sees mainly that it needs to be repaired. The winter ice has been at it, the sun, the rain; it is patched and treacherous, threads of rot are spreading through it. Sometime soon he will take his crowbar to it, rip apart its punky and dangerous boards and the logs excavated by nesting yellow-jackets, and rebuild the whole thing new.

My mother sees it as a place from which to launch canoes, and as a handy repository for soap and towel when, about three in the afternoon, in the lull between the lunch dishes and reactivating the fire for supper, she goes swimming. Into the gelid, heart-stoppingly cold water she wades, over the blackened pine needles lying on the sand and the waterlogged branches, over the shells of clams and the carapaces of crayfish, splashing the tops of her arms, until she finally plunges in and speeds outward, on her back, her neck coming straight up out of the water like an otter's, her head in its white bathing cap encircled by an aureole of black flies, kicking up a small wake behind her and uttering cries of:

Refreshing! Refreshing!

* * *

Today I pry myself loose from my own entropy and lead two children single-file through the woods. We are looking for anything. On the way we gather pieces of fallen birch bark, placing them in paper bags after first shaking them to get out the spiders. They will be useful for lighting the fire. We talk about fires and where they should not be lit. There are charcoal-sided trunks crumbling here and there in the forest, *mementi mori* of an ancient burn-out.

The trail we follow is an old one, blazed by my brother during his trail-making phase thirty years ago and brushed out by him routinely since. The blazes are now weathered and grey; hardened tree blood stands out in welts around them. I teach the children to look on both sides of the trees, to turn once in a while and see where they have come from, so that they will learn how to find their way back, always. They stand under the huge trees in their raincoats, space echoing silently around them; a folklore motif, these children in the woods, potentially lost. They sense it and are hushed.

The Indians did that, I tell them, pointing to an old tree bent when young into knees and elbows. Which, like most history, may or may not be true.

Real ones? they want to know.

Real, I say.

Were they alive? they ask.

We go forward, clambering up a hill, over boulders, past a fallen log ripped open by a bear in search of grubs. They have more orders: they are to keep their eyes open for mushrooms, and especially for puffballs, which even they like to eat. Around here there is no such thing as just a walk. I feel genetics stealing over me: in a minute I will be turning over stones for them, and in fact I am soon on my hands and knees, grubbing a gigantic toad out from under a fallen cedar so old it is almost earth, burnt orange. We discuss the fact that toads will not give you warts but will pee on you when frightened. The toad does this, proving my reliability. For its own good I put it into my pocket and the expedition moves forward.

At right angles there's a smaller trail, a recent one, marked not by blazes but by snapped branches and pieces of fluorescent pink tape tied to bushes. It leads to a yellow birch blown down by the wind—you can tell by the roots, topsoil and leaf-mould still matted on them—now neatly sawn and stacked, ready for splitting. Another earthwork.

On the way back we circle the burn-heap, the garden, going as quietly as we can. The trick, I whisper, is to see things before they see you. Not for the first time I feel that this place is haunted, by the ghosts of those not yet dead, my own included.

*　　*　　*

Nothing goes on forever. Sooner or later I will have to renounce my motionlessness, give up those habits of reverie, speculation, and lethargy by which I currently subsist. I will have to come to grips with the real world, which is composed, I know, not of words but of drainpipes, holes in the ground, furiously multiplying weeds, hunks of granite, stacks of more or less heavy matter which must be moved from one point to the other, usually uphill.

How will I handle it? Only time, which does not by any means tell everything, will tell.

*　　*　　*

This is another evening, later in the year. My parents have returned yet once again from the north. It is fall, the closing-down season. Like the sun my parents have their annual rhythms, which, come to think of it, are not unrelated to that simile. This is the time of the withering of the last bean plants, the faltering of the cabbages, when the final carrot must be prized from the earth, tough and whiskered and forked like a mandrake; when my parents make great altars of rubbish, old cardboard boxes, excess branches lopped from trees, egg cartons, who knows?— and ignite them to salute the fading sun.

But they have done all that and have made a safe journey. Now they have another revelation to make: something portentous, something momentous. Something has happened that does not happen every day.

"I was up on the roof, sweeping off the leaves—" says my mother.

"As she does every fall—" says my father.

It does not alarm me to picture my seventy-three-year-old mother clambering nimbly about on a roof, a roof with a pitch so steep that I myself would go gingerly, toes and fingers suctioned to the asphalt roofing like a treefrog's, adrenelin hazing the sky, through which I can see myself hurtling earthward after a moment of forgetfulness, a misstep, one of those countless slips of the mind and therefore of the body about which I ought to have known better. My mother does these things all the time. She has never fallen off. She will never fall.

"Otherwise trees would grow on it," says my mother.

"And guess what she found?" says my father.

I try to guess, but I cannot. What would my mother have found on the roof? Not a pine cone, not a fungus, not a dead bird. It would not be what anyone else would find there.

In fact it turns out to be a dropping. Now I have to guess what kind of dropping.

"Flying squirrel," I hazard lamely.

No, no. Nothing so ordinary.

"It was about this big," says my father, indicating the length and the circumference. It is not an owl then.

"Brown?" I say, stalling for time.

"Black," says my father. They both regard me, heads a little on one side, eyes shining with the glee of playing this ancient game, the game of riddles, scarcely able to contain the right answer.

"And it had hair in it," says my father, as if now light will break upon me, I must surely guess.

But I am at a loss.

"Too big for a marten," says my father, hinting, waiting. Then he lowers his voice a little. "Fisher," he says.

"Really?" I say.

"Must be," says my father, and we all pause to savour the rarity of this event. There are not many fishers left, not many of those beautiful arboreal voracious predators, and we have never before found the signs of one in our area. For my father, this dropping is an interesting biological phenomenon. He has noted it and filed it, along with all the other scraps of fascinating data he notes and files.

For my mother however, this is something else. For her this dropping—this hand-long, two-fingers-thick, black, hairy dropping—not to put too fine a point on it, this deposit of animal shit—is a miraculous token, a sign of divine grace; as if their mundane, familiar, much-patched but at times still-leaking roof has been visited and made momentarily radiant by an unknown but by no means minor god.

ATWOOD, MARGARET
BLUEBEARD'S EGG

| DATE | | ISSUED TO |